PRAISE FOR *DEEP PURPLE COVER*

"Joel W. Barrows' *Deep Purple Cover* has flavors of mystery and dark motives with fragrant twists. Medium-bodied and knowledgeable of the subject matter, the aroma of the novel is robust in its procedural qualities with just a hint of thriller. Interesting characters also make it perfect for the bookshelf where it will pair nicely with a Baldacci, a Sandford or a Coben. *Deep Purple Cover* is a truly notable vintage."
—Craig Johnson, author of the Walt Longmire Series

"Something's rotten in California wine country, as noted by the discovery of a decapitated head floating in a barrel of fine wine. Whether you're a wine connoisseur or not, you'll dig *Deep Purple Cover*, Joel Barrow's latest twisty, gripping fact-based whodunnit mystery thriller. Watch the sparks fly as FBI agent Rowan Parks hooks up with her former love, AFT undercover agent David Ward, to solve the case."
—Charles Salzberg, twice nominated Shamus Award author of *Second Story Man* and *Swann's Last Song*

DEEP PURPLE COVER

BOOKS BY JOEL W. BARROWS

The Deep Cover Series
Deep White Cover
Deep Green Cover
Deep Red Cover
Deep Purple Cover
Deep Blue Cover (*)
Deep Orange Cover (*)

Other Titles
Poisoned Waters
The Drug Lords

(*) Coming Soon

JOEL W. BARROWS

DEEP PURPLE COVER

A Novel Based on True Events

DOWN & OUT

BOOKS

Down & Out Books
3959 Van Dyke Road, Suite 265
Lutz, FL 33558
DownAndOutBooks.com

The characters and events in this book are fictitious. Any similarity to real persons, living or dead, is coincidental and not intended by the author.

Cover design by Lance Wright

ISBN: 1-64396-263-9
ISBN-13: 978-1-64396-263-4

For Carol

CHAPTER 1

5:37 p.m., Thursday, August 4, Pavesi Vineyards, Napa Valley, California

Martin Pavesi laughed as his old friend, Gino Galli, entertained the group with stories of their youth. Were they embellished? Certainly. But there was more truth than fiction. Growing up in the Bronx during the seventies had provided ample opportunity for mischief, and he and Gino had found their fair share. It was good to have him here now, to see the culmination of his hard work. To own this place was still almost beyond imagination. It was something that he could not have dreamed of back then. Pavesi looked out from the patio onto the rolling vineyard, lovingly nestled into his lush little piece of the valley. Life was good.

"And then Marty says to this mope, 'How's about I just smack that fuckin' smirk off your face?' It's about then that I finally remember how I know this guy. He's a low-level enforcer for the Genovese family. I've seen him hangin' around outside their club." Gino slapped his palms against his forehead. "Holy shit. I look at Marty and mouth the word *Genovese*, which gets his attention. We start backin' up, turn, and haul ass outta there. Fortunately, no shots were fired." Gino laughed, shaking his head. "Later," he explained, gesturing with open hands, "certain

1

apologies had to made."

Pavesi laughed. He remembered the incident well. Not so amusing at the time, but funny as hell now, especially to hear Gino tell it. The guy was a master storyteller. In truth, he and his old friend had been lucky to escape unscathed. It helped that Gino's uncle Frank was a made man. There was always a certain understanding in his neighborhood of how to go along to get along. It was just part of life there. And this episode was the only time that he had even remotely danced along that edge.

Pavesi heard Audra's melodious laugh. He reached for his wife's hand, gave it squeeze. She was delighted with Gino's tales of the old days. She turned to him, smile radiant, the sun illuminating her hazel eyes. She was everything he could have ever hoped for. It took three tries to get the right one, but she was it. His first marriage had basically faded away as they grew apart. When the kids were gone it came to its inevitable conclusion. Then, he married a much younger woman, Marisa. She was magnificent, in many ways. But they had little in common except for the carnal. Conversation became strained. She developed a wandering eye, as did he, but for different reasons. It was then that he found Audra, beautiful, intelligent, cultured. They had been together for eight wonderful years. She was a partner both in life and in business, quickly developing an understanding of all aspects of the industry.

There had been another partner as well. Raymond Amato had invested early, showing faith in the operation when there was little reason to do so. Ray had infused the capital that allowed Pavesi Vineyards to become the highly regarded winery that it was today. It had been just over a month since he vanished. So far, police and private investigators had come up with nothing—no clue, no trace, no explanation. But enough of that, Pavesi thought. He had a surprise for everyone.

"Not to interrupt," Pavesi said, fully intending to do so, "but I have something I'd like to share with all of you, my good friends." He stood. "Follow me."

The group rose as Pavesi led the way. Audra followed, as did Gino and his wife Emma, along with some friends from town, Kyle and Aimee.

"We have a Cabernet Sauvignon that has been aging for just over eighteen months," Pavesi announced. "I think it's going to be our best ever, and I want all of you to be the first to try it."

"Outstanding," Gino exclaimed, rubbing his hands together.

They descended to the barrel room, where wines aging in oak barrels lined the walls. The vineyard also used stainless-steel tanks to age many of its wines, but the traditional oak barrels were still utilized for many of their reds. One barrel had been pulled out and set on a stand in the middle of the walkway.

"This is it," Pavesi proudly announced. He grabbed a wine thief, a glass tube used to extract a sample from the barrel. Pavesi placed one end of the syringe-like instrument into a hole in the top side of the barrel and pulled a small sample. That was deposited into one of six glasses that sat on a nearby cart. He would do the first tasting to ensure that it was as expected.

The glass was approximately one-third full. Pavesi examined it from all angles, holding it to the light, letting it roll toward the edge. Visually, it appeared perfect. He then swirled it in the glass and took a sniff. The aroma was black cherry, the tiniest hint of mint, vanilla from the oak barrel. But something wasn't quite right. He took a taste, intending to swirl it in his mouth, but quickly spat it into a nearby tasting bucket.

"What's wrong, dear?" Audra asked.

"I'm not sure," Pavesi said. He turned to his guests. "My apologies. There appears to be an issue with this barrel." He was embarrassed. "Audra, could you take everyone back out to the patio? I'll have a couple of bottles brought out from an earlier vintage."

"Of course, dear." She led them away, but Gino hung back.

"You okay, buddy?" he asked.

"A little humiliating," Pavesi replied.

Gino put his arm around his old friend's shoulder. "Nonsense,"

3

he said, gesturing toward the barrels that surrounded them. "You've got a beautiful thing here."

Pavesi nodded. Gino was right. "But I still need to find out what went wrong here," he said. "Hopefully, it's just this barrel." The thought of an entire vintage of Cabernet Sauvignon being poured down the drain made him sick.

Pavesi waved over a couple of his workers, Carlos and Jesse. "We need to move this outside, drain it, and remove the top," he said.

The men looked puzzled, but found a dolly, loaded the barrel, and rolled it outside to a storm drain. Once empty, they stood it on its end and used a hammer and chisel to loosen the upper metal bands. That done, they pried the barrel head loose so that it could be tilted and then removed. As Carlos pulled it out, he looked inside. "Oh my God," he said, dropping the barrel head to the ground.

Pavesi stepped forward, Gino alongside. They looked in. Pavesi felt his knees buckle, a wave of nausea hit him like a tsunami. He was staring at what appeared to be the head of Ray Amato, the remaining flesh died a ghoulish, purple hue.

CHAPTER 2

7:13 p.m., Thursday, August 4, Pavesi Vineyards, Napa Valley, California

Detective Joe Adler stepped out of his vehicle and surveyed the scene. Groups of wine country tourists were still there, huddled together on the patio, chatting excitedly, speculating about what must have happened. Patrol units from the Napa County Sheriff's Office had secured the scene. Two deputies stood guard, fending off questions from onlookers. Adler knew both. He approached, nodding his greeting.

"Hey, Joe. Figured they'd send you."

"You figured right," Adler said. Deputy Stacy Webb was a ten-year veteran of the force, and one of Adler's favorites. She was sharp, disciplined, always willing to put in the extra effort on a case. He had tried, unsuccessfully, to recruit her to the Investigations Bureau. But Webb liked the road, wanted to be where the action was. He respected that. With her tonight was Deputy Ryan Conner. He was a lesser light, but still a solid hand.

"Sounds like they found Ray Amato," Webb said, quiet so as not to be overheard.

"Sounds like," Adler replied. Webb knew that he had been working a missing persons case on vineyard owner since he vanished a month earlier.

Webb stepped aside and lifted the crime scene tape so he could pass. "Sorry, Joe."

Adler shrugged. "What can you do?" he asked.

Already familiar with the place, Adler made his way down to the aging room. He spotted Martin and Audra Pavesi standing off to the side, along with a man he did not recognize. An oak wine barrel stood on one end in the middle of hallway, the top removed. From the call out, Adler knew what he would find inside. He approached and looked in. Despite the decay and discoloration, he recognized the severed head of Raymond Amato.

There was that wave of self-doubt, the one that came whenever a case like this did not turn out well. Adler thought about what else he could have done to find the man, find him before this. And one question would not leave his mind. Did Amato know it was coming? God, he hoped not. To Adler, this seemed like a crime motivated less by rage than a desire to send a message. The question was what message...and to whom. He removed a small spiral notebook and pen from his jacket, then turned.

Martin Pavesi was shaken. He leaned against his wife, staring absently at a spot on the floor. Adler approached, unnoticed, until Audra whispered in her husband's ear. When Pavesi looked up, the detective could see that his eyes were red, swollen, still moist.

"I'm sorry for your loss," Adler said.

Pavesi looked at him and nodded, unable to speak.

"Thank you, Detective," Audra said. She turned to the man to her left. "This is our friend, Gino Galli. Gino was here when the barrel was...opened."

"Mr. Galli, Detective Joe Adler, Napa County Sheriff's Office."

"Detective." Galli extended his hand. Adler took it.

"I'd like to ask all three of you a few questions," Adler said. "One at a time, if you don't mind." Adler flipped open his notepad. "Mr. Pavesi, I'd like to start with you."

Audra looked at her husband. He nodded his agreement. She touched Marty's shoulder. "We'll be nearby," she said, then gave him a kiss on the cheek.

Adler waited for them to move out of earshot, then spoke.

"Goes without saying," he said, "but I hoped this would end differently."

"Goes without saying," Pavesi replied.

Adler sighed. "Yeah." Not his best opening.

Adler heard others arrive. It was the crime scene unit. They would immediately begin to process the site. Right behind them was Detective Enrique Estes, known to his colleagues as Double E. Adler acknowledged him, then nodded toward the barrel. He turned back to Pavesi.

"Did Mr. Amato have any enemies?" he asked.

"You asked me that when he went missing," Pavesi replied. "The answer is still the same."

Adler reminded himself to be patient. This had been traumatic for Pavesi. In addition to losing his friend and business partner, he would now have to empty many, if not most, of the barrels that lined the walls...just in case. Adler could only imagine the dollar loss, not to mention the long-term damage to the vineyard's reputation.

"Sorry," Pavesi said. "It's just that..."

"Understood."

"No enemies," Pavesi said. "Certainly, none that I know of."

Estes joined them. Adler made the introductions, then continued his questioning.

"Any problems in his personal life?"

There was a slight snort. "Ray was a ladies' man," Pavesi said, "one girlfriend to the next. There were always problems." He shook his head, then looked toward the barrel. "But nothing that would result in something like this."

"Still," Adler said, "I'll need to get some names."

"Of course."

"Any money problems?" Adler asked.

"Spent too much on his girlfriends," Pavesi replied. "But as far as I know, there were no financial issues. Ray was a successful businessman in the transportation industry."

Adler nodded. Amato Freight Lines was well known up and down the West Coast.

"Was the vineyard having any money problems?" Adler asked.

Pavesi gave him a cool look. "Not until now."

Adler paused for a moment. He knew that the next question would not go over well.

"How'd the two of you get along?"

Pavesi took a step back and met Adler's stare. "Are you kidding me?"

"I have to ask."

"We were good," Pavesi said. "We've always been good."

"Right."

Adler fished out a card and offered it to Pavesi. "Call me if you think of anything else," he said.

"I already have your card," Pavesi said.

That was true, but it was habit, and things got lost. "Fair enough," Adler said. He turned to walk away, then looked back. "Text me those names, the girlfriends."

"I'll do that," Pavesi said.

When they were a safe distance, Estes spoke. "The head's not as decomposed as I would have thought."

"We don't know when he was murdered," Adler said. "Even if it was a month ago, it might have been in somebody's freezer."

Estes nodded. "And I suppose the alcohol in the wine could have helped preserve it."

"Maybe," Adler said.

"So, I hear he disappeared without a trace," Estes said.

"Well," Adler replied, looking toward the barrel, "now we have a trace."

CHAPTER 3

10:17 p.m., Friday, August 5, Boutique Katina, Napa, California

As requested, Martin Pavesi had texted the names of Amato's girlfriends. One name stood out: Katina Orlov. According to the message, she did not respond well to being dumped. Full-on psycho was how Pavesi described it. And that warranted some follow-up. Adler had run across her name before, during the missing persons investigation. But for whatever reason, her obsession with Amato had not been mentioned...by anyone.

Orlov owned a small boutique in Napa, the county seat. Adler asked Double E to come along. Absent the kind of audio/video system found in an interrogation room, it was dangerous to interview a witness by yourself. They could accuse you of things: coaching, intimidation, and worse. It seemed an obvious rule, but people got in a hurry, became sloppy, thought it wouldn't happen to them. But it did. He had seen it many times.

They approached the door. Adler looked inside. Not surprisingly, the place was almost empty at just after ten o'clock in the morning. One customer was rummaging through a dress rack marked fifty percent off. They had pulled a driver's license photo for Orlov. Adler took out his cell and checked the picture. The hairstyle had changed, but she appeared to be the same woman at the back of the store, near the shoe display. Another younger

9

woman, maybe late teens to early twenties, was working the register.

"Showtime," Double E said as he opened the door.

They strode toward the back of the shop, catching an inquisitive look from the woman at the register. Orlov turned from the wall of shoes when they were about ten feet away. She seemed startled.

"Can I help you?" she asked.

She was a striking woman: brunette, dark eyes, perfectly proportioned. Adler guessed she was accustomed to getting what she wanted, especially from men. Her jewelry, assuming it was real, spoke to expensive tastes.

Adler spoke. He would take the lead. "Katina Orlov?"

"Yes," she replied. "Who's asking?"

"Detective Joe Adler, Napa County Sheriff's Office." Adler held up his badge. He gestured toward Double E. "And this is Detective Enrique Estes."

Double E nodded.

"Okay," Orlov said. "Am I in some kind of trouble?"

Adler did a quick glance at Double E to see if he also thought it an odd response. Nothing. But then, Estes was generally impassive in these situations.

"Not that I'm aware of," Adler said. "We'd just like to ask you a few questions."

"About what?"

"Raymond Amato."

A sour expression hit her face. "What about him?" she asked. "Did you find the son of a bitch?"

Adler suppressed a snort. He ignored the question, for the moment. That disclosure would come later. But he could already see that Pavesi was right. There was a certain gleam in her eye.

"I understand the two of you dated," Adler said. It wasn't a question.

"You seem to already know that," Orlov replied, displaying some attitude.

"When did he end it?" Adler asked, trying to provoke her.

"I guess you just assume he ended it?" she asked, putting her hands on her hips, extending a leg. It was a bit of a display, perhaps designed to demonstrate her marketability. That was good. Adler could work with ego.

"Are you saying that you broke it off?" Adler asked.

Her eyes dropped, briefly. "No. I'm not saying that." She crossed her arms, looked away. "He found someone else, some young slut who would do whatever he wanted."

"Did he want you to do things you didn't want to do?"

"That's really none of your business," she replied.

Adler thought it hyperbole, and a bit of rationalization on her part. He moved on.

"So, back to my original question. When did he end it?"

"Eight months ago. Just before Christmas."

"That must have made you angry, the timing."

"It didn't help." She was quiet for a moment, then shook her head. "There was a bracelet. I knew he had purchased for me, for Christmas. Then I saw her, mid-January...wearing the bracelet."

Double E let out a low whistle. She looked at him.

"Exactly," she said.

"Have you contacted him since then?" Adler asked.

"A few times, right after the breakup. Not recently. I have no idea where he is if that's where this is going."

"What if I told you that his phone records show 135 calls from you between January and June of this year? That sounds a bit obsessive, like you couldn't let it go."

Her eyes narrowed. "Is that a question? Because you seem to have all the answers."

"And what about an incident in May, at Uberta's?" Adler had checked with the Napa PD for any call outs involving Orlov. She had been cited for disturbing the peace after upending a table at the local restaurant, a table occupied by Ray Amato and his girlfriend of the moment.

"That was a mistake," she said, looking down.

Adler was quiet for a minute, waiting for more, waiting to see if she would fill the silence. Orlov looked up, meeting his gaze. Her eyes were moist. Seconds later, tears began to roll down her cheeks.

"You don't understand," she said. "Ray loved me. We talked about getting married." Her hands covered her face as she began to softly sob.

Adler felt a pang of guilt. But this was the job. A man was dead, brutally murdered. He had to see it through.

"Just a couple more questions," he said.

Orlov nodded, wiping away the tears.

Adler looked around. "The boutique, did he have anything to do with it? Maybe provide some financing?"

Orlov's mood swung immediately. "I built this business," she said angrily.

"So, he had nothing to do with it?"

She crossed her arms and glared at him. "There was a small amount of seed money, in the beginning. That's it."

"How much?"

Her nostrils flared. Her foot started to tap. Orlov was angry, but thinking, thinking about how much she had to admit.

"Fifty thousand."

Adler pulled out his notepad and jotted it down, as much for dramatic effect as anything.

"You never answered my question," Orlov said. "Did you find him?"

Adler decided it was time. He looked at Double E, who nodded his agreement.

"We did," he said. Adler watched her closely, gauging her reaction.

"Where? Is he okay?"

Adler let the question linger for a moment, then answered, "His severed head was found in a wine barrel at the vineyard."

She caught herself by grabbing the shoe rack. Several pairs

fell to the floor. Hers eyes welled up as collapsed into a chair. Was it an act? Adler wasn't sure. If so, it was a good one.

CHAPTER 4

3:51 p.m., Friday, August 5, Napa County Sheriff's Office, 1535 Airport Blvd, Napa, California

Pavesi had provided them with the username and password to access the cloud storage for the vineyard's surveillance system. Unless downloaded by the subscriber, any recordings were deleted after thirty days. Thankfully, the cameras were motion activated, meaning they did not have to slog through a month's worth of video in real time. Still, it was a chore. Adler had decided to start with the off hours when staff would not normally be present. But four hours in, they had come up with little of value.

"I'm not sure how much more of this I can take," Double E announced.

"Suck it up, brother," Adler said. "We've got a lot more to go through." He rubbed his eyes and reached for his third venti of the afternoon.

"That stuff will stunt your growth," Double E said, eyeing the coffee. He then took another hit from his energy drink.

Adler snorted. "How many of those have you had?"

Double E grinned. "Almost enough to get me through this mind-numbing shit."

Adler raised his cup in acknowledgment.

"Pretty unlikely he was murdered at the winery," Double E

said.

"Agreed. But you never know."

"I'd be surprised if they even put the head in the barrel there."

Adler nodded. "Too risky." He clicked on another video. This one captured the pet cat on a midnight stroll through the aging room.

"What do you really hope to find?" Double E asked.

"Maybe somebody swapping out one barrel for another for no apparent reason."

"Makes sense. Of course, if it was somebody on the inside, they probably turned off the relevant camera beforehand."

"Maybe," Adler said, "if they knew the password."

"Or they just physically disabled it," Double E added, "insider or not."

Adler sighed. It was true. Most likely they were looking for a needle that wasn't even in the haystack. He decided to look at the video around the timeframe in which the body...or part of it...was discovered.

After a few minutes Adler found a video showing two workers pulling the barrel off the rack, presumably getting it ready for the tasting. The time showed it to be about an hour before the incident. "Take a look at this," he said to Estes.

Double E watched the video. Nothing about it seemed suspicious. "Yeah, what about it?" he asked.

"You talked to these guys at the scene, right?"

"Yeah, I talked to them. Why?"

"I'm wondering if anybody told them to pull that specific barrel. I mean, Pavesi's friend, Galli, said they had gone down to sample a particular vintage of Cabernet Sauvignon."

"And there would be many barrels from that harvest," Double E said.

"Exactly."

Double E grabbed his notes. "The names were Carlos Herrera and Jesse Morgan."

Adler looked at his watch. "Let's go have a chat with them."

* * *

They made it to Pavesi Vineyards just before five. Adler hoped the two men were still there. He did not want to call ahead to ask them to stay, which would have eliminated the element of surprise.

They were spotted as soon as they stepped out of the car. Audra Pavesi was on the patio, looking their way. She started toward them, at a brisk clip.

"Detectives," she said. "Do you have some news?"

"I wish we did," Adler replied. "It's very early in the investigation."

Audra nodded. "Of course. It's just that...Marty...he's so upset."

"Understood," Adler said.

"So, what can I do for you?"

"We have a few more questions for two of your employees," Adler replied, "Carlos Herrera and Jesse Morgan. Are they still here?"

"Are they suspects?" Audra asked, startled.

"We just have a few follow-up questions."

"Very well," she said. "I'll go get them."

A few minutes later Audra returned with Herrera and Morgan. Both men appeared nervous. Herrera had removed his cap and was wringing it in his hands. Morgan's squint spoke to a wariness, like a guy who had some experience in the system.

"Gentlemen," Adler said, "I know that Detective Estes talked to you yesterday. We just have a few more questions. Should just take a minute."

"Do I need a lawyer?" Herrera asked.

"That's up to you," Adler said. "But this is just some follow-up. Getting a lawyer will simply delay the investigation."

"And we don't care about your immigration status," Estes added, sensing the concern.

Herrera looked at Audra, who nodded her go-ahead.

"Detectives, why don't we find a more private location," Audra said, glancing back toward the patrons seated on the patio. Some of them were exchanging comments, looking their direction.

"I was going to suggest that very thing," Adler replied.

Audra led them inside and opened the door to a small office, away from any guests or coworkers. "Will this do?" she asked.

Adler looked it over, nodding his approval. "Perfect," he said.

Audra started to usher them into the office. Double E stopped her. "We'll need to talk to them one at a time, ma'am. And you'll need to wait out here."

"Oh," she said, "of course. I'm sorry."

"No worries," Double E said. "Let's start with Mr. Herrera."

Herrera entered the office, followed by the detectives. Audra touched Adler's sleeve before he was fully inside.

"Carlos has been with us for years," she whispered. "He's like family."

Adler nodded, noting she did not say the same for Morgan.

Once inside, Adler took the lead, getting straight to the point. "Did you help pull the barrel down so that Mr. Pavesi and his friends could sample the wine?"

"Yes, sir," Herrera said, nodding. "It was Jesse and I."

"Did anyone ask you to pull a specific barrel of that year's Cabernet?"

Herrera shook his head. "No, sir."

"Okay. Then, between the two of you, who picked that barrel? Was it you or Jesse?"

Herrera thought for a moment. "I guess Jesse went to that barrel."

"You guess?"

"No. I mean, he did, yes."

Adler nodded. "That's all for now. Thank you." He would let things stew with Herrera.

Morgan came in next.

"Just a couple of questions, Mr. Morgan." Adler fished out his notepad and pen. "Did you help pull that barrel from the rack?"

Morgan looked back and forth between the two detectives, the hint of a smirk showing on one corner of his thin-lipped mouth. "Something tells me you already know the answer to that," he said.

Here we go, Adler thought. He just stared at Morgan for a moment, saying nothing.

"Just answer the question," Adler said.

"Yeah, I helped," Morgan said.

"Did anyone tell you to pull that specific barrel?"

"Nope," he answered, looking away for a split second.

Adler made a note. Morgan again looked back and forth between he and Estes.

"So, who picked that barrel? Was it you or Carlos?"

Morgan looked to his left, then up toward the ceiling, as if trying to recall.

"Hmmm. I think it was Carlos. I don't know. It might have been me. Why?"

Adler ignored the question. "Thank you," he said. "That's all...for now."

Morgan's expression of self-satisfaction vanished, replaced by one of puzzlement, maybe concern.

Adler made another note, then looked up. "You can go," he said.

Audra Pavesi showed them out, then excused herself to tend to her guests. On the walk back to their car, Adler turned toward Estes.

"So, Morgan knows more than he's saying."

Double E nodded. "I'm guessing," he said. "That, or it's the standard reflex lying of a low-budget criminal."

Adler knew that was a possibility.

"I'll pull his rap sheet."

CHAPTER 5

5:59 p.m., Friday, August 5, KSFZ TV Studios, San Francisco, California

The six o'clock broadcast was about to start. Marilyn Chen took a deep breath to calm herself as the countdown began. "Five, four, three, two, one, and we're live." She smiled into the camera and went into anchor mode. "Good evening, and welcome to the KSFZ TV Evening News. Tonight, we lead with the details of what appears to be a gruesome murder in wine country."

"That's right, Marilyn." Co-anchor Mark Lane took over. "In a KSFZ TV exclusive report, we go now to Miguel Santos who is live at the scene. Miguel, what can you tell us?"

"Mark, we are just outside Pavesi Vineyards in Napa Valley where sources tell us that late yesterday the severed head of vineyard co-owner, Raymond Amato, was found in an oak wine barrel that had been stored in the winery's aging room. Amato went missing approximately one month ago, vanishing without a trace until the shocking discovery here last evening."

"Do we have any information on possible suspects or a motive?" Lane asked.

"Not at this point," Santos replied, "but a source has informed us that this has all the markings of a hit, one that was meant to send a message. It is unknown whether the surviving co-owner

19

and founder of the vineyard, Martin Pavesi, is considered a person of interest in the investigation."

"A disturbing report out of Napa," Lane said. "We'll stay on top of this developing story. Thank you, Miguel."

"You're welcome. This is Miguel Santos, KSFZ TV, reporting live from Napa Valley."

Special Agent in Charge Thurgood Perry picked up the remote and clicked off the TV. The events in Napa County warranted a look. He grabbed his cell form the desk and punched in a number. It was answered before the second ring.

"Yes, sir."

"Kurt, did you hear about this murder up in Napa, some vineyard owner's head found in a wine barrel?" Perry knew the likely answer. Assistant Special Agent in Charge Kurt Nash didn't miss much.

"Raymond Amato," Nash said. "Been missing about a month. I asked the Santa Rosa office to look into it."

Perry gave a snort. "I should have known. Let me know what you find out."

"Will do."

Perry ended the call. He smiled. Nash was going places. Someday he would head a field office, maybe even a leadership slot at headquarters. Yeah, someday...if his ambition didn't derail him first.

CHAPTER 6

9:07 a.m., Monday, August 8, Napa County District Attorney's Office, Napa, California

It was an adage as old as detective work: follow the money. And that is exactly what Adler intended to do. He had done some of this work before, but it was a shallow dive when just a missing persons case. Now the effort was renewed, and he would need to go deep. One thing seemed clear from talking with Amato's acquaintances over the course of the last month: the man had the resources to vanish if he chose to do so. At least it appeared that way. The other thing that seemed to be understood, if left unsaid, was that it was a possibility. Now it was time to take a closer look at Amato's wealth, see how much was real, how much was show, and if there were financial problems that might provide motive.

From all outward appearances, Amato Freight Lines was an extraordinarily successful enterprise. Its trucks could be seen on interstates and highways across America. But the profit margins of the trucking industry could rise or fall on a variety of factors. The company's books might point him in a new direction. It wouldn't be the first time. And successful or not, how did Amato come up with the money to invest in a vineyard? According to Pavesi, it had been a substantial capital infusion and his new partner had seemed unconcerned with costs. Every proposed improvement had been accepted with something like nonchalance. Yes, Amato was wealthy, but a picture had emerged of a man capable of spending beyond his means, spending to impress.

Adler parked in the ramp across from the Napa District Attorney's Office. He could have simply emailed his subpoena requests but wanted to chat with the deputy district attorney assigned to the case. Caleb Mosley was a solid prosecutor, one with good investigative instincts. In the past it had proved useful to get his perspective at the outset. Adler walked in and was met with a smile from the DA's colorful receptionist, Julie.

"Holy shit," Julie said, her voice as gravelly as a cement truck. "What the fuck, Adler? Where have you been?"

"Nice to see you, too, Jules." He got a kick out of her.

"What are you here about?" she asked, her voice now a raspy whisper. She always had to be in the know.

Adler rested his elbows on the counter, then looked both directions to make sure no one was listening. "Hoffa," he said. "I think I know where they buried the body."

"Oh, fuck you!" Julie exclaimed, sitting back in her chair. She laughed, then refocused and leaned in. "No, seriously. What's up?"

"The Amato case," Adler replied. "You know, the head in the wine barrel."

"I knew it," she said. "Um, um, um. Nasty, nasty, nasty."

Adler drew closer. "I suppose you want to know who did it."

"Tell it."

Adler pushed back from the counter. "No clue. That's why I'm here."

She smiled. "You asshole."

Adler chuckled. "Is Caleb here?"

"Just walked in with one of his lattes," she said. "I'll announce your presence." She picked up the phone.

A few moments later Caleb Mosley appeared, all smiles. "What's up, man?"

"Just taking abuse from your greeting committee," Adler said, eyeing Julie.

"Join the club. It's not very select."

"I believe that," Adler replied. He gave Julie a wink as he and Mosley headed toward the deputy DA's office.

Once they were seated, Mosley began. "The DA has a keen interest in this one," he said.

"I'm sure she does." Adler knew District Attorney Leslie Price to be an astute politician. This one would be high profile, and that meant high stakes. She would monitor every aspect of the case.

"So, do want the good news or the bad news?" Mosley asked.

Adler dropped his head and let out a sigh. "Bad news first."

"DA tells me the FBI has been sniffing around. They're sending over an agent from the Santa Rosa office."

"Shit," Adler said. "That's all I need, the feds bigfooting me on this. You got a name?"

Mosley checked a note on his desk. "Special Agent Rowan Parks. Ever heard of her?"

Adler shook his head. "She must be new. I know most of the agents in that office."

"Sorry, man. Maybe they'll take a pass. No reason to believe this isn't a state case."

"Yeah, well, the FBI could use all the good press they can get right now. If they want it, they'll find a hook."

Mosley nodded. It was a point that could not be denied.

"Any theories?" he asked.

"Not yet," Adler said. "Amato was a big spender: women, expensive toys, vacations. The surviving co-owner says he pumped a lot of money into the vineyard."

"Pavesi, right?"

"Yeah."

"So, KSFZ reported it was unknown whether he was considered a person of interest in the investigation."

"I heard." Adler was pissed off about the report and wondered if anyone in his office had been feeding them information.

"Anything to that?" Mosley asked. "Is Pavesi a viable suspect?"

Adler shrugged. "No more or less than anybody else at this point. But if you want my gut instinct, I'd say no."

"I hear you talked to an ex-girlfriend," Mosley said. "Anything there?"

Adler nodded. "Katina Orlov. Can't rule her out. She was obsessed with the guy. But when Estes and I told her how they found him, she seemed legitimately stunned."

Mosley made a note. "So, you want to start looking at the financials, see if anything points to someone with a possible motive." It wasn't a question.

"You got it."

"Okay," Mosley said, "let's put together a subpoena list."

CHAPTER 7

10:15 a.m., Monday, August 8, on State Route 12, northwest of Napa, California

It was about a half an hour to Napa on Route 12. FBI Special Agent Rowan Parks took in the scenery, reflecting on her decision to transfer to the West Coast. She liked the idea of working in wine country. And so far, it was a much more relaxed vibe than the constant hustle back east. The caseload might be a little different, but there would be plenty of challenging assignments coming out of the field office in San Francisco. Ultimately, she might prefer to be stationed there. But for now, she was content to work out of the satellite office in Santa Rosa.

It was Operation Knock Down that had introduced her to this part of the country. In a joint investigation with ATF, they had managed to decimate a radical environmentalist group known as the Earth Martyrs Brigade. No, *radical environmentalist* was the wrong term, she reminded herself. They were domestic terrorists, plain and simple, jihadists who would employ any tactic to accomplish their aims. It had been one of the most satisfying cases of her career, and one of the most dangerous. What she hadn't known at the beginning was that part of that danger would be to her heart. Maybe that was one of the reasons she was here now, to be close...just in case.

Parks shook her head to snap out of it. There was work to do, and this was a case with potential. It had already acquired significant media attention. She was sure that was why Nash had asked her to check it out. Still, she was new here. The vote of confidence was appreciated, particularly on a case that had garnered the attention of the SAC, Thurgood Perry. He was on the way up. This was a chance to make a good impression.

She planned to make the sheriff's office her first stop. It was a courtesy call. They were the lead agency on the investigation. Parks was sensitive to the concerns of the locals, at least she told herself that. She had been a cop, Chicago PD. But she had to admit, there were times when she took charge, forcefully if necessary. And sometimes it was necessary. She hoped this would not have to be one of those times.

Route 12 took Parks to the southern section of Napa. Parks turned right on Airport Boulevard and quickly found the sheriff's office. She had made a call on the way over, asking if she could meet with the lead investigator, a Detective Joe Adler. Parks had been told that the request would be passed along, whatever that meant. She hoped he would show. But if not, she could live with it. Her colleagues said Adler was solid, and that he would not be receptive to an FBI takeover. That was nothing new. She had her approach. The first step would be to attempt a good impression. After that, it was up to him.

Parks found a spot for her government ride, slipped out the driver's door, and headed inside. She flashed her credentials and was waved through with directions to the correct office. There, she was met with a skeptical look from the receptionist.

"Can I help you?" the woman asked.

"Special Agent Rowan Parks, FBI." She again displayed her credentials. "I'm here to see Detective Joe Adler."

The woman studied her for a moment before speaking. "He's been delayed," she said.

Parks took a breath. "Any idea how long?" she asked, pleasant as possible.

"Nope," the woman said, now studying something on her desk. "But you can have a seat over there." Without looking, she pointed to a small waiting area.

"Fine," Parks said. She took a seat, so far underwhelmed by the hospitality.

About ten minutes later a guy walked in. Parks could tell by the way he carried himself that he was law enforcement. She guessed it was Adler. He looked at the receptionist, who jerked her toward Parks. He walked toward her.

"You Parks?" he asked.

She stood. "I am."

"Detective Joe Adler." He extended his hand. "But I guess you knew that."

They shook. It was quick. Adler broke it off.

"So, are the feds here to poach my case?" he asked.

Parks stifled a sigh. "The SAC says to look into it, we look into it. Just want to find out if there is a federal angle, or if we can be of assistance."

"I've been the beneficiary of the FBI's *assistance* in the past," Adler said. "More like a hostile takeover."

Parks was losing patience. She took a step forward and placed her hands on her hips. "Look, I didn't have to make this *courtesy* call. You know damn well we can just step right in and what the Napa County Sheriff's Office thinks about it won't mean shit."

Parks caught a glimpse of the receptionist who had now sat up in her chair, eyebrows raised.

Adler chuckled. It wasn't the reaction she was expecting. He raised his hands as if in surrender. "Okay, okay," he said. "Guess I could have been a little more...open-minded. Follow me. I'll tell what we've got."

Adler led her down the hall to a small conference room and waved her in.

"Have a seat," he said, gesturing toward one of the chairs. He sat directly across from her. "I've had a couple bad experiences with the feds," he said.

Parks couldn't tell if it was a bad attempt at an apology, an explanation, or the start of another rant. She decided to give him the benefit of the doubt, and to cut it off before it went any further.

"I was a cop," she said, "Chicago PD. My dad was a cop. Nobody here was hatched a fed."

Adler looked her in the eye, nodded. The comment seemed to resonate. She sensed an opening.

"So, Raymond Amato," she said, getting down to it. "Tell me where you're at."

Adler summarized the investigation for her, the scene, the interviews, what he had learned about the guy. "We're about to start a deep dive into his finances," he said. "There's a motive in there somewhere."

Parks nodded. "Maybe we can help with that." She had to admit, it sounded as if Adler was off to a good start, and that he knew what he was doing. "So, it was a hit," she said, "and one meant to send a message."

"Looks like it," Adler replied.

"The question," Parks said, "is what message, and to whom."

CHAPTER 8

10:32 a.m., Wednesday, August 10, Amato Freight Lines Corporate Headquarters, Sacramento, California

Adler flipped through a magazine in the waiting area. He had been told that the comptroller would be with him shortly. The quick response was a surprise, the subpoena having been sent over shortly after noon on Monday. Normally, it took several days, if not weeks, to respond to a demand for this much data. Even Pavesi Vineyards' accountant said it would likely take them until at least Friday to put everything together. The state's attorney had asked for a broad spectrum of financial documents from Amato Freight Lines going back nine years, two full years before their founder had even invested in Pavesi Vineyards. From previous discussions with corporate officials, Adler had the impression that management was eager to help. That, and the fast turnaround, told him that the company probably had little to hide. But he knew better than to let appearances lead to presumptions or influence his path. You could trust your gut to an extent, but you still needed to run every lead to ground. Tunnel vision was the enemy of any good detective, a shortcut that provided fodder for defense attorneys. And Adler knew that a subpoena never guaranteed full compliance. Clever lawyers could construe them in endless ways, finding language that was *subject to interpretation*, even when the words seemed abundantly clear to anyone else. Besides that, it was the company that controlled the spigot on the flow of information, at least initially.

"Detective Adler?"

Adler turned to see a slender, balding man walking toward him, hand outstretched.

"Bob Ferguson, company controller."

They shook. "Yes, we spoke on the phone a few weeks ago after Ray went missing," Adler said.

"I recall," Ferguson said. "As you can imagine, everyone here is heartbroken that it ended like this."

"I'm sorry for your loss," Adler said. "And I appreciate the rapid compliance with our request."

"Well, it wasn't so much a request," Ferguson said, a half smile on his face. "Nonetheless, we're happy to help."

"Fair enough," Adler replied. "So, do you have some boxes for me?"

"Boxes?" Ferguson asked, seeming puzzled. "The subpoena didn't say anything about hard copies." He removed a flash drive from his shirt pocket. "It's all on here, almost a terabyte of information." He shook his head. "If we had printed this out, you would have needed a semi."

Adler sighed. He took the flash drive. The thought of the FBI's assistance on the forensic accounting was suddenly sounding more appealing.

"Wondered why you drove over," Ferguson said. "I could have just overnighted this to you."

"Sacramento isn't much of a drive," Adler replied. "And as long as I'm here, mind if I ask you a few questions?" It had been his plan to interview the accountant all along.

"Not at all," Ferguson answered. "Like I said, happy to help."

Adler looked around. There had been consistent foot traffic through the area while they had talked. "Can we go someplace more private?"

"Oh, of course," Ferguson said. "Apologies. Follow me."

They reached a small office. Pictures of the comptroller and his family were propped up here and there. The room was heavy on computer monitors, but not on paper.

"Have a seat," Ferguson said, gesturing toward a chair.

Adler sat down and pulled a notepad and pen. "I know we've talked before, but just a few follow-up questions in case anything else has occurred to you. Did Ray have any enemies, anyone who might want to do him harm?"

Ferguson shook his head. "Not that I'm aware of. He was generally well-liked by everyone here and respected in the industry."

"Generally?" Adler asked.

"Oh, you know, there are always those people who are chronic malcontents, some of whom you have to let go."

"Sure," Adler said, nodding. "Any of them make threats or seem like they were capable of violence?"

"Nobody springs to mind," Ferguson said. "Most of us in management have been here for years. And any firings of drivers, warehouse workers, that sort of thing, would have been handled by someone else."

"Okay," Adler said. He paused for a moment, then leaned in a bit. "I'm sorry to have to ask you this, but I'm sure you'll understand why it's important. Did you ever come across any evidence that Ray might be stealing from the company?"

The beginnings of a smile curled up on one side of Ferguson's mouth. "You gotta understand, Ray started this business, built it from nothing. It's a closely held corporation, with most of the stock held by his family. I doubt you could find any chief executive under those circumstances who hasn't used a few company assets for personal pleasure. But if you mean real theft, siphoning off corporate profits, that sort of thing...No, never."

"Understood," Adler said. He made a note, wondering if what Ferguson said was true, or if it was an example of admitting only what you had to. It occurred to him that the one terabyte data dump might be designed to bury something.

"One more question," Adler continued. "Did Ray ever ask you anything about the company's finances or, for that matter, his personal finances that you found to be...suspicious?" He looked up from the notepad, watching Ferguson's response.

"No, no," Ferguson said, smiling, both hands raised as if to ward off the question. "Nothing like that."

The smile was too quick, like a nervous habit. Adler thought the response exaggerated. A simple *no* would have sufficed. He closed his notepad.

"Very good." Adler rose from the chair. "Thank you. I'll show myself out."

CHAPTER 9

3:38 p.m., Friday, August 12, Napa County Sheriff's Office, 1535 Airport Blvd, Napa, California

Adler sat back in his chair. He clasped his hands behind his head and closed his eyes. A long sigh escaped.

"Yes?" Estes asked, the hint of a smirk on his face.

"I got a C plus in accounting," Adler said. "I might be in a little over my head." He hated to admit it, but it was true. Double E had pushed for enlisting the FBI's assistance. Now, he was going to have to hear the *I told you so*, even if it wasn't said in so many words.

"Not gonna say it," Estes announced. "Not gonna say it."

Adler looked at him. "I think you've said enough."

"You gonna call her?" Estes asked.

Adler rubbed his forehead. He was through maybe one percent of the content on the flash drive Ferguson gave him. That morning, he had received the documents requested from the accounting firm for Pavesi Vineyards, also on a memory stick. And now there was a package on his desk from Amato's personal accountant.

"No más," Adler exclaimed, raising his hands in the air. "I'm done. You win."

"We all win," Estes said.

Adler fished the phone out of his jacket pocket and pulled up

33

his contacts. There she was, *Parks, Rowan*. He hesitated for a second, then tapped her number, raising the cell to his ear.

"Good boy," Estes said.

Adler shot him a look that said, *don't push it*.

Parks didn't answer right away. There was one ring, two, three. He envisioned her staring at the name on the screen, a smug look on her face, taking satisfaction in another local begging for help. He was about to terminate the call when she picked up.

"Detective Adler," she said. "What can I do for you?"

Adler took a deep breath. "We could use some help with the accounting," he mumbled.

"I'm sorry. What's that?"

Adler sighed. "We could use some help with the forensic accounting," he said. "Does your offer still stand?" He glanced at Double E, who was grinning a little too broadly. Adler flipped him off.

"Sure," Parks replied. "I just have to sell it to management. But that won't be a problem."

"Thanks," Adler said. Even he was underwhelmed with his lack of enthusiasm and thought better of it. "Seriously. Thank you."

"Anything new since our last talk?" Parks asked. "I want to be able to give them the complete picture, just in case I get some unexpected resistance."

"Maybe," Adler replied. He described Ferguson's reaction to his question about any suspicious inquiries from Amato.

"Noted," Parks said. "Anything else?"

Adler picked up the rap sheet on his desk. "I mentioned that we interviewed the two workers who pulled the wine barrel off the rack."

"Yeah, I recall that," Parks said. "One of them gave you some attitude, might have been holding back."

"Right," Adler said. "Jesse Morgan. Don't know if this is anything or not, but he has an assault conviction out of Brooklyn. There are also a couple of arrests on theft charges. Both of those cases were dropped."

"Interesting," Parks said. "I'll make a call to the New York office."

"I thought you might."

"I'll be in touch," Parks said. She ended the call.

It was a short walk to the office of Supervisory Special Agent Brad Harrison. Even though ASAC Nash outranked him and had called her directly about looking into the case, a line agent followed protocol, and that meant going through the chain of command. Harrison ran the Santa Rosa office. She had to wonder if the call from Nash to her rankled him. She was guessing yes. It was an affront. Maybe there was some history between the two. All Parks knew was that she had seen this sort of bypass maneuver before. It could cause problems for the field agent involved, and that was not how she wanted to start her detail here.

Harrison's door was open. Parks could see him at the desk. She knocked. He looked up and waved her in.

"Got a minute to talk about the Amato case?" she asked.

"There's no case yet," Harrison replied. He pointed to a chair. "Have a seat."

Parks didn't like the way this was starting out. She wanted to try to get ahead of it. "Nash should have called you first," she said.

Harrison just stared at her for what seemed like ten minutes. "Not your fault," he finally said. "But if you're gonna brief me, we better get Nash on the phone."

Parks nodded. Harrison picked up the phone and dialed.

"Kurt? It's Brad Harrison. I've got Special Agent Parks here. She wants to talk about the Amato situation over in Napa."

Parks noted the terminology, *situation* not *case*. She again wondered if Harrison was going to push back against FBI involvement.

"Mind if I put you on speaker?" Harrison asked. "Okay. Hold on." He hit the speaker button and put the handset down.

"Rowan, how are you?" Nash asked over the speaker. Parks wished he had stuck with *special agent*.

"I'm good."

"Give us your assessment," Nash said.

Parks summarized what she had learned from Adler, including his impressions from interviewing the comptroller, Ferguson, and Jesse Morgan. "Turns out Morgan has some history," she said. "There's an assault conviction in Brooklyn, and a couple of theft charges that were later dropped."

"Have you called New York?" Nash asked.

"Next thing on my list," Parks said, "assuming I get the go-ahead."

"So, what's the federal hook?" Harrison asked.

"Don't know yet," Parks replied. She had a thought but didn't want to put herself out there with some unsubstantiated speculation. If it didn't pan out, Harrison might be inclined to use it against her later. "Right now, I would call this more of an assist to the locals. They clearly need some help with the forensic accounting."

"Okay," Nash said. "Open a case. I've got an agent over here who is a CPA. This is right up her alley. I'll have her get in touch." He hung up.

"Well," Harrison said, "I guess it's a case now."

Parks wanted to leave before there was any further discussion. "Right," she said. "I'll go make that phone call to New York."

CHAPTER 10

6:14 a.m., Saturday, August 13, Jake's Peak, West Shore, Lake Tahoe, California

It was widely considered to be the best view of the lake, one of the few spots from which the entire body of water was visible, and Special Agent David Ward now witnessed its majesty at sunrise. The clouds were yellow, orange, and purple, casting their reflection across the water and framing the mountains with their vivid hues. In *Roughing It*, Mark Twain had said of Lake Tahoe, "It must surely be the fairest picture the whole world affords." And to Ward, there could be no fairer picture than what he saw before him. It had been well worth the effort of climbing the 9,187-foot peak the day before and camping overnight.

Ward breathed in the crisp mountain air, slowly inhaling and exhaling. A calm settled over him. It had long been his tradition to seek peace and rejuvenation in the wilderness following a long undercover mission. This time the pilgrimage had been delayed. His infiltration of the Ozark Militia had ended months earlier, but the ramifications of what transpired continued to resonate throughout Washington and the nation. It had been a case of modest beginnings that ended as possibly the most significant of his career. But now, finally, he was where he needed to be.

The plan was to hike the Tahoe Rim Trail, a 165-mile journey that he hoped would condition his body and start to soothe his mind. There was a darkness that hovered near, ever-present, fueled by the evil that he too often witnessed up close. How much was more than a person could bear, enough to break a mind. He wondered when this cycle of going undercover, becoming a wholly different person, each time losing a bit of himself, would end. There would come a time, either by burnout, breakdown...or violence. And there was the loneliness that came with it, one unique to the deep cover operative. Like many, he had no family to welcome him home. Maria had left long ago, weary of their empty, childless home, not knowing if he would live or die, not knowing if he would return at all.

The sunrise reminded him of his mother. She was always awake long before the rest of the family, coffee made, out on her porch listening to the dawn chorus of birds chirping at the first light of day. He smiled at the memory. But the view also caused him to recall another dawn, that of the new millennium, when the leader of a cult known as The Church of the Father Eye convinced his followers to commit mass suicide. One of those followers was his sister, Lori. His parents never recovered, never returned to anything like a normal life. And neither had he. The group's leader, Reverend Jeremiah Boothe, had exploited the members, both financially and sexually. Lori was no exception. Boothe's hold on her was complete. At his urging, she completely severed ties with the family. Their many attempts to save her all ended the same way, total failure. It reminded Ward again that there were bad people in the world, people who had to be dealt with...and that he had the skills to do so.

Ward took another deep breath and shook it off. Now was not the time, and this was certainly not the place. He would enjoy the moment, try to live in it. Still, he knew that when duty called, he would answer.

CHAPTER 11

10:32 a.m., Monday, August 15, on Interstate 680 north of San Jose, California

Parks had offered to drive, picking up Adler on the way south. They had been in the car for almost an hour. The trip down had forced them to get to know more about each other. Being trapped together in a moving vehicle could do that. Adler had clearly been uncomfortable at first, but Parks got him to open up, talk about his family. That was the plan. It helped. She could sense the beginnings of something like trust.

They had an appointment to interview Amato's ex-wife, Gloria. She was a marketing executive for Starbird Technologies at their headquarters in San Jose. Parks had arranged the meeting. The request had been received with a hint of puzzlement, as if she could have nothing to offer. But Parks knew better. A former spouse, even if not a suspect, could provide insight unlike anyone else.

"You know anything about this company?" Adler asked.

"Mid-tier cybersecurity firm," Parks said. "Not a big player, but a solid book of business. Wall Street sees them as a buy."

Adler nodded approvingly. "Sounds like you did your homework."

Parks looked at him. "I always do."

"I have no doubt."

Interstate 680 turned into 280. A few minutes later, Parks found her exit and headed north into downtown. Starbird was located on two floors of a small office building in the middle of the city, having not quite risen to the level of its own campus. The flashing blue dot on the vehicle's navigation system showed that they were getting close.

"There it is," Parks said.

She circled the block and found a spot. They exited and made their way to the building. A security guard was stationed near the door. Parks flashed her badge, eliminating inquiry. She checked the building directory, then headed for the elevator. The doors opened onto the fifth floor and a workspace that screamed Silicon Valley. There were no individual offices. Nap pods were scattered here and there. Attire was beyond casual. No receptionist could be seen. Eventually, a young man rolled up to them on a skateboard.

"I'm Marcus," the young man said. Then there was silence. It was apparently their turn.

Parks looked at Adler and then back to Marcus. "Hello, Marcus. I'm Special Agent Rowan Parks." She held up her credentials.

Marcus seemed unimpressed. He stepped on the back of his skateboard causing the front to pop up and caught it with his hand, all in one seamless move.

"Okay," he said.

Parks let out a soft sigh. "We have an appointment with Gloria Amato."

Marcus nodded. "Okay." There was no movement.

Parks stared at him for a moment. "Could you go get her?"

"Oh, yeah." He dropped the skateboard to the floor and rolled away.

Parks turned to Adler. "What the fuck?"

Adler shook his head.

Moments later, a statuesque brunette approached. Parks

guess her to be in her mid-fifties. Her jeans, blouse, and jacket were casual, but certainly more professional than anything worn by her counterparts.

"Special Agent Parks?" She extended a hand. "I'm Gloria Amato."

Parks shook. "This is Detective Joe Adler of the Napa County Sheriff's Office."

Adler nodded.

"Detective," Gloria said. "So, you want to talk about Ray. Of course, I've heard what happened, the details. The kids are just in shock. I don't know that I can be of much help, but I'm happy to provide any information that I can."

"We appreciate that," Parks said. She looked around. "Is there any place we can talk that isn't so...out in the open?"

Gloria smiled and nodded. "Of course."

She led them to a large, glass-walled conference room. Parks was pleased to see that it had a door.

"Please have a seat," Gloria said.

Parks and Adler sat on one side of a long table. Gloria sat facing them.

"Can I get you something to drink?" Gloria asked. "Coffee, juice, water?"

"No, thank you," Parks said.

Adler waved his hand. "Nothing for me, thanks."

Parks sat her phone on the table. "Would you mind if I record this?" she asked.

Gloria's brow furrowed. "Well, I guess not," she replied.

"It's just easier and more accurate than taking notes," Parks said.

"Okay."

"So, how long ago were you and Ray divorced?" Parks asked.

"It's been seventeen years," Gloria replied. "The kids were little, four and six."

"And you kept his last name?" Parks asked.

"Because of the kids."

Parks nodded. "I know this is not a simple question, but what led to the divorce?"

Gloria snorted. "A lot of things," she said. "Ray had just started the company. He was consumed with it, spent less and less time with the family. And I, admittedly, was not the risk-taker that he was, something he frequently pointed out. We were always on the financial edge, one step from bankruptcy. I wanted him to find something with a stable paycheck. I mean, we had little kids."

"It seems he was eventually quite successful," Parks noted. "Did you resent that?"

Gloria tipped her head to one side, a slight squint to her eyes. "Maybe...just a little."

"Were you surprised by his success?" Adler asked.

"Not really. Ray always did find a way to make it happen, get the next contract, pay off the loan."

"About that," Parks said. "Who were his creditors back then?"

Gloria shrugged. "He had bank loans, a business line of credit."

"Anything unusual about his financing?" Parks asked.

"I can remember a time when things were pretty bleak," Gloria replied. "There wasn't much business. He was having a hard time getting any of the banks to lend to him."

"What happened?"

"All of a sudden it was okay," she said. "I can remember asking him about it. He would change the subject, tell me not to worry about it."

Parks looked at Adler, then back to Gloria. "Did you ever learn more about what happened, where the money came from?"

Gloria shook her head. "No. Ray was very vague about it. He always did keep a lot of details to himself. That was one of our problems, lack of communication." She paused. "That, and the secrets."

"What kinds of secrets?" Parks asked.

Gloria looked her in the eye. "An affair," she said. "And the money—our money—that he was spending on the bitch."

"Got it," Parks said. "How have things been between the two of you since the divorce?"

"Okay, I guess," Gloria replied. "It wasn't good at first, but things improved. We tried to get along for the kids' sake."

"And what was his involvement with them?"

"Limited. Visitation was spotty. At first, he did okay. But as they got older, it tapered off, almost completely. He paid his child support. Or, I should say, he paid it once he was successful. When Ray had a little money, he liked to throw it around. And that was a lot of his involvement with the kids, trying to buy their affection. Not the greatest parenting technique"

"Understood," Parks said. "And what are the kids doing now?"

Gloria smiled. "Andrea will be a senior at Stanford," she said. "Nathan is a set designer in Los Angeles." The smile faded a bit. "Wouldn't have been my first choice of a career for him. Ray, on the other hand, supported the idea. It was his way of currying favor, trying to build some sort of bond with Nate."

"Did that make you angry?" Parks asked.

"Well, the bonding sort of centered around making Mom the enemy. Yeah, it aggravated me. But it's something most divorced couples deal with."

"Did he ever try to bring the kids into the business?" Adler asked.

"Andrea worked for him one summer," Gloria replied. "It didn't work out. She got tired of seeing her dad drunk all the time, a new bimbo on his arm every month."

"How did the kids feel about their dad?" Parks asked.

Gloria sighed and looked away, a sadness in her eyes. "They loved their dad," she said. "They just learned to lower their expectations."

Parks paused to give her a moment. It was time to wrap this up.

"Do you know of anyone who would want to hurt Ray?" Parks asked.

Gloria looked at her. "May be one of his ex-girlfriends. Other than that, I would have no idea." She leaned forward. "Like I said, we got along fine after the divorce. It was a lot easier to be his ex than it was to be his wife."

CHAPTER 12

12:35 p.m., Wednesday, August 17, Napa County Sheriff's Office, 1535 Airport Blvd, Napa, California

Adler looked at his watch. Morgan was late, of course. He was asked to come over the lunch hour. They just had a few follow-up questions. At least, that's what they told him. That, and it would be best to avoid any embarrassment at the vineyard. Basically, the message was you come to us or we'll come to you. The reality was they simply didn't want to draw too much attention to the fact that they were taking another run at him. Right now, everybody was a suspect and there was no reason to put an exclamation point on who was being pressured.

Parks had driven over for the interview. Double E was in the building, so Adler had asked him to sit in as well. The show of force could sometimes cause a subject to crack. You just had to make sure that everybody played their part.

"Looks like a no-show," Estes said, standing to stretch. "He might force our hand, make us go to the vineyard."

"I don't want to do that," Adler said. They couldn't force him to come in, not at this point. Besides, that had its own complications. As it was, even if he did show they would have to make it clear that he was free to leave at any time. The alternative was to read him his Miranda rights, something that had caused many an interview to auger in right out of the gate.

"If he doesn't show, we'll find a place away from work," Parks said. "I don't want anybody there to know we're working him. And it might not hurt to catch him off guard."

Estes nodded. "Understood."

Adler turned to Parks. "Tell him what you found about our friend," he said. She had briefed him on what she learned about Morgan from the New York office but wanted Estes to hear it from her.

"You know about his rap sheet, right?" Parks asked.

Estes nodded. "An assault. A couple of thefts that got dropped."

"Right," Parks said. "Dropped because the victims refused to come forward. And word is, the assault was on a store owner who refused to pay protection money."

"Are you telling me this guy is Mafia?" Estes asked.

"New York thinks he's a low-level associate of the Genovese family," Parks said.

"The guy's name is *Morgan*," Estes said.

"His mom is a Bellomo," Parks replied. "Liborio Salvatore Bellomo is the current head of the family."

"Well, that raises some interesting questions," Estes said. "Doesn't it?"

The phone on Adler's desk started to ring. He picked it up. "Okay," he said. "I'll be out in a minute."

"He showed?" Parks asked.

"He did." Adler stood up. "Everybody ready?" he asked.

"Ready," Parks said.

"Let's do it," Estes agreed.

"Okay," Adler said. "I'll bring him to interview room two."

Estes nodded. "We'll be waiting."

Adler walked out to the lobby. Morgan was there, smug look already planted on his face.

"Thanks for coming," Adler said. He did not extend a hand.

Morgan snorted. "Like I had a choice."

Adler was now picking up on the Brooklyn accent that he had missed before. "Totally voluntary," he said. "You can leave at any time."

"And then what?" Morgan asked. "You harass me at the vineyard? I know how this works."

I doubt that, Adler thought. The way he figured it, Morgan was just a brain stem that would follow orders.

"Follow me," Adler said. He led Morgan to the interview room and pushed open the door. "After you."

"Who's the chick?" Morgan asked.

Parks raised her eyebrows. Adler hoped she didn't pistol whip the dumbass right out of the gate.

"Special Agent Rowan Parks," she said, "FBI."

Adler pulled out a chair for Morgan. "Have a seat," he said. He then took his place with the others on the opposite side of the table.

"Why are the feds involved?" Morgan asked, looking at Adler.

"We'll ask the questions," Adler said.

Parks pulled out her phone and placed it in the middle of the table. "I'll be recording this interview," she announced.

Adler knew she had to be aware of the video system in the interview room. He wondered if it was an FBI thing, not trusting the locals to hit the record button.

Parks glanced at him, apparently reading his mind. "I like to have my own copy," she explained. "It helps when I'm writing reports."

Adler nodded but was skeptical.

"What if I'm not okay with that?" Morgan asked.

"It's for your protection and mine," Parks said. She started the recording, noted the date and time, and began some introductory remarks. "This is Special Agent Rowan Parks. We are present for the interview of Jesse Morgan. Also present are Napa County Sheriff's Office detectives Joe Adler and Enrique Estes. Mr. Morgan, this is a voluntary interview. You are free to leave at any time. Do you understand that?"

Morgan smirked. "Yeah, I understand that."

"Good," Parks said. "Now, you work at Pavesi Vineyards, is that correct?"

"You already know that," Morgan replied.

Parks stared at him. "Do you work at Pavesi Vineyards?"

Morgan shrugged. "Yeah, I guess so."

"You guess so?"

Morgan leaned forward. "Yeah, I work there. So what?"

Adler could see this was not going to go well.

"How'd you get the job?" Parks asked.

Morgan sat back in the chair and crossed his arms. "Friend of a friend," he said.

"Either of these friends got a name?" Parks asked.

"Yeah, Paul and Shorty."

Parks sighed. "Last names?"

"I don't recall."

"Seriously?" Estes asked.

Morgan looked at him. "I don't recall."

"Do you recall how you got to California?" Parks asked.

"How do you know I wasn't born here?" Morgan asked.

"Okay," Parks said, "let's talk about how I know that." She pulled out a copy of his rap sheet and tossed it on the table. "An assault conviction in Brooklyn. Two theft charges that were dropped, likely due to witness intimidation. You would be that same Jesse Morgan, correct?"

"Youthful indiscretions," Morgan announced. "I've changed my ways."

"Have you?" Parks asked. "So, you're no longer affiliated with the Genovese crime family?"

Morgan laughed. "Unsubstantiated rumors," he said.

"So, it's not true?" Adler asked.

"I don't even know what you're talkin' about," Morgan said.

"Let's lay it all out there," Parks said. "We think you had something to do with what happened to Ray Amato. We don't necessarily think you killed him. Maybe you just helped dispose of the body, you know, send a message."

"And let me guess," Morgan said, "this is where you give me a chance to help myself."

"This is your chance," Parks said.

"No," Morgan said, "this is bullshit. I don't know nothin' about nothin'." He stood. "I believe you said I'm free to leave."

"Correct," Parks said.

"Well, I'm leavin'."

Adler looked at Parks and shook his head. He got up and escorted Morgan from the building.

CHAPTER 13

*10:23 p.m., Friday, August 19, Federal Bureau of Investigation,
Santa Rosa Resident Agency, Santa Rosa, California*

Parks escorted Adler and Estes into a conference room. Official
photographs of the president and vice president adorned the
wall at one end of the room. The director's photo stared at
them from the opposite wall. A U.S. flag stood in the corner.
The furniture was, to put it mildly, of a higher quality than that
found in the sheriff's office. And it occurred to Adler that this
was just a resident agency. He wondered what the Bureau had
for furnishings in San Francisco.

A diminutive, bookish woman stood as they entered. Two
laptops were opened on the table before her, and one of those
was connected to an external monitor. The eyes behind her
glasses were bright, lively with intelligence. She seemed to exude
competence.

"This is Special Agent Carly Holt," Parks said. "She is a
CPA and one of our best forensic accountants."

Holt nodded pleasantly. She seemed happy to be there, eager
to share her findings.

"Detectives Adler and Estes," Parks continued, "Napa County
Sheriff's Office." She gestured for them to take a seat.

"So," Holt began, getting right to it, "I have burrowed into these records. Two things are interesting, what I did find and what I didn't find."

"What do you mean?" Adler asked.

"Well, Amato was clearly a man who lived beyond his means," Holt said, "even though his means were considerable."

"That seemed to be the consensus of everyone we talked to," Adler replied. "That doesn't make him unusual. Living on credit has replaced baseball as the national pastime."

"No doubt," Holt said. "But his personal spending and business investments are only partially covered by his income, credit card debt, or any standard loans."

Estes leaned forward, resting his elbows on the table. "And by partially you mean...?"

"Just over a third," Holt replied. "At most, forty percent." She looked at them expectantly, waiting for the next question.

"So, where's the money coming from?" Adler asked.

"Where it's not coming from," Holt said, "is the business. He is not stealing from Amato Freight Lines. I have to admit, I was a little surprised by that."

"As am I," Adler said. "Begs the question, who was his creditor?"

"And what was the interest rate?" Parks added.

Holt shrugged. "There's no record of it here," she said, her hands gesturing toward the laptops.

"When he went missing, was there any financial or digital trail at all?" Parks asked.

Adler shook his head. "No debit or credit card activity, no phone calls to or from any of his friends or family, no ATM withdrawals. There was nothing. The guy just vanished."

"Until the head showed up," Parks said, "in a way clearly calculated to send a message." She looked around the room. "Are we all thinking the same thing?"

CHAPTER 14

9:52 a.m., Tuesday, August 23, Pavesi Vineyards, Napa Valley, California

Parks pulled into the guest lot at the vineyard. It was a beautiful morning in wine country, seventy-two degrees under a cobalt blue sky. But for a murder investigation, it would be a great day to take leave and tour the valley. As it was, the forensic examination of Amato's financial records made it clear that they would need to take another run at Martin Pavesi. There were tough questions that needed to be asked. And this time they were showing up unannounced, allowing Pavesi no time to prepare. Maybe they could rattle him and shake loose some previously undisclosed truths.

Parks turned to Adler. "You ready?"

"Born ready," he replied.

The way he said it, so matter-of-fact, Parks believed it to be true.

"Showtime," she said.

They exited her government ride and headed toward the main entrance. Parks spotted a woman on the patio, rearranging chairs. They headed her way.

"Is that Audra Pavesi?" she asked.

"It is," Adler replied. "I'll warn you. She's the protective type."

"Understood."

"Good morning, Ms. Pavesi," Adler called out.

Audra spun around. Her eyebrows raised. She seemed surprised, not in a good way.

"Good morning, Detective." She hesitated, now looking concerned. "Do you have some news?"

"I'm afraid not," Adler said. "We'd like to speak with Mr. Pavesi. Just a few follow-up questions."

"And who is we?" Audra asked, looking at Parks.

"My apologies," Adler said. "This is…"

"Special Agent Rowan Parks, Federal Bureau of Investigation," Parks interjected. She displayed her credentials. "Pleasure to meet you."

"I wasn't aware the FBI was involved," Audra said.

"We neglected to send out a press release," Parks replied. Her dad had always said she was a natural born smartass.

Adler shot Parks a look, then turned back to Audra. "Is Mr. Pavesi available?" he asked. "It should only take a few minutes."

"I'll check," Audra replied, eyeing Parks. She left and went inside.

"Apparently, I'll be playing good cop today," Adler observed.

"Sorry," Parks said. She was…sort of.

A few minutes later, Martin Pavesi emerged, Audra at his side.

"Detective," he said.

"And this is Special Agent Parks," Audra proclaimed, gesturing.

"Pleased to have the FBI's involvement," Pavesi said. He turned to Adler. "No offense."

"None taken," Adler replied. He glanced at Parks. "Always happy to work with our federal *partners*."

"Is there somewhere we can talk in private?" Parks asked.

Pavesi looked around. "We can talk here on the patio," he said. "I wouldn't anticipate any guests for another hour or so."

Parks looked at Audra. "I mean…*in private*."

Audra turned to her husband and touched his arm. "Marty?"

"It's fine, dear," Pavesi said, patting her hand.

Audra excused herself as they all took seats at one of the patio tables.

"Our forensic analysis of Mr. Amato's financial records raised some questions," Parks began.

"Okay," Pavesi replied. "That doesn't have anything to do with me, or the vineyard."

"I'm not necessarily saying that it does," Parks said. "But he did invest a lot of money here, correct?"

"He did."

"And that money came from somewhere, correct?"

"Obviously."

"Well, Mr. Amato appears to have been greatly overextended. And that raises some questions."

Pavesi's brow furrowed. "I wasn't aware," he said.

"And that's why we're here," Parks said, "to see if there were any indicators of trouble that you might have noticed, or that he may have alluded to."

Pavesi nodded. "Nothing comes to mind," he said. "But please, ask your questions. Maybe it will jar something loose."

Parks pulled out a notepad and pen. They seemed to be off on a positive foot. She decided to forego recording the interview, thinking it might make Pavesi less cooperative.

"Did Mr. Amato ever talk to you about any financial problems, mention that money's a little tight, anything like that?"

Pavesi shook his head. "Not that I can recall."

"Not that you can recall?" Parks repeated. It wasn't her favorite answer, often indicating deception. Or at least a willful blindness.

"Ray was so self-assured," Pavesi replied, a half smile appearing on his face. "Everything was always great with him, positive. He was an upbeat guy. Some of that was salesmanship, no question. But you believed it, you know? He just wasn't the type to show a chink in that armor. I doubt he would have mentioned it if there was a problem." Pavesi lowered his head and paused, then looked back up at Parks. "Well, I guess he didn't, did he?"

"I guess not," Parks replied. "Did he ever say where he got the money to invest in the vineyard?"

"I just assumed it was income and profits from the trucking company," Pavesi answered. "Maybe I should have asked more questions. I don't know. We were just happy to have the injection of capital."

"Were you having problems?" Adler asked.

Pavesi shrugged. "I would just say that it came at the right time."

"Did he gamble?" Parks asked.

Pavesi gave a little snort. "Ray liked to bet on sports, football games mostly. And he would head over to Reno about once a month. No high-stakes poker or anything like that, no ponies."

Parks nodded. "Vegas?" she asked.

"Yeah," Pavesi answered. "Maybe once a year."

"So, there was at least the possibility of a problem?"

"He never mentioned any gambling losses," Pavesi replied. "But yeah, I guess so."

"You ever go with him?" Adler asked.

"Not my thing. The money was too hard to come by in the first place."

Adler nodded. "I hear that."

"What about threats?" Parks asked. "Did he ever say anything about being threatened?"

Pavesi shook his head. "No. I never heard anything like that."

Parks thought for a moment. "Did he ever act like he thought someone was following him, watching him?"

Pavesi sat forward, resting his elbows on the table. "You know, he did. I never really gave it much thought until now. But when we would go out to a bar or restaurant, he would scan the room, repeatedly. I thought he was just checking out the women, seeing if any clients were there, that sort of thing. But in retrospect, maybe he was doing some kind of security check."

Parks made a note, then continued. "When you were in the car with him, did he ever do anything that, looking back on it, might have been an evasive maneuver?"

"Such as?"

"Inexplicably circling the block, suddenly accelerating, hitting the brakes for no apparent reason, something like that?"

Pavesi thought for a moment. "I can't recall anything like that. But then, we didn't ride together that often. We usually just met at whatever establishment we were going to."

"Did he do drugs?" Adler asked.

"Smoked a little pot," Pavesi said, "like a lot of people these days."

"Do you know where he got it?" Adler continued.

Pavesi shook his head. "Didn't ask. And I don't partake."

"Understood," Adler said. "I have to ask: did he know any drug dealers? I mean, they're not unknown to Napa Valley."

"No, they're not," Pavesi acknowledged. "But I'm not aware of him having any associations like that. And I do not, if that's your next question."

"Fair enough," Adler said.

Parks leaned in, studying Pavesi. "What about any Mafia types? Are you aware of any *associations* along those lines?"

Pavesi was silent for a moment, giving her a cool look. When he spoke, it was clear that he meant his words to be taken seriously. "First of all," he said, "I'm not aware of any such *associations*. Furthermore, I grew up around that and wanted nothing to do with it. If I thought that Ray was involved with the Mob in any way, we would not have been partners." He sat back in his chair. "You can write *that* in your little notebook. Got it?"

"Yeah," Parks said, "I got it."

Parks waited until they were close to the car, out of earshot. "You think he was a little *too* defensive on the Mafia thing?" she asked.

"I don't know, maybe," Adler replied. "Maybe he was just pissed off because he's Italian and thought you were making assumptions."

Parks nodded. She might have handled it better. But then, rattling the interview subject was what often yielded the best results. And it was a question that had to be asked.

CHAPTER 15

Parks waited outside the office of Special Agent in Charge Thurgood Perry. Her supervisor, Brad Harrison, sat two chairs down. They had driven over separately. It was telling. Harrison gave some bullshit excuse about wanting to make a couple of stops in town before heading back. It was fine with Parks. Here and back, it would have been two hours of painful, forced conversation. Instead, she had enjoyed the scenery and listened to reggae. It calmed her.

The door opened. Assistant Special Agent in Charge Kurt Nash appeared. He smiled at Parks. The smile faded slightly when he nodded his greeting to Harrison.

"He's ready to see you," Nash said, waving them in.

Harrison maneuvered around Parks so that he could enter first. Parks ignored it, but Nash noticed. There was a sigh, a shake of the head. Harrison was oblivious, too consumed with getting to his audience with the SAC. He charged in.

Perry stood, extending his hand. "Brad. Good to see you." The affect was flat.

"Great to see you, Thurgood," Harrison said, exuberant. "Always happy to come to Frisco."

Parks winced. She glanced at Nash in time to see him roll his eyes.

"Rowan," Perry said, coming around the desk. "Glad to have you here." They shook hands. "Please, have a seat."

Parks was directed to one of the two chairs directly in front of the SAC's desk. Nash took the other. Harrison was relegated to a couch along the wall. He sank in, sitting nearly a foot lower than everyone else. Perry moved back behind his desk.

"So," Perry said, looking at Parks, "why should we stay in this, not turn it back over to the locals?"

Right to the point, Parks thought. But then, they all knew why they were there.

"Amato had a lot of debt," Parks said. "After a thorough forensic analysis of his finances, we cannot determine where he got the money to invest in the winery. The investigators all believe that Amato's creditor had to be the Mob or one of the cartels."

"I've read your reports," Perry said. "Where's the evidence for that, other than a head in a barrel?"

Parks knew this was coming. It was a fair question.

"We know the cartels have put money into the wine industry in the past. And, of course, the Mob and booze go back to the days of Prohibition. Amato's funds clearly did not come from legitimate sources. It's the only explanation that makes sense. Besides, both of them are all about sending a message, and Amato's head in a wine barrel sure seems like it was meant to send a message to somebody."

"Who?" Harrison asked, scooting forward to the edge of the couch.

"That's one of the things we need to find out," Parks replied.

Harrison shook his head. "All speculation," he said. "We've got bigger battles to fight. I say our resources are better used elsewhere."

Parks took a breath, then another. She couldn't react to Harrison.

"I think Rowan's right," Nash said. "There's something

significant here. I can smell it."

Perry nodded. Parks could already tell that he respected Nash's opinion. She was happy to have the ASAC's support, even though she knew it was going to complicate her relationship with Harrison.

Perry rested his chin in his hand, studying Parks. "You've done a lot of good work for the Bureau," he said. "I'm inclined to trust your instincts."

Parks couldn't help the smile that crept onto one corner of her mouth. She glanced at Harrison. He was studying his feet, clearly unhappy.

"So," Perry continued, "if I okay this, what's our plan of action?"

Parks knew that Perry had done undercover work and valued it. "I think we need someone on the inside," she said.

"Inside what?" Harrison asked, his disgust apparent.

"The wine industry," Parks said, "in Napa. Somebody who knows how to work their way in, be in the right place, ask the right questions, keep their ears open."

"That sounds like an open-ended path to nothing," Harrison said.

Parks knew that she was out on a limb here but saw no other way forward. "There's something here," she said. "I know it. I can feel it. The way Martin Pavesi described Amato's behavior, looking over his shoulder, always aware of his surroundings. He was afraid of someone. There is some dark presence at work in this industry. And I want to know what it is."

Perry looked at Nash, who nodded his agreement.

"Okay," Perry said. "I'll let you run with this...for a while."

Parks could her a faint groan coming from Harrison. She suppressed a smile.

Perry leveled a look at Harrison, then turned back to Parks. "Now, who do we have in mind as the undercover?" he asked.

"I worked with an ATF agent by the name of David Ward in Operation Knock Down," Parks said. "I know you're familiar with the case. It resulted in the dismantling of the Earth Martyrs Brigade."

"I am familiar with it," Perry said, "and your contribution to the case. It was good work."

"Thank you," Parks replied, "but it was mostly Ward. I worked closely with him on the case. He's simply the best."

"Very closely," Harrison interjected, "at least that's what I hear."

Parks's blood started to boil. Suddenly, she did not give a shit that Harrison was her immediate supervisor.

"No need to insinuate," she said, now staring at Harrison. "What's the concern?"

"Several," Harrison answered. "I'm *concerned* that you're too close to him to be the case agent on this. Perhaps more importantly, I see no reason to involve ATF. Why cede any control to them? Why not use one of our people?"

Parks could see Perry studying her, waiting for an answer. "First of all," she said, "we did have a relationship. That is no longer the case. That fact does not stop me from recognizing that he is one of the most talented undercover operatives in the country. He is the one who brought down The Nation, a white supremacist, anti-immigrant vigilante group that tried to assassinate President Buckley."

"Legendary work," Perry said, "quite familiar to those of us who have worked deep cover." He looked at Harrison as if to say, *unlike you.*

Parks was making headway with Perry. It was time for the closing pitch. "In addition," she said, "the case does involve the wine industry." She looked at Harrison. "It is the Bureau of *Alcohol*, Tobacco, Firearms and Explosives. They have jurisdiction and expertise in this area."

Perry nodded. He looked at Harrison. "She's right, Brad. I can't believe I'm saying this, but ATF should be involved. And we would be lucky to get Ward."

Parks looked at Nash. He gave her a wink. Suddenly, she

understood that he had set the stage for her before she even entered the room. She just had to bring it home.

"Of course, you'll be the case agent," Perry told her, "reporting to ASAC Nash."

Parks glanced at Harrison. His mouth hung open. Perry had just taken him out of the chain of command. It was a rare move, a slap in the face. While part of her was pleased that she would not have to report to him on this investigation, she also knew that he would now make trouble for her in other ways. This also had Nash's fingerprints all over it. What had happened between the two of them?

"Who is Ward's boss?" Perry asked.

Parks had his name and number in her phone. She pulled it up. "That would be..."

"Leroy Wheeler," Nash said, cutting her off. "He's the special agent in charge of ATF's Denver Field Division."

Parks remained deadpan. Nash's interruption was not intended to be rude. It was meant to send a message. The fact he had that information at his fingertips told Harrison that Nash was *his* supervisor and that this was how it was going to go from the start. There was the hint of a smirk on Nash's face.

"Very good," Perry said. "I'll give Wheeler a call this afternoon and let you know how it goes." He stood, signifying that the meeting was adjourned.

CHAPTER 16

7:22 p.m., Friday, August 26, Parks's condominium, Santa Rosa, California

The phone sat on the coffee table, staring back at her. *What are you waiting for?* Parks reached for it, but stopped halfway, slumping back into her sofa. *Come on, you wanted this.* She looked around her empty condo. The furniture was sparse, family photos almost nonexistent, little present that indicated any sort of personal life. It was the residence of an agent, one who had moved often to further her career, never establishing roots. Suddenly, it looked sad, lonely. Parks again stared at the phone. Was she doing this for the right reasons? Or did Harrison's comments sting because there was an element of truth to them? Thinking of him made her angry all over again. *Fuck Harrison. I know what I'm doing.* Parks snatched the phone before she could change her mind. The contact was already pulled up. She tapped the number and heard it ring once, twice...

"Hello, Rowan."

She could feel her heart pound, her pulse quickened.

"Hi, David."

There was a pause. "How are you?"

"I'm good. You?" She dropped her head, mortified.

"No complaints."

Parks was frozen. It was becoming awkward. *Say something.* "I've got a case...and I could really use your help." There, she'd said it. She held her breath.

"Just name it," Ward replied.

Parks exhaled. "Thank you." This might go okay after all.

"I will need to check with Wheeler," Ward continued.

"Well...that's already been taken care of."

Ward chuckled. "Of course."

"I have to be honest," Parks confessed, "he okayed it, but said it's up to you."

"What have you got?"

Parks began to relax. He was as easy to talk to as ever. She remembered the nights at their undercover apartment in Portland, the effortless banter, the humor. It had seemed so natural. Playing the role of the girlfriend as they infiltrated the Earth Martyrs Brigade had been one of her most enjoyable and challenging assignments. And then it became something more, for both of them. But after the case was over, separated by a continent, enduring the strains that came with working undercover...Neither of them really ended it. It just sort of faded away. Maybe that was for the best. Maybe.

"Rowan?"

Parks snapped out of it. "Sorry. My thoughts wandered for a moment."

"I understand," Ward replied. "Happens to me all the time."

She wondered if they were talking about the same thing.

"So," he continued, "tell me about the case."

Right, the case. Tell him about the case. Parks began, "You may have seen the news stories about a missing co-owner of a Napa vineyard whose head showed up in one of the wine barrels. The guy's name was Raymond Amato. Happened about three weeks ago. It got some attention from the national press."

"Yeah, I think I remember hearing something about that," Ward said. "What's the FBI's hook?"

"At first, just a request for assistance from the locals," Parks said. "Forensic accounting."

"And what did that show?"

"Some real questions about the funding source for Amato's investment in the vineyard. It's unexplained, maybe drug money or the Mob. One of the winery's employees may have a connection to the Genovese family. And he helped pull the barrel for the tasting that led to the discovery of the severed head."

"Tasting?"

"I know, right."

"Sounds a little vague."

"Maybe...a little." Parks waited for the verdict, eyes closed.

"Wine country and the Mob. How could I say no?"

Parks pumped her fist. *Yes.*

"I was hoping you'd feel that way," she said.

"Who's the case agent?"

"Um...that would be me." Parks closed her eyes. "You okay with that?"

There was no hesitation. "Yeah," Ward replied, "I'm okay with that. Can't think of anybody better."

Parks could feel her heart thud in her chest. This was going to happen. "I'll set up a meeting and text you the particulars."

"Just tell me where and when," Ward said, "and I'll be there."

CHAPTER 17

9:57 a.m., Tuesday, August 30, Federal Bureau of Investigation, San Francisco Field Office, San Francisco, California

Ward entered the Phillip Burton Federal Building and United States Courthouse. It looked much like many of the federal buildings he had entered over the course of his career, monolithic. He badged his way through security and walked to the elevator. Not a fan of such mechanisms, he entered warily and hit the button for the thirteenth floor, home to the FBI's San Francisco Field Office. Of course, he thought, the thirteenth floor. There was a disturbing number of creaks and shudders as he rose toward the intended target. Once there, Ward quickly disembarked, looking back over his shoulder at a death trap undoubtedly installed and maintained by the lowest bidder.

"Can I help you?"

Ward turned to see a receptionist studying him.

"The elevator always sound like that?" he asked.

"Afraid so," she said, now smiling. "But no fatalities...yet."

Ward gave a snort.

"Thirteen flights is a lot of stairs," she added.

"Not that many," Ward replied. "I could use the exercise."

"Oh, I don't know," she said, her eyes giving him the once-over. "You look like you're in pretty good shape."

66

Ward smiled. The receptionist was attractive, and he might normally engage in some playful banter. But today, all he could think about was the woman he was there to meet.

"David Ward," he said by way of introduction.

"I figured," she said. "I'm Carla."

"Nice to meet you, Carla."

"Same." She gave him another look. "You better get back there. Everyone else is here."

"Sounds like I'm off to another good start," Ward replied.

"Good enough for me," she shot back. Carla picked up the phone. "He's here," she said.

Moments later, a man appeared, clearly an agent. He was right out of central casting.

"Special Agent Ward," the man said, extending his hand. "Kurt Nash, Assistant Special Agent in Charge."

Ward nodded, shook his hand. "My pleasure."

"Let's go on back," Nash said. "Everyone is eager to meet you...or see you again."

Ward wondered if that was supposed to mean something. Probably not. Nash struck him as the type of guy who was very precise in how he employed the English language.

They came to a small waiting area outside what Ward assumed to be the SAC's office.

"Ready?" Nash asked, smiling.

"Born so," Ward replied.

Nash chuckled, then opened the door.

Ward walked in. His eyes immediately went to her. He remembered the first time he saw Rowan Parks. It was at the Portland International Airport. He was waiting for her to disembark the plane just in from Chicago. Their cover story had them as reunited lovers. When she appeared, he was stunned by her natural beauty. She was tall, five-ten, athletic, but womanly. Her hazel eyes sparkled with intelligence and a passion for life. They were framed by dark eyebrows and high cheekbones. Thick brunette hair was fashioned in a ponytail flipped up on her shoulder. Full, sensuous lips completed the look. It was a first impression that one didn't forget, didn't want to forget. And if that weren't enough, being fully in character, she rushed to embrace him, delivering a lingering, passionate kiss. At least, it seemed passionate. That is, until she told him not to get any ideas. It was all part of the act. Ward smiled at the memory. He smiled at her. She smiled back. It was Nash who returned him to reality.

"This is Special Agent in Charge Thurgood Perry," Nash said, gesturing at the man behind the desk.

Perry came around the desk and held out his hand. "Special Agent Ward, it's a pleasure to meet you," he said. "You're a bit of a legend."

Ward shook Perry's hand. The grip was firm, sincere. "Most legends are dead," Ward replied. "I'll pass on that status."

Perry chuckled. "Fair enough."

"This," Nash continued, "is Special Agent Ralph Mancuso."

Mancuso nodded, then stepped forward to offer a handshake. Once that was accomplished, he stepped back. Nothing was said.

"Ralph has some experience with Mob investigations from his time in the New York office," Nash said. "We thought he would be a good addition to the backup team."

Ward nodded. Mancuso's experience could be useful, as long it didn't cause him to try to take over.

"And, of course, you know Special Agent Parks," Nash said.

Ward wasn't sure how to greet here. A hug was obviously inappropriate. A handshake seemed too formal. "Hello, Rowan," he said. It was enough.

"Good to see you again, David."

Ward thought he saw just the hint of a blush. Maybe he imagined it. He looked elsewhere, hoping to remove any focus on the two of them. There was another man in the room. Something about him seemed uncomfortable, out of place.

"Finally," Nash said, "we have Detective Joe Adler from the

Napa County Sheriff's Office."

As Adler stepped forward, Ward noticed a disapproving look from Mancuso. Ward guessed that Mancuso was one of those agents who preferred a federal-only operation that kept the locals out of it. Ward understood the sentiment. Sometimes working with state and local law enforcement brought risks, especially in an undercover operation. But in his experience, the benefits of having them involved usually outweighed those risks. They knew the players, the terrain. The key was gauging the competence of who you invited in.

Adler shook Ward's hand. "It's good to meet you," he said.

"You as well," Ward replied. There was no hint that Adler was awed, or even impressed, by his federal surroundings. Ward liked that. The man was simply here to do his job, and probably not too keen on anything that looked like a federal takeover.

"Joe is here at my invitation," Parks said, a hint of defiance in her voice. "He has been working Amato's disappearance, and now murder, since the beginning."

"Have a seat, everyone," Perry said. "Now, let's discuss the plan."

CHAPTER 18

7:27 p.m., Thursday, September 1, Menfi Vineyards, Napa Valley, California

Massimiliano Rizzo relaxed on the patio as he watched another exquisite Napa Valley sunset. Hues of orange and purple painted the high clouds that hovered over the horizon. The moment was perfected by the exceptional 2016 Pinot Noir that swirled in his glass. This was a place where he found peace, at least temporarily. Named for the region in Sicily where his mother was born, Menfi Vineyards was a place she would have loved. He wished that she had lived to see this.

A latecomer to the wine industry, Rizzo found that the agrarian lifestyle suited him. Well, agrarian with certain comforts. He looked to the nearby Spanish colonial that he called home; a sprawling estate fitted with every modern convenience. Its Old-World charm gave no hint of the state-of-the-art surveillance system and smart home technology throughout. As a kid, he loved gadgets of every kind. It was no surprise that he grew up to be tech-savvy, one of those people compelled to buy the latest version of everything as soon as it came out. The billionaires of Silicon Valley were the dealers who supplied that drug and fed his addiction. He wondered how many of them had financed vacation homes from his purchases alone.

"Max. Come back to the party. We have guests."

He turned to see his wife, Geneva. She was smiling. That was good.

"Sorry, dear. I'll be there in just a second."

"Don't be long. It's Elliot's birthday."

Max smiled. "You're right," he said, "it is." He took Gena's hand and followed her back to the celebration. A long table under the pergola was laden with food and drink. Patio lights illuminated the festivities with an almost magical golden glow. A dozen friends laughed and drank toasts to Elliot, each other, and anything else they could think of. He smiled at the scene, then turned the smile toward Gena. He raised his glass to her.

"To my sweet bride of many happy years and many more to come."

Gena squeezed his hand, then went up on her toes to give him a kiss. He escorted her to the table and pulled out her chair. They had been together since their high school days back in Brooklyn, sweethearts then and now. Together, they had raised three children. And with their daughter Anna pregnant, their first grandchild, a girl, was on the way. Rizzo looked forward to the day when he could chase her through the vineyard, play hide and seek, spoil her in the way that only a grandpa can.

Before he sat, Gena touched his forearm. "Max, make a toast," she whispered.

"Of course," he said. Rizzo tapped a fork on his wineglass. The revelry subsided briefly as their guests turned their attention to him.

"To Elliot," Rizzo announced. "Happy birthday to he who slays the taxman."

"Hear, hear," cheered one of the guests.

"*Bevo alla tua salute*," Rizzo continued. "I drink to your health," he added for those who did not speak Italian.

"Grazie," Elliot replied, nodding his appreciation.

Rizzo had always wondered if his accountant had been named for the famed Prohibition agent Eliot Ness. He had never asked. It would be ironic, given Elliot's mastery of moving money around to minimize the winery's tax consequences. Most of it was avoidance, the legitimate arrangement of finances to lessen liability. Other times, it slid closer to what *might* be called evasion. They had to be careful. There was no desire to bring unwanted attention.

Rizzo took a seat. He put his arm around Gena's shoulder, then leaned over to kiss her cheek. "It's a beautiful night, my love," he whispered in her ear. "Almost as beautiful as you."

"Oh, stop it," she said, smiling. Gena turned to look him in the eye, her hand resting on his. "It is a beautiful night, isn't it?"

CHAPTER 19

2:21 p.m., Monday, September 5, Federal Bureau of Investigation, San Francisco Field Office, San Francisco, California

It was a short walk from the hotel. Ward had to admit, the FBI provided excellent accommodations, much better than he was used to. With little to do prior to the development of his legend, he spent the last few days seeing the sights and enjoying San Francisco's legendary cuisine. The rest of his time involved studying the wine industry, which made him quickly find that he knew next to nothing about it. There would be training, but he had a long way to go before he could feign any expertise.

Ward had resisted the desire to call Rowan. He knew he couldn't, but the temptation was undeniable. At one point, he had even picked up the phone. It took a long moment before he sat it back down. There had been that spark when he saw her, the rush of feelings. Did she feel it? He thought so. Was he just fooling himself? Ultimately, it didn't matter. Feelings could compromise judgment. They had crossed that line before, lucky that it didn't derail the investigation. Besides, she was the case agent on this. It wouldn't be fair to her. And what if he completely misread the situation? What if she rebuffed him? Whether due to professionalism or lack of interest, the result could be the same. It could completely undermine their working relationship. No, he had made the right decision.

Ward nodded to the court security officers as he entered the Phillip Burton Federal Building. Known as CSOs, they worked for a private firm that held a security contract with the United States Marshals Service. Most were retired state and local law enforcement. It was a good gig that allowed them to double dip after securing a state pension. It also helped fill the void that came when you were no longer on the job. Ward always shared a little gossip. And the CSOs, sometimes referred to as blue coats, were happy to reciprocate. Once done with the chit-chat, he headed for the elevator.

He thought about talking the stairs. Ward looked at his watch. He was supposed to be there in two minutes. He closed his eyes and took a breath, then opened them and hit the up button. The death trap clanked open. He could swear there was a groan as it beckoned him to enter. He took another breath, then stepped inside, quickly pushing the button for the thirteenth floor. Again, the thirteenth floor. Why? The door rumbled shut as the beast shuddered and began its ascent. Ward clutched the handrail as it creaked and rattled upward. He felt clammy, lightheaded. What the hell was taking so long? Thankfully, there was no one else onboard.

After what he was sure was a good twenty minutes, there was one final lurch. It had stopped. He looked up. They had made it, the thirteenth floor. There was an unsettling screech as the doors opened. He stepped off quickly, a prayer of thanks on his lips. Ward looked to his left. The receptionist, Carla, was watching him, a bemused look on her face.

"I don't like elevators," Ward announced.

"I remember," she said. Carla stood up. "C'mon. They're waiting for you." She gestured for him to follow her. They walked down the hall, where she opened the door to a small conference room. Inside sat Rowan, Special Agent Mancuso, and another individual Ward had never met.

"I'll leave you to it," Carla said. She looked back over her shoulder as she walked away.

Ward noticed the quizzical arch of Rowan's eyebrows.

He smiled. "Hi, Rowan."

"David."

Mancuso looked back and forth between the two of them.

"Special Agent Mancuso," Ward said, nodding his greeting.

"Seriously? Let's go with Ralph," Mancuso said.

"Ralph it is."

"And this is Special Agent Lola Reed," Parks announced.

Reed stood. She approached Ward and handed him a manila folder. "Nice to meet you, Mr. Ricard." She extended a hand.

Ward shook it as he glanced at Rowan, then Mancuso. Both had an amused look.

"Okay," he said. "So, my last name is Ricard."

"Harley Anson Ricard," Reed announced.

Ward had never used an undercover persona, or legend, developed by the FBI. He wondered if it always began like this.

"Have a seat," Reed said.

Ward sat. "And what does Harley Ricard do for a living?" he asked.

"You are a wine buyer for a large supermarket chain," Reed said, "Coastal Foods."

"They're a big operation," Ward said. In his experience, undercover work normally involved employment with a fictitious company. That made it easier to control the story and deal with any inquiries.

"We have everything in place," Reed said. "One aspect of the cover is that Coastal is contemplating setting up online wine sales. They're not, at least not right now, but certain executives there know what to say if they're asked."

Ward wasn't sure he liked that. The fewer civilians involved the better.

"I know what you're thinking," Reed said, "but trust us on this. To make this work in the wine business there has to be an actual presence."

It made sense. Ward just hoped these executives were reliable.

"The upside is that in a position like this the vineyards will try to court you," Reed said. "It's a ready-made entrée."

Ward nodded. "I like it," he said. "Problem is, everything I know about wine could fit in a beer glass."

Mancuso chuckled. Ward glanced at Rowan and caught her smile. He almost gave her a wink but suppressed the urge.

"There'll be training," Reed assured him.

"That sounds like it could be fun," Ward observed.

"I'm sure," Reed replied, her tone flat.

As Special Agent Reed didn't seem to have much of a sense of humor, Ward moved on. "What's my background?" he asked.

Reed nodded at the folder. "It's all in there," she said. "Basically, your ancestors were vintners involved in the French wine industry. But your background will be in sales and marketing. You will be sufficiently familiar with winemaking for purposes of this job. We didn't want to put you in anything that required real expertise."

"Good choice," Ward agreed. He grabbed the manila folder and emptied the contents onto the table. "I guess I better get to work."

CHAPTER 20

9:42 a.m., Wednesday, September 7, Foster Road, Napa, California

"This is it," Parks said, "your undercover residence."

She pulled into the driveway of a house in a quiet residential neighborhood. Ward liked the looks of the place, even the white picket fence that surrounded the front yard. It was an older home, but well kept. A massive evergreen dominated the backyard.

"Does the FBI own it or rent it?" Ward asked.

"We own it," Mancuso said from the backseat, "through a front company. We have a few other properties in the area as well, but the city of Napa just made sense for your cover. It's close to the action for someone in Harley Ricard's position. You'll meet the people you need to meet, and probably be courted by more than a few of them after they learn your occupation."

Ward agreed. It did make sense. So far, he was impressed by the thought that had gone into developing his undercover persona, particularly given that the decision to bring him aboard had occurred a mere two weeks ago.

They exited the car and went inside. The interior was painted a bright white.

"Are all the rooms this color?" Ward asked.

"I'm afraid so," Parks replied. "Too cheery for you?" she

asked.

"It's a lot of white."

"It is," Parks agreed. "But the bathrooms and kitchen were all recently updated, and there's a great backyard."

"You sound like a real estate agent," Ward observed.

"Not enough action," Parks shot back.

Ward chuckled. Rowan was a woman of action. No doubt about it. His thoughts drifted back to the undercover apartment they had shared in Portland. That had been a different kind of action.

"Let's take the tour," Mancuso said.

The living room opened into a kitchen. There was a bathroom on the first floor and two bedrooms, one of which had been set up as a home office. There were two additional bedrooms and another bath upstairs. The entire house had been furnished and looked lived in. Not in the messy, careworn way, but comfortable, homey.

"How did you pull this together so fast?" Ward asked.

"We've had this place for a couple of years," Mancuso replied. "It was previously used as a safehouse."

Ward nodded. A repurposed safehouse should be okay. He was confident that the Bureau had done what was necessary to keep it from being comprised.

"Given that history," Ward said, "I imagine there is a some-what sophisticated surveillance system."

"State-of-the-art," Mancuso replied. He motioned for Ward and Parks to follow him. They walked the property, inside and out, as Mancuso pointed out security cameras, many of which would have been almost impossible to spot without the guided tour.

"Impressive," Ward said.

"There's more." Mancuso led them back inside to the spare bedroom that had been converted into an office.

"Of course, you'll be able to monitor the cameras from your laptop or from an app on your phone," he said, "but we also have this."

Mancuso opened a closet door and flipped on the lights. It was a sizable space. Ward guessed it at eighty square feet. Inside were a dozen monitors covering all entrances and exits, as well as several other strategic locations around the perimeter.

"I'll certainly be able to see what's coming," Ward said.

"Hopefully, it won't come to that," Mancuso replied. "But if it does, and for whatever reason you are unable to immediately terminate the threat, this space doubles as a safe room. Fully fortified, it is bulletproof against anything short of a .50 caliber." He pointed to a vent on the ceiling. "The space has its own ventilation system." He then opened one door of a cabinet that sat along the wall. "Communications equipment, water, and a first aid kit are in here."

Ward nodded. "Seems you've thought of everything."

Mancuso smiled. "We have." He opened the other cabinet door, exposing a small arsenal of assorted weaponry. "Just in case," he said.

"Just in case," Ward repeated. This was easily shaping up to be the most secure undercover residence he had ever utilized.

"Oh, and one last thing," Parks said.

She guided them back through the living room and into the kitchen, stopping at a door on the south wall. Ward assumed it led to the garage, the only thing they had not yet covered on their tour.

"We couldn't have you driving just anything," Parks said as she opened the door and flipped the switch. "Harley Ricard needs to make an impression."

A 1966 Corvette convertible gleamed under the lights. It was in immaculate condition. Ward could feel his mouth hanging open.

"Forfeited in a wire fraud case," Parks added.

"Original Rally Red paint," Mancuso said in obvious admiration. He looked at Ward. "I'm a bit of a car buff."

Rowan put her hand on Ward's shoulder and smiled at him.

Then, as if realizing their audience, she quickly removed it. Ward looked at Mancuso. He seemed not to notice, still enamored with the car.

CHAPTER 21

7:18 p.m., Wednesday, September 7, Menfi Vineyards, Napa Valley, California

Rizzo swirled the 2007 Cabernet Sauvignon in his glass and then brought it to his nose, savoring the aroma of sweet cassis and black currant. It had been a good year for Napa Cabs, and this bottle should probably have been saved for a special occasion. But thirteen years was enough. He was in the mood for something special. And he needed no better reason than to simply share it with Gena.

"What do you think?" he asked as she took her first sip.

"Oh, Max," she sighed. "It's exquisite."

"Almost worthy of you," he said, raising his glass.

"Stop," she said, smiling.

They were silent for a moment, watching the golden sunset backlight the mountains and illuminate the vineyard.

"What a beautiful evening," Gena said.

"They're all beautiful here," Rizzo observed.

"It's heavenly." She took his hand. "More than I could have ever imagined for us."

Rizzo understood her point. But in truth, he had always imagined the world for her.

A wet nose nuzzled their clasped hands. It was Molly, their

border collie, trying to worm her way into the moment.

"Jealous?" Gena asked the dog.

Molly let out a whiney yip, then maneuvered her head under their hands.

"She's terrible," Rizzo said, now stroking the dog's head. "Who's a good girl?" he asked her.

Molly sat, enjoying the attention, making sure that the focus was where it should be, on her.

"Hey, boss."

Rizzo turned to see his longtime associate Nunzio Moretti step onto the patio.

"Sorry to interrupt, Gena," Moretti said as he approached.

"It's no trouble, Rudy," Gena said. "Sit. Join us."

Moretti found a chair and lowered himself into it. At six foot three and two hundred eighty pounds it strained under his bulk. Rudy, as Gena called him, was short for Rudolph, a nickname he had earned because of his rather large red nose, a color made more prominent by his fondness for drink. He was built like a wine barrel: thick, strong. Overall, Nunzio Moretti was an intimidating presence. Rizzo wondered if his parents had somehow known at birth, Nunzio meaning *messenger* in Italian.

Molly perked up at the big man's arrival. She jumped up, wagging her tail so hard that it almost threw off her balance. She ran to Moretti and sat directly in front of him, eyes alert. Moretti reached into a jacket pocket.

"How's my good girl?" Moretti asked, producing a dog treat. Molly was so excited that she could barely contain herself, whimpering and scooting forward. Moretti held it out in the palm of his hand. The dog gently removed it, then scarfed it down as he scratched her ears. When she was done, she looked up at him, longingly. He held up both hands, as if to say, *no more*. Molly knew the sign. Recognizing that further attempts were futile, she lay at Moretti's feet, rolling to her side so that he could rub her belly. Moretti obliged.

"Try this," Gena said, pouring him a glass of the Cabernet.

"Grazie," Moretti replied, taking it from her.

He made a show of savoring the bouquet before taking an oversized swallow. Moretti was many things, but Rizzo knew he was no oenophile.

"Magnifico," Moretti said, raising his glass.

Gena smiled. Rizzo knew how she loved to share. And he was glad it made her happy, because a 2007 Cabernet Sauvignon was wasted on a guy who would be happy to drink nothing other than inexpensive Chianti. But it didn't matter. Rudy was a friend, one who had proven himself loyal on many occasions.

CHAPTER 22

10:03 a.m., Friday, September 9, U.S. Route 101, San Francisco, California

Haze from nearby forest fires obscured the view as Parks drove over the Golden Gate Bridge and into downtown, staying on Route 101. Mancuso said the place was at the corner of Bush and Larkin, just a couple blocks off the highway. It had been used by the San Francisco Field Office for several years. Located in Nob Hill, one of the city's most exclusive neighborhoods, the condominium was another asset seized through use of the federal forfeiture laws. Now it would serve as the safehouse for this operation, a place they could all meet far from Napa Valley, thus minimizing the risk of detection.

As Parks listened to the news on the radio her thoughts drifted back to the murder of her father. He and another officer were shot dead by members of Chicago's notorious El Rukn gang. It happened during an early morning drug raid. She was twelve at the time. After that, there was no question that she would carry on the family tradition. First came the Chicago PD, then the Bureau. But truth was, there had never been much doubt about where she would end up. At age six she announced that she was going to catch bad guys, like her daddy. Parks smiled, recalling the moment, sitting on her dad's lap. He was proud. But he also wanted to keep his daughter safe. Over the years that followed, he did everything he could to dissuade her, to no avail.

She found Bush Street and turned left onto the one-way. The building was two blocks down and on the right. It took a while to find a parking spot, but she managed to squeeze into one that was still within close walking distance. Minutes later, she was there. A video intercom system allowed Mancuso to see her and buzz her in. Parks went to the elevator, entered, and hit the button for the seventh floor. She knew that David was up there. Part of her wondered why he hadn't called. But the other part knew it was probably for the best.

The elevator stopped on seven and Parks stepped out. She found the condo and knocked. Mancuso opened the door. David stood behind him.

"C'mon in," Mancuso said, stepping aside to make way.

"Hello, Rowan," David said. His smile told Parks that he was glad to see her.

"Hi, David."

"Ralph was just showing me around," Ward announced.

Parks surveyed the place. It was small, but nice. There were beautiful mahogany floors that complemented the modern style. But the most prominent feature was the bright red cabinets. She walked into the kitchen area, nodding her approval.

"I like it," Parks said. She caressed the oven. "Italian?" she asked.

"As are all the appliances," Mancuso replied, smiling. "Only the best."

"If you say so," Parks replied. "Let's see the rest of the place."

Mancuso showed them the layout. It was one bedroom, one bath. The tour did not take long.

"Small as it is," Mancuso said, "I'm told it would list for almost seven hundred thousand dollars in this neighborhood."

Ward let out a low whistle. "I'll stick to Montana."

"The building does have a decent security system," Mancuso added. "Obviously, we've beefed that up for this condo."

"The thought is that we can all meet here when you ostensibly travel back to corporate headquarters," Parks said. "Coastal Foods' main office is in San Francisco."

Ward nodded. "I've been researching the company, online wine sales, the wine industry as a whole."

Parks was sure that was true. She had seen him prepare before, totally immersing himself in the subject areas related to an investigation.

"About that," Mancuso said, "I've arranged for some specialized training by a vintner and a viticulturalist. They'll be here tomorrow. They can teach you anything you need to know about the business and production of wine."

Parks saw David's brow furrow, his mouth tighten. She understood the concern, the risk of bringing in outsiders.

"I know what you're thinking," Mancuso said, eyeing Ward. "But you know as well as anybody that your credibility in this area is essential. These wine people live and breathe this stuff. They'll spot an imposter."

Ward nodded. "You're right. How well do we know these people?"

"Well enough," Mancuso replied. "They owe me a favor. And they know not to ask questions."

"Understood," Ward said.

"Besides," Mancuso added, "it's not like the FBI has resident experts on the wine industry."

"Huh. I thought you guys were experts on everything."

"Almost everything," Parks interjected.

"Oh, and on the subject of research," Mancuso said, "I almost forgot." He motioned for them to follow him back into the kitchen. There, he opened a cabinet door to expose a small wine rack. "Some of my favorites," he said. "You know, to complete your studies."

"Nice," Ward said. "Very generous."

Parks gave Mancuso a nod of approval.

CHAPTER 23

4:06 p.m., Saturday, September 10, Federal Bureau of Investigation, San Francisco Field Office, San Francisco, California

Ward stared out the window of the conference room, taking in the city. He briefly allowed himself to fantasize about seeing the sights with Rowan, taking her to dinner, and other things. Then he shook it off. It was better to keep those thoughts out of his mind, stay focused. He needed to become Harley Ricard, removing himself from the world of David Ward and all that went with it.

Ward looked at his watch. They would be here soon, Mancuso and his two experts. Saturday was the only day that both were available and in the city. Both would be needed. Based on his studies so far, wine was proving to be a far more complicated subject than he had ever imagined. He would need to pay attention, drinking in everything that these oenophiles had to offer. Ward groaned at his poor joke, promising to do better. The critique was interrupted when the door opened, and Mancuso walked in. He was followed by a man and a woman, both impeccably dressed. The woman was youngish, maybe mid-thirties, attractive. The man was older, silver-haired, somewhat regal in his bearing. He carried a bag in one hand. Another carrying case of some sort hung from his shoulder. He noticed Ward looking.

"It's a wine tote," the man said, stepping forward. He held out his hand. "Justin." There was no offer of a last name.

"Well, this training session is taking on a whole new appeal," Ward announced, shaking hands. He provided no name, alias or otherwise.

"And I'm Colette."

Ward shook her hand, as well. She had long slender fingers that lingered slightly as they pulled away. Her smile was impish, one that could lead a man to trouble.

Ward turned to Mancuso. "Didn't think the Bureau allowed alcohol on the premises."

"It is Saturday," he replied. Mancuso then addressed Justin and Colette. "My apologies. I'm needed elsewhere." He looked to Ward. "I'm sure you'll find this gentleman to be a very attentive student."

"I'm counting on it," Colette said, a twinkle in her piercing blue eyes.

Mancuso gave Ward an advisory look, then headed out the door.

Justin sat his wine tote on the table and pulled out two bottles, one a red, the other a white. On closer inspection, Ward could see that the red was a Cabernet Sauvignon, the white a Chardonnay.

"We'll hold off a bit on the tasting," Justin announced. "Something to look forward to after we discuss the winemaking process."

"And I'm afraid we only have two hours," Colette added. "Justin and I need to be at an event at the Harriet Smithson Gallery this evening." She smiled. "But I'm sure we could arrange a follow-up session if needed...or desired."

Justin chuckled. "Let's see how it goes, shall we?" He gestured for everyone to take a seat.

Ward grabbed a legal pad and pen, then took his place.

Colette removed a laptop from her bag and proceeded to power it up. She tapped a few keys, then spun it around so Ward could see the screen. A photo of a vineyard was displayed.

"So, I'm the viticulturalist," she said, "someone who cultivates grapevines, and grapes, that are suitable for winemaking."

"And I'm the vintner," Justin added. "In other words, I'm a winemaker."

"And, of course, this is where it all starts," Colette said, nodding toward the picture. "Actually, that's not true. There is a long discussion about which vines work in certain regions based on climate, soil conditions, and a host of other factors." She smiled. "But we don't have time for me to go all horticultural on you."

Ward returned the smile. Colette was hard not to like. But the thought of Rowan made him want to behave himself. That surprised him a bit, given all the impediments to any kind of relationship with her. Or maybe it didn't.

"So, let's start with the basic steps involved during the winemaking process," Colette said. She tapped a key to move to another image, this one showing a worker picking grapes off the vine. "The harvesting can be done by hand but is increasingly done by machine." She then pulled up an image a large blue farm implement, the vines disappearing into a vertical opening in its front as it drove down the rows. "Of course, the grapes must be at just the right stage of ripeness. This typically happens sometime in late August or early September, depending upon the climate that year."

Ward made some notes. He had researched much of this online but could already tell that this would be a cogent presentation that would fill in the gaps.

"The next step is sorting and destemming," Colette said, clicking on the next image. "Usually, this is done by hand. The objective is to remove the rotten or shriveled grapes. After that, the nice, plump grapes are run through a machine that removes the stems."

Ward nodded, scribbling away in his legal pad.

"After the grapes are destemmed," Colette continued, "the

process moves to crushing. You may recall that in the old days this was done by stomping on the grapes. Now it's done by using a press." She pulled up a picture. "The pressing process is much faster with white wine, leaving only the juice. The seeds, skins, and other solids are separated so that any undesirable colors and tannins do not get into the wine. With red wine they are left in during the fermentation process to add color and tannins, which contributes to giving the wine the desired flavor." She paused. "Any questions so far?"

Ward shook his head. "Not yet."

The next image appeared to be a large stainless-steel tank containing the pressed grapes. "The next step is fermentation," Colette explained. "Fermentation converts the sugars into alcohol and carbon dioxide. Wine will begin to ferment from airborne yeast, but yeast is added to control the process and flavor. With red wine the skins float on top during fermentation, so the winemaker must dip or push the skins into the wine several times a day. After fermentation, the red wine is pressed again to remove the grape skins and other solids."

She was moving fast. "Hold on a second," Ward said. "Let me catch up."

"I know it's a lot," Colette said. "I'll slow down." She waited.

"Okay, go ahead," Ward said.

"Following fermentation, the wine is transferred into oak barrels or another stainless fermenter for clarification. This does occur naturally, but winemakers also use other methods. Fining involves adding an adsorbent that helps captures undesirable particles, causing them to sink to the bottom of the tank. They also use filtration."

"Quite a process," Ward observed.

"And these are just the basics," Colette said. "The oak barrels are expensive," she added. "Stainless steel is by far the most common. During fermentation in the stainless tanks many winemakers will add oak chips which produces a distinctive oak flavor."

"And then aging?" Ward asked.

"Correct," Colette replied. "And this can be done in another stainless tank, oak barrels, or even bottles."

"Your preference?" Ward asked.

"Oak barrels. No question."

"I concur," Justin interjected.

Colette gestured for Justin to go ahead.

"Okay, now it's my turn," he said. "I was told to focus on the Napa region, so let's cover the wines produced there. The primary reds would include Cabernet Sauvignon, Merlot, Pinot Noir, and Zinfandel. The whites are Chardonnay, Sauvignon Blanc, Pinot Grigio, and Viognier. Pinot Grigio is sometimes referred to as Pinot Gris."

Justin picked up the bag he had carried in and removed six glasses. Three of them had shorter stems and a much larger bowl. The other three had longer stems and a narrower opening.

"Different stemware for red and white," he said. "Red wine glasses have a wider rim and larger bowl to allow the wine to breathe. More oxygen opens up the aroma and flavor of these bolder wines. White wines, on the other hand, do not need as much breathing space. The narrower glass concentrates the wine's qualities and subtle aroma. Also, whites are normally served at a much lower temperature. That is the reason for the long stem. It keeps the drinker's hand away from the bowl, which could warm the wine."

Justin uncorked the Cabernet Sauvignon and poured a small amount into the three red wine glasses, leaving them about one-third full. He served one to Colette and another to Ward.

"There is far more to this than you will likely need to know, so I'll stick to the basics,' Justin said. "Follow along as I demonstrate." Colette picked up her glass. Ward followed suit. "First, you would evaluate the wine by sight in three ways: by looking straight into the glass, a side view, and a tilted view. These allow you to examine the wine's color range, clarity, age, and weight." He lifted his glass, looking first down into the opening, then lifting it up to the light and finally tilting it, causing the wine to roll near the edge. "These steps let you examine the complete color range of the wine. The depth of color is an indication of the wine's density." Justin then viewed the wine through the side of the glass. "Here" he said, "I am looking for clarity. A murky wine is indicative of problems during the fermentation process." He then tilted the glass again. "If the wine looks watery along the edge it may lack flavor. A brownish color in a white wine or rusty orange in a red means the wine may have oxidized."

"Meaning it's past it's prime?" Ward asked.

"Absolutely correct," Justin said, looking pleased with his student's question. He swirled the Cabernet, then hovered his nose over the opening. "The first purpose of the sniff is to detect flaws," he said. "If the wine smells musty it is spoiled. A vinegar scent is also obviously a problem. These would be two of the primary indicators that there is a problem." He gave the wine another sniff. "Next, the wine's nose is checked for fruit aromas, those of flowers, herbs, or spices, as well as wine barrel aromas. A few examples of the latter might be smoke, chocolate, or roasted nuts. You may also have heard the term bouquet. That usually refers to the secondary scents."

"What about this Cabernet?" Ward asked.

"Rather complex," Justin announced. "I'm picking up blackberry, crème de cassis, vanilla bean, and cocoa, with a slight cedar aroma as well."

Ward detected little of that and hoped that he hadn't rolled his eyes. "What about the tasting?" he asked.

"Of course," Justin said. "Take a sip. Then suck on it, the same as you might if using a straw." He demonstrated. "This aerates the wine and spreads it round in your mouth."

Ward did his best. He could sense how it enhanced the taste.

"Flavor should follow aroma," Justin said. "We are also tasting for balance, harmony, and complexity. For balance, there should be a good proportion of sweet and sour, meaning residual sugars and acidity. It should not be too astringent, nor should it leave the taste of alcohol. Harmonious means well integrated, with the flavors in proportion. Complexity has to do with the way the flavors linger, the subtlety. A wine is referred to as complete if it combines all of these things."

Ward looked down at his legal pad. He had managed to take eight pages of notes.

"Any questions?" Justin asked.

Ward wasn't sure where to begin.

CHAPTER 24

8:22 a.m., Monday, September 12, Evans Creek Vineyards, Napa Valley, California

The call had come into dispatch early that morning. Adler heard about it and called his sergeant, volunteering to respond. He then contacted Estes, who asked to ride along. Whoever phoned it in reported that someone had dumped thousands of gallons, flooding both the fermentation and barrel rooms. It had to be one helluva mess.

"There it is, up ahead," Estes said, pointing to the entrance. Double E looked back down at this phone. "Says here that Evans Creek has won numerous awards for their wines, particularly their Pinot Noir."

"That so?"

"Sounds like they are serious players in the industry."

Adler wondered if professional jealousy might be a motive, maybe taking out the competition. That, or a disgruntled worker. Of course, plain old criminal mischief was also always a possibility. And there was always the insurance angle, though this did not seem like a place that would be having problems with profitability.

"Maybe whoever's Pinot Noir got second place," Estes offered.

"Exactly what I was thinking."

They parked in front of the winery, stepped out, and walked toward the main door. A man was standing there, waiting for them.

"You from the sheriff's office?" he asked.

"Detective Joe Adler." He showed his badge.

"Detective Enrique Estes."

"Henry Evans," the man said, offering his hand. "Thanks for coming out."

"Of course," Adler replied. "Hope we can help find out who did this."

Evans shook his head and sighed. "Maybe," he said. "But I have no idea who would want to do something like this."

"I did a little research," Estes said. "Your vineyard has been very successful."

Evans nodded. "Thank you," he said. "A lot of hard work went into this place, and we've been fortunate. We'll recover from this, but it will be a financial blow for sure."

"Do you think one of your competitors could have done this?" Estes asked.

Evans shook his head. "No. It's a competitive business, but I don't see any of them doing something like this. We all have too much respect for each other and for the effort that goes into making good wine. I just don't think that's possible."

"Any disgruntled employees?" Adler asked. "Anyone you recently had to let go?"

"All of my regulars have been with me for years," Evans replied. "They're a pretty dedicated bunch."

"Why don't you show us where it happened," Adler said.

"Sure. Follow me."

They went through the main doors, passed through a wine bar, then entered the production area, stopping at an opening that led into a room filled with large stainless-steel tanks. They rose out of a sea of purple.

"Unless you brought boots, I would suggest you stop here," Evans said.

Estes shook his head. "What a mess."

"Barrel room's the same," Evans added.

"Who called it in?' Adler asked.

"One of the workers, Walt. He opens up every morning. Called you guys before talking to me."

Adler studied Evans. "Why would you want him to call you first?" he asked.

"Oh, I just mean, you know, it's my business. I should have been the one to make the call." He paused. "Besides, I would have cleaned up a bit before you got here."

"Crime scene's more useful when it's fresh," Adler pointed out. "We always to arrive before the cleanup."

Adler watched for a reaction.

"Sure," Evans said. "That makes sense. I just meant, you know, you would need waders to go in there."

"We'll want to talk to Walt," Estes said.

"He's not here," Evans replied. "He ran into town to get some supplies."

Adler didn't say anything. He looked at Estes, who gave him a quizzical look.

"I assume you have some kind of surveillance system?" Adler asked.

"Sure," Evans replied, "of course."

"We'll want to see everything from close of business yesterday through this morning."

"It's stored in the cloud," Evans said. "I'll get you the username and password so you can download it."

"You do that," Adler said. He handed Evans a card. "And have Walt give me a call."

"Okay," Evans replied, "but I don't think he'll know any more than I do."

"We'll see."

Adler glanced at Estes, then looked back the way they came, indicating the two of them should talk alone. Estes nodded.

"The crime scene unit will be here in a few minutes," Adler

said. "They'll take photos, check for prints, that sort of thing."

"Okay," Evans said. "But my guess is this was just vandalism. Probably a bunch of kids."

"But you'd still want them caught, right?" Adler asked.

"Well, yeah...sure."

Adler's phone rang. He pulled it from his jacket. It was Estes, a little trick they used when they needed to confer without drawing suspicion.

"I need to take this," Adler said. He looked at Estes. "It's about the Tyler case." It was total bullshit. There was no Tyler case.

Adler turned to Evans. "Could you excuse us for a minute?"

"Of course."

They walked back toward the main entrance, Adler pretending to talk on the phone. Once outside, he checked to see if anyone was in earshot. Nobody was around.

"What did you make of that?" Adler asked.

"It's almost like he doesn't want us to investigate."

Adler nodded in agreement. "Pretty damned odd." He smiled. "Well, too bad. Let's get back in there and do some interviews."

CHAPTER 25

1:12 p.m., Monday, September 12, Napa County Sheriff's Office, 1535 Airport Blvd, Napa, California

Before they left the vineyard that morning, Henry Evans had provided them with the username and password for the surveillance system. That is, after he was reminded, twice. Adler wasn't sure if Evans had something to hide, but he was certainly acting like he did.

The surveillance system's cameras were motion activated. Any significant movement caused them to record, with the video then being stored in the cloud. Adler was able to access the library of clips which were grouped by date. Here, there was only one night in question. It was a much simpler task than slogging through the thirty days of video from Pavesi Vineyards. So far, there was nothing. Apparently, there were long periods of time during which absolutely nothing moved in Evans Creek's fermentation or barrel rooms. That seemed a little hard to believe.

Double E walked in with two coffees, handing one to Adler. "Anything yet?" he asked.

"Nada," Adler replied. "Makes me wonder why Evans was so hesitant to fork over his password."

"Assuming he had something to do with it," Estes said.

"Fair enough," Adler replied.

"But it was strange."

"And nobody there saw or heard anything?"

"So they say."

"Yeah, so they say."

Adler clicked on the next video. A bird had apparently found its way into the barrel room and set off the camera. The time was 3:07 a.m. There was no wine on the floor. Only three clips remained before the time Walt supposedly arrived to open the facility, which Evans said was usually around six thirty. Those three videos showed start times of 3:17 a.m., 3:42 a.m., and 4:06 a.m. After that, there was nothing until 6:32 a.m., which Adler guessed was Walt arriving to discover the flooded winery. He continued through the videos. The bird made another fleeting appearance. There was nothing else. The others were similar. When the last clip ended at 4:08 a.m., there was no flooding to be seen.

"Anything?" Estes asked.

Adler shook his head. "About to play the last one, which I assume is Walt showing up to fine Lake Pinot."

Estes snorted. "Nice." He stepped closer to watch.

Adler hit play. The video showed a man arriving in the fermentation room. He seemed panicked, not sure what to do. Adler saw him check the valves on a couple of the stainless-steel tanks, then reach into a pocket and pull out a cell phone. He punched in a number and then engaged in what appeared to be an animated conversation. The time was 6:35 a.m. Adler checked his notes. It was the exact time the call had come into dispatch. It appeared that Walt was not their guy, or he was an incredible actor in an elaborate production. Adler was putting his money on the former.

"Looks legitimately surprised," Estes observed.

"I agree." Adler sat back in his chair and let out a sigh. "So, what the hell happened between the time the last video ended at 4:08 and this one?" he asked.

"I'd say somebody turned off the system or went in later to delete the videos," Estes replied.

"Somebody with the username and password," Adler said. "Evans was not too eager to hand those over."

"We might be able to subpoena the vendor," Estes said, "see if there was any activity on the account between 4:08 and the time we talked to Evans."

Adler nodded. "Good idea. There may or may not be a record of shutting off the system or deleting videos, but it sure doesn't hurt to ask."

"I'll take care of it," Estes offered.

"Thanks, man."

Adler replayed the 6:32 video. He was halfway through when his phone rang. He didn't recognize the number.

"Detective Adler," he answered.

"Detective, this is Walt Jenkins. I was told to give you a call."

"Thanks for contacting me, Mr. Jenkins." Adler grabbed a notepad and pen. "I just have a few questions about what happened this morning."

"Yes, sir."

"Did you see anybody coming or going around the time you arrived this morning?"

"No, sir," Jenkins replied. "I'm usually in around six thirty. Ain't much else movin' around that time."

"Understood," Adler said. "Any idea who might want to do this?" he asked.

"Not a clue. Everybody likes Mr. Evans."

Well, apparently not everybody, Adler thought. "He's a good boss, I take it?"

"Yes, sir. Most of us here been with him for a long time."

"Have there been any recent hires?" Adler asked.

"No," Jenkins replied. "I mean, the field workers come and go, of course. But last person hired on staff was just over a year ago. Before that, you're probably goin' back four or five years."

Adler recalled Evans saying that all his regulars had been with him for years. Jenkins's answer was not entirely consistent with that.

100

"Who was it who was hired about a year ago?" Adler asked.

"That would be Tommy Serra," Jenkins replied. "Good kid."

"Okay," Adler said. He made some notes.

"Anybody fired recently?" he asked.

"No, sir."

"So," Adler continued, "Mr. Evans said he wished you had talked to him before calling the sheriff's office. Did he say anything to you about that?"

"He did. Said I should have talked to him first. Said he's the owner and that he should have been the one to call it in."

"Did he say anything else?"

"Not really."

"Not really?"

"Well, he said something about cleaning up a little before you guys got there."

"Yeah, we discussed that," Adler said. He was beginning to wonder what exactly was meant by *cleaning up*. "Anything else you think I should know?" he asked.

"No, sir," Jenkins replied.

"Okay," Adler said. "You think of anything else, you give me a call."

"Yes, sir."

Adler ended the call. He pulled up his contacts and found the number for Special Agent Rowan Parks.

CHAPTER 26

9:53 a.m., Tuesday, September 13, the safehouse, San Francisco, California

Ward and Mancuso waited for Rowan to arrive. She wanted to share the details of a call she had received from Detective Adler. Something about wine being dumped at a Napa vineyard. Ward wasn't sure why it needed to be in person, but he was happy for any chance to see her. He checked his watch.

"What time did she tell you?" he asked.

"Nine thirty," Mancuso replied. He took a sip of coffee, then rubbed his forehead.

Ward walked to the window, checking the street. He wanted to hear from Rowan about whatever it was Adler had to say. But then he wanted to talk to her and Mancuso about getting things moving. There had been enough training. It was time to act.

"Sorry I'm late," said a voice over the video intercom system. "Traffic was a bitch." It was Rowan.

Mancuso got up to check the screen.

"Fuck me," he said.

"What?" Ward asked.

"She has Adler with her."

It was considered a breach of protocol to bring a local to the safehouse, that is, unless they were highly trusted. Ward had faith in Rowan's instincts. But if she was wrong, it was his ass on the line.

Mancuso buzzed them in. He looked at Ward, shaking his head.

"If she trusts him," Ward said, "that's good enough for me."

Mancuso did not respond. He clearly did not agree.

Minutes later, Rowan walked in, followed by Adler. Mancuso glanced at the detective, then give Rowan a cool look.

"Relax," Parks said. "He rode with me. And no, I wasn't followed. Besides, I wanted you to hear this straight from the horse's mouth."

Ward suppressed a chuckle. He knew Rowan, and he knew she wouldn't give a shit about Mancuso's opinion if she didn't agree with it. He got up to get the new arrivals some coffee.

"Let's have a seat," Mancuso said, defeated. They moved to the kitchen table.

Ward returned with the coffees. He knew Rowan liked hers black.

"There's cream and sugar," he said, handing a cup to Adler.

"This'll do," Adler replied.

Rowan took a sip, then turned to Adler. "Go ahead. Tell 'em."

"We got a call out to an Evans Creek Vineyards," Adler began. "Sometime early Monday morning someone dumped all the wine in their fermentation and barrel rooms. Of course, there are several possibilities in a situation like that. It could be a bogus insurance claim, if that sort of thing were even covered, a disgruntled employee, or just straight up criminal mischief. Evans Creek is successful operation, or so it would appear. That raises the possibility of sabotage by one of their competitors."

"Anything causing you to lean toward one of those theories?" Mancuso asked.

"That's just it," Adler said, "there's a problem with all of them. The owner, Henry Evans, seemed decidedly unenthusiastic about our investigation. Then there's the surveillance system. After Evans reluctantly turned over the username and password, we accessed the stored videos. There was an inexplicable gap from approximately four o'clock through six thirty. Everything looked fine around four. At six thirty, there was wine all over the place. One of the regulars came in to open up and found it. He called it in, which apparently pissed off Evans. He gave us some bullshit story about being the one who should've contacted us because he's the owner. Then, he said something about wanting to clean the place up before we got there."

Rowan looked at Ward, then Mancuso. "Pretty suspicious, huh?"

"So, not likely to be some random criminal mischief or a competitor," Mancuso observed.

"Right," Adler said, "unless the competitor somehow had access to the surveillances system, which seems unlikely. But what benefit would really come from it? There are a lot of players in the wine industry."

"And I take it you could not identify a suspect employee?" Ward asked.

Adler shook his head. "Not at this point. Looks like most of the workers have been there for a long time. I talked to the guy who opened up that morning, Walt Jenkins. Seemed like a straight shooter. He told me that the most recent hire was over a year ago. He also said Evans was a good boss."

"And you think insurance fraud is out because the place is so successful?" Parks asked.

"Correct," Adler replied. "Obviously, I haven't seen their books, but right now it doesn't look like money was a problem."

"You never know," Mancuso said.

Adler nodded. "Agreed," he said. "I can't rule it out, not at this point."

"It's not impossible that it could be a loan from the wrong people," Parks added, "with one too many late payments."

Ward understood the connection she was trying to make. "Or maybe something else involving the wrong people," he said.

"Like what?" Mancuso asked.

"That's what I'm here to find out," Ward replied. "I don't believe in coincidences."

I don't know if it's connected to Amato's murder or not," Adler said, "but there does seem to be someone sending messages. And in the case of Henry Evans, I'm thinking that message was received."

"Along those lines," Parks said. "We would like you to give the impression that the Amato murder investigation has hit a dead end. If everyone's radar goes down a few levels it will make it easier for us to do our undercover operation."

Adler nodded. "That shouldn't be a problem," he said. "It has hit a dead end. That's why all of you are here."

"Can you do the same on the Evans Creek investigation?" Parks asked.

Adler shook his head. "I don't know," he said. "I mean, I did call you because of the possibility of a connection between the two cases. But even if Henry Evans doesn't want me to investigate, the sheriff is going to expect me to follow up." Adler paused for a moment, looking from face-to-face. "Unless you want me to tell the sheriff the feds asked me to back off?"

Rowan looked at Ward. He shook his head. She turned to Mancuso. He did the same.

"Let's hold off on that," she said. "How about this? You go through the motions until the sheriff is satisfied. At that point, you tell Evans you've run out of leads."

Adler took a breath. "I'm not a go through the motions type of guy. This is a big ask."

"I know it is," Parks said. "But lowering the antennae of those who may be involved is mission critical."

"Understood," Adler said. He smiled. "But what if I inadvertently solve the case?"

"Well," Ward said, "something tells me that's not going to happen without someone on the inside."

CHAPTER 27

10:02 a.m., Tuesday, September 13, Three Peaks Vineyards, Napa Valley, California

Ward's call to the owner was initially received with guarded skepticism. But when he explained that he was a buyer for Coastal Foods, and that the supermarket giant was considering setting up an online platform to sell wine, the mood turned positively buoyant. That was a good sign, one that told him the FBI might have had some idea what they were doing when they developed his legend.

It was a beautiful day, seventy-five degrees, the sky clear. Ward had the top down, the wind whipping through his hair. It had grown long since his last case. He always changed his look afterwards. He also did his best to avoid subsequent operations in the same part of the country. But that was sometimes beyond his control. Wine country, however, was new turf.

Ward spotted the entrance to Three Peaks and slowed down. As he rumbled up the drive, he saw several workers stop and take notice. The car was an eye-catcher for sure. It occurred to him that he might need a cover story for the car. A mint '66 Corvette would be out of range for a buyer from a supermarket chain. He glided into a parking spot and stepped out, slipping his sunglasses into his jacket pocket. A man was walking down the path from the winery, headed his way. He assumed it was the owner, George Reidel.

"Mr. Ricard, I assume," Reidel said, hand outstretched.

"Call me Harley," Ward replied. "Good to meet you."

"Beautiful car," Reidel said. "A '66, correct?"

"Correct," Ward said. "You know your cars." He patted the hood affectionately. "I inherited it from my dad. She was his baby."

Reidel nodded. "C'mon," he said, "let me show you around."

They walked back up the path to an expansive deck that overlooked an enormous vineyard. It spread down the hillside into a lush valley, a small lake in the distance completing the postcard view.

"Magnificent," Ward said, taking it in. "It's hard to imagine anything more picturesque."

Reidel smiled proudly, looking out over his land. "I'm a lucky man, no doubt."

"It's a lot more than luck," Ward said. "You're the owner of one of the most successful labels in the business. You don't get there without a lot of hard work and talent." It was true. Three Peaks was a major player. Their wines had won countless awards. There was a reason Ward had decided to start here. If he impressed an industry leader like Reidel, it would do a great deal to establish his reputation in Napa Valley.

Reidel turned to him. "Thank you, Harley." He gestured toward the door. "Let's go inside, tour the operation."

They walked through large double doors, swung open to accept the September air. Ward noted the hand carved grapevines that framed stained glass depictions of the valley below.

"This is impressive work," he said.

"Impressive, and damned expensive," Reidel said. "But the entry needs to make a statement, don't you agree?"

"I do," Ward replied. "And this makes quite a statement."

They entered the tasting room. Its masonry and woodwork were even beyond what Ward might have expected, creating a warm, beckoning environment that pulled you in and made you want to stay. He could almost hear the clinking glasses and laughter, even though it was midmorning on Tuesday, and no one was there.

"I think I could settle in here and never leave," he observed.

Reidel laughed. "Well," he said, "that's kind of the idea."

They passed through. Stone steps led down to the barrel room. Hundreds of oak casks were stacked on racks lining the walls.

"As you know," Reidel began, "this is where the wine is aged, the end of the process. We still prefer the oak barrels, despite the added cost."

Ward nodded approvingly.

"But let me take you through the whole facility," Reidel continued. "we'll start at the beginning."

Ward could already see from the attention he was receiving that there was interest in supplying product for Coastal's online platform. He had to admit, the role of buyer was shaping up to be the perfect undercover entrée into this world. He followed as Reidel led him to the sorting tables, there describing the process by which the acceptable grapes were separated and destemmed. They then examined a grape crusher and a press before moving to the fermentation room, Reidel explaining Three Peaks methodology every step of the way.

"I know you're familiar with all of this," Reidel said, almost apologetically. "But I wanted you to see how we do it, the little things that set us apart."

"I appreciate it," Ward said. "My ancestors were vintners in the French wine industry, so I guess that, to some extent, it's in my DNA. But my background is sales and marketing. The refresher course is always helpful to me. And, as you say, every vineyard has their approach. Yours is clearly one that works."

"Thank you," Reidel said. He put his hand on Ward's shoulder, a gesture of sincerity. "Perhaps, a tasting would be in order."

"I would have been disappointed had you not offered."

"Excellent," Reidel said.

He led the way back to the tasting room. Once there, he slipped on a pair of readers and selected a bottle from a rack behind the bar.

"As you're undoubtedly aware," Reidel said, "we're know for our Cabernet Sauvignon."

He deftly opened the bottle, then selected two glasses, pouring them about one-third full. Ward watched as Reidel went through an abbreviated version of the sampling steps that had been explained by Justin, Mancuso's expert.

"This is from the 2013 vintage," Reidel said, "an almost perfect growing season." He slid the glass to Ward.

The trick was to demonstrate the proper technique, but without undue commentary. To do otherwise would be to insult the man. Indeed, he could not be seen to check for irregularities in a wine of which Reidel was justifiably proud. His approach could only be one of savoring the experience. This was a critical moment.

Ward bypassed the examination by sight. He swirled the wine around the glass, then hovered his nose over the opening, breathing in the bouquet. Nodding his approval, he then took a sip, light sucking on it for aeration and to spread it throughout his mouth. He sighed.

"Simply sublime," Ward announced.

Reidel smiled, pleased. "Perhaps, I could entice you to stay for lunch?' he asked.

"I would like that," Ward replied.

CHAPTER 28

11:37 a.m., Tuesday, September 13, Pavesi Vineyards, Napa Valley, California

Adler had called ahead. This was the kind of news best delivered face-to-face. Besides, it would help sell the story. He wondered how Marty Pavesi would take it. By now, his expectations had to be low, didn't they? Amato had been missing for months before he was discovered. Well, before part of him was discovered. Still, there was a strong possibility that it would not go well. And there was one reason why.

The vineyard was just around the corner. Adler slowed and turned in at the gate. He parked in the visitor lot, stepped out, and headed for the main entrance. He was no more than halfway there when the reason appeared. Audra Pavesi, ever her husband's protector, emerged to meet him.

"Good morning, Detective," she said coolly. "Marty informed me that you wished to discuss the investigation."

"That's correct," Adler replied.

"Might I ask what, specifically, you wish to discuss?"

Adler wasn't in the mood to deal with Audra as gatekeeper. She could hear what he had to say at the same time Marty heard it. He looked as if to check behind her. "Is he here?"

She studied him for a moment. "Follow me," she finally said.

They went through the tasting room and down a hallway, eventually stopping at a closed door. Audra opened it, gesturing for Adler to go inside. Marty Pavesi was seated at a desk. It appeared to be his office, one befitting the owner of a vineyard. Memorabilia was scattered about on the walnut furnishings. Awards sat on the bookshelves. Framed articles from various wine magazines covered the walls. Whether true or not, it gave the impression of success. Pavesi stood, extending his hand. Adler took it.

"Please, have a seat," Pavesi said, pointing him toward a chair. "I take it you have news?"

Adler looked at Audra. She remained standing. She looked at the chair as if telling him to sit. He did.

"I'm afraid no good news," Adler began. "The fact is, we seem to have hit a dead end."

"How is that possible?" Audra asked, appearing agitated. "It was just a few weeks ago that you were here with that FBI agent, Parks. We thought that something might finally happen with this investigation."

Adler tried not to take the comment personally. He failed.

"The forensic accounting produced no solid leads," Adler said, looking directly at Audra. "We've talked to everyone. There are no viable suspects. While his personal finances raise some questions, in the end they lead to nothing more than speculation." He turned back to Marty. "I'm sorry. I know the two of you were close. The case will not be closed. It will never be closed, not while I work at the sheriff's office. But the reality is there's just not much more we can do." He stood. "I wanted you to hear it from me." Adler wanted to get out of there. He had done what Parks asked, and he didn't like it.

Pavesi lowered his head, a hand covering his eyes. "I appreciate that, Detective. I know you've done everything you could." He was silent for a moment, then stood. "I'll show you out."

"Marty, I'll walk him out," Audra said. "You need to..."

"I'll do it," Pavesi said, interrupting her.

It was as forceful as Adler had ever seen Pavesi toward his wife. She appeared stunned.

"Let's walk," Pavesi said, gesturing toward the door.

They entered the hall and walked back toward the tasting room. Pavesi looked back over his shoulder, checking for Audra. When they were out of earshot, he spoke.

"She's a good woman, Detective. And I love her dearly." He paused. "But she can be overly protective."

No shit, Adler thought.

"I just wanted to tell you how grateful I am for everything you've done," Pavesi continued. "I mean it."

Adler knew he did. It made him feel like hell.

"Just doing my job," he said.

Pavesi stopped and turned to look Adler in the eye. "No," he said, "it was more than that. I can see the dedication in you, the desire to find the truth and do justice. You have my thanks."

Adler felt as if he might falter. This was killing him. He so desperately wanted to tell Pavesi that they had in no way given up. But he would not do that. The undercover operation was the way to proceed. And this was his small part in making it a success.

"Thank you, Mr. Pavesi," he said. "I wish I could have done more."

Pavesi smiled and patted him on the shoulder. They walked on, through the tasting room and onto the patio. Once outside, Adler immediately saw him, Jesse Morgan, standing no more than twenty yards away. Adler avoided eye contact. He had a thought. Certain that Morgan had seen them, he stopped and turned to Pavesi.

"Again, I wish there was more we could do," he said, speaking just loudly enough to be overheard, but not so loud as to appear that was what he wanted. "I hoped to find justice for Ray, and also for you."

Pavesi took his hand, cupping it in both of his own.

"Bless you for all that you've done."

They parted ways. Adler turned to walk back to his car. Out of the corner of his eye he could see Morgan watching him.

CHAPTER 29

8:11 p.m., Tuesday, September 13, Menfi Vineyards, Napa Valley, California

It was a small dinner party, with a few special guests. None more special than the one who sat on Rizzo's lap, his granddaughter, Sofia. He kissed her cheek, holding a cannoli while she dipped her fingers into the creamy filling. The little girl made a mess, smearing it all over both of them. Rizzo didn't mind. Every moment with her was a joy.

His grandson, Marco, was chasing Molly. The boy was the only one Rizzo knew who could match the border collie's energy. They had chased each other around the patio for an hour. Just watching it made Rizzo tired. Boy and dog would both sleep good tonight.

"More wine, Dad?"

"Always," Rizzo replied. He smiled at his daughter, Julia, as she filled his glass. It had been a surprise visit, up from San Jose. She had moved there after the divorce, taking a job as a software developer. She had always been the smart one.

"So, with your job, you can work remotely, right?" he asked.

"Theoretically," Julia replied, "I suppose so." She studied him, her eyes narrowing. "Why?"

"Look around," Rizzo said, smiling. "What better place to

be. Move up here. Get out of the city. Enjoy nature."

"The key word was *theoretically*," she said. "If you want to move up, you need to be near the seat of power."

"Always the ambitious one," Rizzo said, raising his glass to her. He took a sip. "Can't blame an old man for asking."

"Can't blame him at all," Julia replied. "Maybe someday."

"I'll take what I can get," Rizzo said. He grabbed a napkin and wiped some dessert off Sofia's nose.

The ring of silverware on crystal caught his ear. A toast was imminent. Rizzo looked up to see Stuart Boyd standing, his glass lifted high. Boyd was a carefully cultivated friend, and a writer for *The Wine Observer*. He was an important person to have in your camp.

"To our gracious hosts, Max and Gena. A beautiful evening of family and friends."

Rizzo gave a quick bow of the head, then stood, handing Sofia to her mother. "Grazie," he said. "It is our privilege to have all of you here. Enjoy in abundance."

"Hear, hear," said of the guests.

"And if you need to stay the night," Rizzo said in response, smiling, "we have an excellent breakfast."

There was laughter around the table. Rizzo watched as Rudy Moretti helped himself to more wine. So far, the big man was jovial. But Rizzo knew to keep an eye on him. Rudy could get loud, and worse.

The conversation eventually moved to business, as it often did. Rizzo had invited several vineyard and winery owners to dinner, something he had done for years. When he arrived in Napa, it was a surprise to learn how many of those in the industry were willing to offer advice. Rizzo had taken advantage of those offers, absorbing everything he could about the winemaking process and the business of getting product to market. Several of those who had helped him in the early days were here tonight.

"A guy stopped to see me today."

Rizzo turned to listen. The comment came from George

Reidel, one of those who had been a real mentor in the beginning. Reidel was a leader in the industry, his advice always worthy of careful consideration.

"Harley Ricard," Reidel continued. "Said he was a buyer for Coastal Foods. Apparently, they're thinking about getting into online wine sales."

Rizzo leaned forward. Selling wine online was not new. There were several major players. But if a supermarket giant like Coastal got into the game, they could immediately move to the top of the heap.

"Guy seemed to know his stuff," Reidel said. "I was impressed. I just mention it in case he makes contact. He's worth a listen."

Rizzo nodded. "Good to know." He also knew that a lot of people would have kept that to themselves, made sure they were in on the ground floor before letting anyone else in on it. But that wasn't Reidel's style. Besides, he was such a presence in the industry that he could share with impunity. At this point, there was almost nothing that could affect the success of Three Peaks Vineyards.

"I don't know," Rudy said. "Buyin' wine on the computer. I don't like it."

And there it was, Rizzo thought. The first signs. Rudy was starting to get sloppy, argumentative.

"I think it's a great idea," Rizzo said, staring at his associate. It was meant to be definitive, to end it. Rudy looked at him and shrugged. That meant message received.

"Too bad about what happened over at Evans Creek," Reidel said. "They won't be selling any wine from this vintage online or anywhere else."

There were nods around the table.

"Why would somebody do that?" Boyd asked.

"Who knows?" Rizzo replied. He stared at the glass in his hand and sighed. "Who knows?"

CHAPTER 30

9:32 a.m., Thursday, September 15, Cahill Estates, Napa Valley, California

Ward continued working his way through the vineyards and wineries of Napa Valley. This morning, it was Cahill Estates. When he talked to the owner yesterday afternoon, he led right off with the story about being a buyer from Coastal Foods and the prospective online wine store. Ashton Cahill immediately agreed to meet, the sooner the better. Ward was increasingly impressed with the entrée provided by his undercover persona. It was almost too good to be true. And when that was the case, it made him nervous.

Cahill Estates was another big player in the valley, known particularly for their Pinot Grigio. Ward preferred reds. In truth, he preferred beer. But he had done some extra homework on white wine the night before to prepare for this meeting. That included sampling Cahill's product, which he enjoyed more than anticipated.

The gate was just ahead. Ward turned in, the Corvette slowly rumbling toward the winery. The sound must have announced his presence. A man he assumed to be Ashton Cahill emerged, smile as wide as the sky.

"Harley Ricard?" he asked, marching across the parking lot

at a brisk pace.

Ward was barely out of the car before Cahill arrived.

"Thanks for agreeing to meet me so soon," Ward said, extending his hand.

"My pleasure," Cahill replied. "Coastal is a good customer. I was happy to hear they're thinking of taking things online."

"Still in the planning stages," Ward said. "But when we get ready to launch, we want to have all of the pieces in place." Ward knew that Coastal had carried Cahill's wines for some time. That made him nervous. Cahill would presumably be familiar with people who worked there. He hoped that the FBI was right when they told him that certain corporate executives would know what to say if asked.

"Of course," Cahill replied. "An operation like that does not happen overnight."

"No, it doesn't," Ward said. "In fact, there's only a handful of people at corporate who know this is coming."

"No point in alerting the competition," Cahill said with a wink.

"Exactly," Ward replied.

"Well, c'mon in," Cahill said. "Let me show you around."

"I'd like that."

They walked back toward the winery, bypassing the tasting room, and heading straight into the production facility.

"This is our destemming machine," Cahill said, starting the tour. "We harvest early in the day when the grapes are still cool. In fact, we sometimes rig lighting so the workers can start before sunrise. As I'm sure you know, freshness is crucial, so we get the grapes here as fast as we can. We want them destemmed and pressed within a few hours."

Ward nodded. He knew that it was important to remove the juice and pulp from the skins as quickly as possible. Unlike with reds, white wine was fermented with the skins and seeds removed.

"And this is our press," Cahill said, leading Ward to a large steel tank. "We use a bladder press. The bladder inside inflates and pushes the grapes to the side, causing the juice to flow through screens."

He walked on, motioning for Ward to follow.

"After pressing, we pump the wine into this chilled tank," Cahill explained. "There, it can settle for a bit, letting any remaining debris sink to the bottom. After a few hours, the somewhat clarified juice can be moved to other tanks or barrels where it begins the fermentation process."

They next went to several larger stainless-steel tanks.

"These are the fermentation tanks," Cahill continued. "Here, as you know, we add yeast to begin the process. Of course, the wine also goes through a fining process to remove any haziness." He turned and pointed to several slightly smaller tanks down the line. "We also age most of our wine in stainless."

They moved on to what Ward recognized as a bottling machine.

"Our bottling process is highly automated," Cahill said. "That helps limit the exposure to oxygen. Different machines then affix the labels and place the bottles in boxes to be shipped," he added.

"It's an impressive operation," Ward observed. He turned to Cahill. "Coastal believes that the online platform will significantly expand their sales, as well as the demand for featured labels." He knew that Cahill would understand that to include his product. "Will it be a problem for you to meet the increased demand?"

Cahill smiled. "If it is, that's a problem I'd like to have." He put his hands on his hips, looked back over the facility, then turned to Ward. "Mr. Ricard, we can produce whatever you need."

"That's what I wanted to hear," Ward replied.

"Do you have time for a sample?" Cahill asked.

"Always," Ward replied.

Cahill led the way to the tasting room. It was not the masterpiece of design that Ward had encountered at Three Peaks but was still quite inviting in its own way. Ward watched as Cahill selected a bottle and uncorked it, pouring two glasses a third full. He rather quickly examined it by sight, breathed in the aroma, then took a sip, a satisfied look appearing on his face.

"I think you'll find this Pino Grigio to your liking," Cahill said, sliding the other glass to Ward.

As he had done at Three Peaks, Ward skipped the examination by sight. He swirled the wine, breathed in the bouquet, then took a sip, lightly sucking on it for aeration.

"Just incredible," he said.

Cahill raised his glass in a toast. "To our future business endeavors."

"Indeed," Ward replied. He felt some guilt. Cahill, like Reidel, seemed to be a nice guy. But this was part of the job, the way he worked himself into the industry.

"Say," Cahill continued, "there's an industry event this weekend, the Napa Valley Harvest Gala. Most of the major players will be there, and I think a lot of them would like to talk to you. Any interest?"

"Absolutely," Ward replied. "Just tell me when and where."

CHAPTER 31

10:07 a.m., Thursday, September 15, Napa County Sheriff's Office, 1535 Airport Blvd, Napa, California

"How's it going with that Evans Creek investigation?"

Adler looked up to see Sheriff Calvin Beeler approaching on his left.

"Got a couple calls from some local vineyard owners," Beeler said. "They're nervous. Hoping this wasn't some sort of environmental protest statement, or maybe something about exploiting migrant workers."

Adler shook his head. "It's nothing like that," he said. "Besides, those groups take credit, seek publicity for their cause. I haven't heard anything along those lines."

Adler wondered if these vineyard owners had called Beeler, or if it was the other way around. The sheriff was always looking for an opportunity to contact campaign doners, give the impression that he was doing everything possible to keep the county safe, calling to alleviate any concerns. Standard political bullshit. And that was what had worried Adler when Special Agent Parks asked him to *go through the motions*.

"Got any leads?" Beeler asked.

"Not really." Adler summarized the state of the investigation, including the dead spot in the surveillance camera timeline and

Henry Evans' seeming lack of interest in the investigation.

"Odd," Beeler observed. "Inside job?"

"Always a possibility," Adler replied. "Right now, I can't point to anything solid to indicate that." He knew he should tell the sheriff about the federal involvement, but he also knew that Beeler had a hard time keeping his mouth shut. The sheriff was aware of the FBI's forensic accounting in the Amato case, but nothing else. Parks and Ward had shown some real trust in him. Adler wanted to prove he deserved it.

"Any recent hires out there?" Beeler asked.

"Evans told me his people had all been with him for years," Adler replied. "But when I talked to the guy who opened up that day, a Walt Jenkins, he did say that there was somebody hired just over a year ago."

"Got a name?"

"Yeah." Adler checked a note on his desk. "Tommy Serra. Jenkins described him as a good kid."

"Have you talked to him?"

"Planned on doing that today," Adler replied. At least, that was the plan now.

Adler called Henry Evans right before he arrived but left out the reason for the visit. The owner was already waiting for him when he pulled into the parking lot.

"What's this about, Detective?" Evans asked, alongside Adler's vehicle before he had even stepped out the door.

"Just a little follow up," Adler replied. "I'd like to speak with Tommy Serra."

Evan's brow furrowed. The look on his face was one of surprise, maybe a hint of concern.

"Tommy? You don't think he had something to do with this?" Evans shook his head. "Tommy's a good kid. You're wasting your time."

"Is there a reason you don't want me to talk to him?" Adler

asked. He was becoming exasperated with Evans' attitude.

"What? No. Of course not," Evans replied. "I just don't think Tommy was involved. He's a great employee. Seems to enjoy working here."

"Then it shouldn't be a problem," Adler shot back. "Look," he said, "I'm just covering the bases. He is your most reason hire, right? A little over a year ago?" Adler put some emphasis on the last part. He wanted Evans to know that he was aware of that.

"Um, yeah. That's true," Evans replied. "I guess there's no harm. Wait here. I'll go get him."

"I'll be here," Adler said. He watched Evans walk off, pondering the man's motivation.

A few minutes later Evans returned. Adler guessed the young man with him to be in his early to mid-twenties.

"Tommy, this is Detective Adler," Evans said. "He wants to ask you some questions."

Adler nodded his greeting. "Should just take a few minutes."

Serra shrugged. "Okay," he said.

Evans did not move. Adler looked at him. He either didn't to get the message or had to be told.

"In private," Adler said.

Evans held up his hands. "Just trying to help."

Adler doubted it. He waited until Evans was well out of earshot.

"How long you been workin' here?" Adler asked. He took out a small notepad and pen.

"About fourteen months," Serra replied.

"Like it?"

Serra shrugged. "Yeah. I mean, it's not my life's ambition, but I'm learning a lot."

"What is your life's ambition?" Adler asked, smiling.

Serra smiled back. "I don't know. Guess I'm tryin' to figure that out."

Adler chuckled. "Sure. I get that." He felt the same at Serra's age, at least before he found that law enforcement was a good fit for him.

"So, how do you get along with Mr. Evans?" he asked.

"Good," Serra replied. "No complaints."

"Any idea who might have done this?" Adler asked. "Hear any talk among the employees, anything like that?"

Serra shook his head. "Nope. Most everybody seems pretty happy to be here."

"Most everybody?"

"I mean, nothing beyond the usual grumbling. But even that is pretty minimal compared to most places."

Adler nodded. He jotted a couple notes, then looked up at Serra. "Did you have anything to do with this?" he asked.

"No, sir," Serra replied. There was no break in eye contact, no visible tell that Adler could pick up on.

Adler closed his notepad and pulled out a business card, handing it to Serra. "Give me a call if you hear anything, okay?"

Serra tucked the card in his shirt pocket. "Will do."

He waited until the detective's car was well down the road before making the call. The number was not in his contacts. He had it memorized.

"Yeah," answered the voice on the other end.

"That guy from the sheriff's office was here again today."

"You think he knows anything?"

"I don't think so."

"Keep it that way."

CHAPTER 32

7:03 p.m., Saturday, September 17, the Napa Valley Harvest Gala, Marroquin Winery, Napa Valley, California

"I wouldn't have agreed to this if I'd known it was black tie," Ward said into his phone. It had been a long time since he was in a tuxedo.

"That's not true," Parks replied. "But I am a little surprised that you could manage a bow-tie."

"You can learn how to do anything from watching YouTube videos," Ward said.

She laughed. "No doubt."

Ward could see the entrance to Marroquin Winery ahead. There was a line of cars pulling in, all high-end luxury models. Here, the Corvette would fit in, maybe even be a bit understated.

"I'm almost there," Ward said. "Have to let you go."

"Good luck."

"Thanks." Ward terminated the call." He wished that Rowan could be there with him. But that was impossible.

Ward found a spot and parked. His neck chaffed under the starched collar as he walked toward the entrance. A dozen guests, dressed to the nines, had arrived at the same time. They walked alongside him, chattering excitedly about what the night entailed. It was clear to Ward that this was, indeed, one of the

125

premier social events of wine country.

The Tuscan style Marroquin Winery was beautifully illuminated, a beacon of warmth and hospitality. The expertly manicured grounds were extraordinary. Laughter and music drifted across the lawn as Ward approached, drawing him in. He had to remind himself that he was there to do a job. Still, it was okay to have a good time. That made the performance all the more convincing.

As Ward followed the crowd toward the back of the main building, an enormous tent appeared. Inside were dozens of tables. The settings were those of a fine restaurant. A sizable wait staff scurried about with final preparations. No buffet style here. Someone had gone to tremendous expense to put all of this together.

Ward scoured the crowd, hoping to see Cahill. After a few minutes he spotted him, talking to another man. They were clearly in a high mood, wine glasses in hand, enjoying themselves to the fullest.

"Mr. Cahill," Ward said, announcing his approach.

Cahill turned. A smile lit his face. "Harley, so glad you could make it." He reached out to shake Ward's hand, then turned to the other man. "Pete, this is the fellow I was telling you about."

Pete extended his hand. "Pedro Marroquin," the man said. "My friends call me Pete."

"Harley Ricard," Ward responded. "Pleased to meet you, Pete."

"Pete is our host this evening," Cahill added, "if that wasn't obvious."

"It's magnificent," Ward said, surveying the festivities. "Simply, magnificent."

"Gracias," Marroquin said with a nod. "I'm sure you will enjoy yourself."

"I have no doubt," Ward said with a smile.

"Pete was quite interested to hear that Coastal is moving into online wine sales," Cahill added.

Marroquin waved his hand. "We can discuss business later. This is a night of celebration."

"Agreed," Cahill replied. He turned to Ward. "Let's get you a drink."

They walked to one of several tables that had been set up as a bar. Marroquin selected a bottle. "May I offer you one of our Cabernets?"

"I would be delighted," Ward replied.

Marroquin poured, then handed him the glass. Ward gently swirled the wine, breathed it in, then took a sip, holding it in his mouth.

"Sublime," he said. "Just exceptional."

Marroquin bowed. "I am pleased that you approve." He gestured toward the tent, which was more of a big-top. "Tonight, our meal is prepared by my good friend, Chef Alessandro Ricci. I think you will find it to be a most extraordinary gastronomical experience."

"Chef Ricci holds seven Michelin stars," Cahill added. "He is truly one of the best. A meal prepared by him is like no other."

"I am honored to have this opportunity," Ward replied. "This will be a night to remember."

At that moment, the band took the stage.

"You're in for a treat," Cahill said. "Napa Sunrise. They're an Eagles tribute band, and a damned good one."

Ward listened as they broke into an astonishing version of "Hotel California." He was blown away. "Wow."

"Right?" Cahill asked.

"It's like they're here," Ward replied. The song reminded of his own informal group of bandmates back home, and why they never attempted anything by The Eagles.

Moments later, his listening was interrupted by the approach of two men coming from their right. As they drew closer, Ward recognized one of them as George Reidel.

"I thought I recognized this guy," Reidel said. "Nice to see you, Harley. Did you drive that '66 Vette?"

"I did."

Reidel turned to Cahill. "You should see it, Ashton. It's a beauty."

"Actually," Cahill replied, "I already have."

Reidel eyed Ward. "Makin' the rounds, I see." He chuckled. "Well, your online selection would not be complete without the Cahill label."

"Indeed," Marroquin added.

"Thank you, gentlemen," Cahill said with a bow.

Reidel turned to the man next to him. "Stuart, this is Harley Ricard from Coastal Foods."

The man extended his hand. "Stuart Boyd, with *The Wine Observer*."

They shook.

"George has been telling me about Coastal's move into online sales," Boyd said. "We might be interested in doing a piece on that."

Ward had to nip this in the bud. Certain executives at Coastal might be aware of what to say if asked about the prospect of launching internet wine sales, but an article in a publication as well known as *The Wine Observer* could cause discussions and raise questions.

"It's still classified as exploratory at this point," Ward said. "We're just trying to gauge interest. Coastal is by no means ready to go public." He hoped that was enough to fend off Boyd but still keep the vineyard owners interested.

"Fair enough," Boyd said. "We'll call it industry rumors."

Ward made a note to check the next edition for any reference to Coastal's plans. For now, he wanted to get away from Boyd before there were any more questions.

Cahill seemed to sense the discomfort. He motioned for Ward to follow him. "Let's mingle," he said. "I've got a few people I want to introduce you to."

"Nice to meet everyone," Ward said. "If you'll excuse us."

When they were out of earshot, Cahill leaned in. "Boyd's a

pain in the ass," he said. "I can't stand the pompous fuck. But he's...necessary."

Ward chuckled. "Understood."

As they wandered the grounds, Cahill introduced Harley Ricard to any number of players in the industry. Aside from the encounter with Boyd, the night was shaping up to be very productive.

CHAPTER 33

8:47 a.m., Monday, September 19, Federal Bureau of Investigation, Santa Rosa Resident Agency, Santa Rosa, California

"Anything happening with the Amato case?"

Parks looked up to see Brad Harrison approaching. She took a breath, reminding herself to stay calm.

"That's what I thought," Harrison said before she could answer. "Just curious." There was the hint of a smirk on his face.

"My recollection is that the SAC said I should report to ASAC Nash on this." Parks knew that she shouldn't have gone there, but it just had to be done.

Harrison's expression turned sour. "So be it," he said, then turned to leave.

"Fuck," Parks said under her breath. She did not want it to go like this with her supervisor, but she also wasn't going to put up with his bullshit. That was not in her DNA.

Parks looked at her cell. There was a message indicator on the phone icon. She pulled up her voicemail. The area code was 973, Newark, New Jersey. Joe Adler had called her after his interview of Tommy Serra, the most recent hire at Evans Creek. According to Adler, the interview didn't produce much. But he also mentioned that Serra had been hired just over a year ago. That was inconsistent with a statement by the owner, Henry Evans, who told him that all his regular employees had been there for years. Maybe it was just a misstatement, but given Evans seeming disinterest in the investigation of the incident at his winery, it was worth some follow-up. Parks pulled the kid's rap sheet. There wasn't much, but there was an arrest for disorderly conduct in Newark, a Mob haven. The charge was eventually dismissed. Still, on a hunch, she put in call to the Newark Field Office. This had to be them. Parks played the message.

This is Special Agent Lou Chambers, Newark. I've got something on the Serra kid. Give me a call.

Parks smiled. Fuck Harrison. She hit the callback number. One ring, two...

"Chambers."

"This is Parks, Santa Rosa. Thanks for the quick turnaround. What've you got?"

"I dug into that disorderly arrest," Chambers said.

"Yeah?"

"Your boy was picked up with a low-level member of the Lucchese family."

Parks sat back in her chair. The Lucchese crime family was one of the Five Families who made up the Commission, the governing body of the New York Mob.

"Might mean something, might not," Chambers continued. "I'll send you an email with the details."

"I appreciate it," Parks said.

"No problem." Chambers terminated the call.

This, combined with Jesse Morgan's connection to the Genovese family? It had to be more than a coincidence. Parks was pleased. She thought about it for a moment, but then changed her mind. Fuck Harrison. She picked up the phone to call Nash.

CHAPTER 34

*7:12 p.m., Monday, September 19, Ward's undercover residence,
Foster Road, Napa, California*

Ward sat down to some Chinese takeout from a nearby restaurant.
It had been another day on the wine trail, making connections,
establishing his persona. Things were going well, so well that it
made him nervous. But maybe that was just his nature, one that
helped keep him alive.

Tonight, it was Kung Pao chicken, with a side of wonton
dumplings in chili sauce. Ward opened a bottle of Pinot Grigio
from Cahill Estates. He had no idea if this was an appropriate
pairing, but he liked Ashton Cahill and had developed a taste
for the wine. Ward poured a glass and settled in. He flipped on
the television and prepared for another dinner alone in another
undercover residence.

The FBI had surprisingly subscribed to just about every major
streaming service. Ward searched for one of his favorites shows,
then scrolled down to where he had left off in the series. As he
was about to hit play, his phone rang. He looked at the number.
It wasn't in his contacts, but he immediately recognized it as the
cell Rowan was using to contact him. He answered.

"Hi, Rowan."

"Hello, David."

"What's up?" he asked. Hearing her voice only put an exclamation point on his loneliness. Part of him wanted to invite her over, but he knew that was impossible.

"I have some news about one of the workers at Evans Creek Vineyards," she said, "Tommy Serra."

"What've you got?" He was disappointed that she went straight to business.

"He was the most recent hire there, just over a year ago. That was inconsistent with Henry Evans' statement to Adler that all of his regulars had been there for years."

"So, you took it upon yourself to do a little digging," Ward proffered.

"You know me so well."

He could hear the hint of laughter in her voice. It warmed him.

"And what did you turn up?"

"An arrest in Newark, New Jersey, for disorderly conduct."

"And...?"

"He was arrested with some low-level functionary in the Lucchese family."

"You the mean the Mob family?"

"The same."

Ward's wheels stared to turn. They already had Jesse Morgan's connection to the Genovese family. Now this.

"So, you think the Mob is putting their people at some of these wineries?"

"I don't know," she replied. "But it's a helluva coincidence."

"I don't believe in coincidences."

"I thought you might say that."

CHAPTER 35

7:33 p.m., Monday, September 19, Dash Estates, Napa Valley, California

Rory Stone surveyed the usual group of hangers-on and C-listers. It was yet another night of partying, and he didn't know how to stop it. But honestly, even if he could, wouldn't he miss it? The glory days, if you could call them that, were becoming a distant memory. That's why he needed these people, to remind him that he was once a star. Hollywood had quit calling twenty years ago, but this group still treated him as if he had just won an Emmy.

The place drew its name from his biggest success. *Dash*, a crime drama about a private investigator who plied his trade on the streets of Las Vegas, had run for five years in the mid-eighties. The ratings were never great, but the show hung in there. Few parts came after. Then, a disastrous role on a vapid 1993 sitcom ended his career when the show was canceled midseason.

Fortunately, the looks had remained. Stone fucked his way through LA with panache, quickly realizing that his key to survival was women of means. And that is how he came to own Dash Estates. His wife, Madeline, had come from a wealthy family. Rory tried to convince her, and himself, that there was love, at least in the beginning. But his wayward eye got the best of him. He tried to keep it discreet. But she knew, and she put up with it. Or so he thought. Madeline had died just over a year ago. When her attorney read the will, Stone learned that she had left him her share of the vineyard they bought together, but little else. The bulk of her estate went to her two children from a previous marriage. The fine print in a prenup that he had neglected to read carefully cemented his fate. There was no way to challenge the will. And even if he had, her offspring would have used their considerable resources to ensure his defeat. Now, the never particularly profitable Dash Estates had no backup funding. And things were going downhill...fast.

"Rory! Great party, my man!"

Stone turned to see Ned Henderson, glass in hand, sloppy drunk, as per usual. Ned meandered a good fifteen yards to cover the five between them, twice nearly falling over.

"Thanks, Ned," Stone replied, already plotting his exit strategy.

"Do you remember that episode of *Dash*," Ned slurred, stopping to catch his breath, "the one where you stopped that terrorist from blowing up the casino?"

"Yeah, Ned. I remember."

"Oh, man. I love that one." Ned grabbed the back of a sofa to steady himself. "That was the *best* show ever."

"Thanks, Ned."

"They just don't make 'em like that anymore."

"I guess not."

"The so-called actors today, they *suck*. Couldn't act their way out of a fuckin' wet paper bag."

Stone wasn't exactly sure what that meant but nodded his agreement. It was best to just go along with Ned's pronouncements, then escape when he got distracted or passed out.

"Hey, Ned!" someone yelled. "C'mere and see this. There are some weird lights in the sky. It looks like a UFO."

"No shit!" Ned let go of the coach, almost toppling over. He righted himself and blasted off in the general direction of the aliens. "On my way!" he announced.

Ned staggered toward the window. The UFO had been spotted by Stone's alleged agent, the irrepressible and wildly unsuccessful Harvey Koppel. As soon as he had Ned safely pointed in the direction of the fictitious spaceship, Koppel headed toward Stone, a bemused smirk on his face.

"You're welcome," Koppel said as he drew near.

"What would I ever do without you?" Stone asked.

"According to you, win an Oscar."

Stone laughed. Koppel was a quick wit. He had to give him that.

"Does this crowd ever change?" Koppel asked, looking around the room.

"Sadly, no," Stone replied. "But it might not matter much longer."

"Why's that?"

Stone took a drink, then looked his old friend in the eye. "Things aren't goin' so well, Harvey."

"What do you mean?" Koppel asked, concerned. "Is it your health? Are you sick?"

"No," Stone replied, "nothin' like that." He paused, looking around to see if anyone was listening. "It's the vineyard. This place is hemorrhaging money. It's going under."

"I'm sorry to hear that."

"I can't lose this place, Harvey. It's the only thing I have left."

"Can you get a loan?"

"You mean another one?" Stone asked. "No bank is going to lend me money, not when they see the balance sheet."

"I didn't know."

"If I just got one good infusion of cash," Stone said, "I could make some changes, turn things around."

Koppel was silent for a moment, staring into his drink. When he looked up, his eyes were serious as death. "How bad to you want to keep the place?" he asked.

"I don't know what I would do without it," Stone replied. "I'm desperate."

Koppel nodded. "Okay," he said. "I know a guy. He might be able to help."

CHAPTER 36

12:43 p.m., Tuesday, September 20, Menfi Vineyards, Napa Valley, California

"Most people know nothing of wine," Rizzo said. "Someone tells them that it's good and they believe it."

Stuart Boyd grimaced. He held up his glass. "Wine is life," he announced. "I cannot imagine such a thing...unless I'm the one telling them."

Rizzo chuckled. "You know it's true. If *The Wine Observer* gave a ninety-eight-point rating to some swill, people would rave about it." He took a bite from his antipasto plate and a sip of Chianti Classico.

"Perhaps," Boyd acknowledged. "If it came from *The Wine Observer*."

"Of course, they would never do that," Rizzo noted. "I'm just saying."

It was a play to Boyd's vanity. In truth, Rizzo found the man tolerable in nothing beyond small doses. But he was good for business.

"By the way," Boyd said, "I didn't see you at the Harvest Gala."

"I'm sorry to have missed it. Other obligations." He was sorry. The dinner was always exceptional, and it was a great place to gather intelligence.

"George Reidel introduced to me to Harley Ricard, that buyer from Coastal."

"The one who's setting up the online platform?"

"The same. I suggested that the magazine might be interested in doing an article. I thought he would jump at it."

"He didn't?"

"Not at all. He characterized their efforts as exploratory, an attempt to gauge interest. He told me that Coastal was not ready to go public with it."

"I'm surprised," Rizzo said. "I had the impression that they were full speed ahead. Still, I'd like to meet him."

"You should. Maybe Reidel can arrange it."

"I'll talk to George."

"Ashton Cahill seemed to be showing Ricard around, making introductions. So, that might be another avenue. Do you know Ashton?"

"We've met," Rizzo replied. "Polite banter at industry events. Nothing more."

"What do you think of the Chianti?" Rizzo asked, nodding at Boyd's glass.

"Graceful," Boyd observed, "balanced. The cherry aroma and acidity pair perfectly with antipasto."

"I thought you would approve." Rizzo wondered if Boyd had ever simply said that he liked a particular wine. Not likely. It was more probable that he had commented on the bouquet and tannin structure of the first glass that ever passed his lips.

"Sorry to interrupt, boss."

Rizzo turned to see Rudy Moretti rumble onto the patio.

Moretti nodded at Boyd. "Stuart, how you doin'?"

Boyd raised his glass. "A lovely afternoon at Menfi Vineyards, as always."

"Rudy, would you care to join us?" Rizzo asked.

"No, thanks." Moretti jerked his head to the side. "Could I talk to you for a second?" He turned to Boyd. "No offense,

Stuart. It's a business thing."

"None taken."

"If you'll excuse us," Rizzo said, rising from his chair.

"Of course."

They stepped off the patio and walked a safe distance, out of Boyd's earshot.

"What is it?" Rizzo asked.

Moretti looked around, then turned back to Rizzo. "There's this thing that's come up."

CHAPTER 37

11:29 a.m., Wednesday, September 21, outside of Sadie's Diner, Sonoma, California

The meeting was to take place at eleven thirty sharp. He had been told to look for a black Cadillac sedan parked near the diner. The instructions included to not approach the vehicle from the rear. Koppel was quite specific on that point. It brought to mind a scene in an episode of *Dash*, one that did not end well for the character who got in the car.

Stone spotted the Cadillac. It was parked around the corner from the main entrance, on the opposite side of the street, facing him. He pulled down his cap and adjusted his sunglasses, certain that he would be recognized without them, then approached. When he was within fifteen feet, the darkly tinted driver's window lowered a few inches.

"Get in," came a gruff voice from inside.

Stone felt movement in his bowels, like an animal was crawling through them. He considered walking by, never looking back. But that wasn't really an option. He took a breath. Drawing on his acting experience, he conjured up the appearance of confidence. Then, stepping around to the passenger side, he got in.

"How you doin'?" the driver asked. He was a big man, thick, dangerous.

"I'm okay," Stone replied. He thought about extending a hand but decided against it.

"I remember your show," the man said. "*Dash*, right?"

"That's right." The comment made Stone feel slightly more at ease.

"That was a good show."

"Thanks."

"So, I hear the wine business ain't goin' so good," the man said, staring out the window. He had yet to make eye contact. It was disconcerting.

"It's a tough business," Stone observed.

"Yeah, and everybody wants to get into it."

"True," Stone replied. He couldn't deny it. Sometimes it seemed like every successful entrepreneur who liked wine and had a little cash wanted to buy in. And then there were the celebrities. He was far from the first actor to invest in a vineyard.

The big man turned toward Stone, giving him the once-over. "Problem is, half of 'em don't know shit about makin' wine," he said. "How 'bout you? Do you know shit about makin' wine?"

Any hint of being at ease had now evaporated. Loan officers had pored over his financial statements in the past. It always made him nervous, approval hinging on their analysis. But this was a different kind of assessment, no less important, and far more intimidating.

"The vineyard needs some capital investment to upgrade operations," Stone said, struggling to appear calm. "We have a good product, but it can be better. Our grapes are excellent. I'd like to hire a new vintner, one who can bring us to our full potential. We also need to boost our marketing."

The big man nodded, saying nothing, then turned away, looking out the windshield. The silence was terrifying.

"How much do you need?" he finally asked.

Stone had no idea what was possible. "How much can you loan me?" he asked.

The big man grunted. "That's not the question," he said.

"One point five," Stone answered, holding his breath.

"That's a lot of money," the man replied. "But I think we can do business."

Stone exhaled. "What's the interest rate?" he asked.

"I like you," the man said. "We'll make it ten percent."

"Ten percent?" Stone asked, surprised. He had expected something much higher.

The man turned to look at him. "That's per month."

"Oh."

"And we may ask for an occasional...favor."

"I see."

"That a problem?"

Stone looked away, wondering how he had ever gotten himself in this position.

"No," he replied. "That's not a problem."

"Good," the man said. "We'll be in touch."

The meeting was clearly over. Stone grabbed the door handle, preparing to exit, then stopped. "What's your name?" he asked, instantly regretting the question.

The big man started the car, then jerked his head toward the passenger door, signaling for Stone to get out.

"We'll worry about names later," he replied.

Stone stepped out. He shut the door. Within seconds, the Cadillac turned the corner and was gone.

CHAPTER 38

6:01 p.m., Wednesday, September 21, the safehouse, San Francisco, California

Ward found a spot three blocks away, a good distance from the safehouse. He was sure that no one had followed him. There had been no sign of a tail. It was not surprising. At this point, not a single soul seemed suspicious of his cover. It was too comfortable, the kind of thing that caused you to let your guard down. And that was one reason he had driven a rental. The Corvette was an exclamation mark; fine for visiting vineyards, not so good for flying under the radar.

As an additional precaution, Ward casually mentioned his need to visit Coastal's headquarters to Ashton Cahill. The amiable vintner had, of course, accepted this at face value. The two of them were becoming friends, at least to the extent that any undercover agent could befriend someone in their assumed world. Cahill seemed a legitimately good man. Once again, Ward felt guilty about deceiving an innocent player in the game. But it was a necessary part of creating his legend, and a skill at which he had become almost disturbingly adept.

Ward checked his surroundings. Seeing nothing out of place, he adjusted his sunglasses, pulled down his cap, and stepped out of the car. It was a short walk to the building. Before he could even access the video intercom system, he was buzzed in. Ward walked to the elevator, entered, and hit number seven. Rowan was waiting, with Mancuso. The plan was to debrief, provide information for their 302s, the FBI version of the case report. Aside from being needed for any ultimate prosecution, they were also necessary to demonstrate progress to leadership, and keep them onboard.

As he stepped of the elevator, Ward was surprised to find himself slightly nervous about seeing Rowan. Suddenly he had a flashback, to a hallway outside the apartment of his ex-wife, Maria. He was there to pick her up for their second date, quite anxious about making a good impression. The memory, the sudden realization, startled him. He took a breath, then knocked on the door.

Rowan opened it. Her eyes lit up when she saw him. A radiant smile spread across her beautiful face; the reaction so natural, sincere. Ward suddenly found himself unable to speak. Why was this happening now? Say something, idiot, he thought.

"Hi, Rowan." Genius.

"C'mon in," she said, swinging the door open.

Ward entered. Mancuso sat at the table, typing away on his laptop. He stood when Ward approached, extending a hand.

"How are things in Napa?" Mancuso asked.

"I have to give you guys some credit," Ward admitted. "My cover story has worked brilliantly."

"Mark your calendars," Parks said. "ATF just admitted that FBI did something right."

Ward chuckled and took a seat. Rowan came around to her laptop.

"Want something to drink?" she asked before sitting. "A coffee maybe?"

Ward held up his hand. "I'm good. Had one on the way over."

"Well, bring us up to speed," Mancuso said, ready to type.

Ward spent the next hour taking them through his visits to

the vineyards, his friendship with Cahill, the night at the Harvest Gala, including the suggestion of an interview by the writer from *The Wine Observer*.

"We'll make sure that our people at Coastal are prepared for any inquiry," Mancuso said.

"Please do," Ward replied.

Just then, Mancuso's cell rang. He picked it up.

"Sorry, hon," he said. "I'm leaving now." He terminated the call.

Rowan looked at him, raising her eyebrows. "Are you in trouble?" she asked.

"A little bit," Mancuso replied, looking at his watch. "We have dinner reservations at eight. I need to get going." He turned to Ward. "Anything else?"

"No, that's about it for now."

"Okay," Mancuso said, shutting his laptop. "I'm outta here." He gathered his things and headed for the door.

As Mancuso left, Ward realized that he was now alone with Rowan for the first time since it had ended between them. He wasn't sure what to do.

"Are you going to head back?" Rowan asked. Always so self-assured, she seemed uncharacteristically nervous.

"I thought I might spend the night here," Ward replied. "Change of scenery, and it fits better with the excuse for the trip."

She nodded. "Makes sense."

They were silent for a moment. It started to become awkward.

"I could pick up some dinner," she offered. "You know, if that's alright."

Ward didn't want to read something into it that wasn't there. Maybe she was just being polite. He wanted to say yes, but knew it was probably a bad idea. On the other hand, he didn't want to offend her.

"I'd like that," Ward said. It sounded like he was accepting a date. Stupid. "I mean, sure. Why not?"

He saw the hint of a knowing smile curl up on one corner of her mouth.

"There's a great Thai place just around the corner," she said. "How does that sound? Do you like Thai?"

"Absolutely." Right now, he would have been fine with anything.

She typed in a search and quickly navigated to the restaurant's menu, then spun the toward him so that they could look at it together. Ward found the choices a bit overwhelming, and his mind was elsewhere.

"I'll just have the pad Thai," he said.

"And pad kee mao for me," Rowan announced.

Ward reached for his wallet. "Let me pay," he offered.

"Too late," Rowan replied. "Already ordered and paid for."

Ward smiled and put his wallet away. "Thank you."

Rowan got up and went into the kitchen. She returned with an opened bottle of Pinot Gris and two glasses.

"This seemed the best pairing," she said. "But then, you're the expert."

"Hardly," Ward replied. "Still, an excellent choice."

"Thank you." Rowan slipped on her jacket and checked her weapon. "I'll be right back."

After she left, Ward found the bathroom. He splashed some water on his face, dried off, then ran his fingers through his hair. It would have to do. By the time he was back at the kitchen table she was coming through the door.

The food was delicious, as was the wine. They talked about her career, the case, not about the past. Ward briefly considered going there, but this was not the time. He tried to just enjoy the evening. Both knew there was much unsaid.

When they were done, both got up to clear their dishes at the same time. Ward found himself face-to-face with Rowan, inches away. He sat his plate back on the table. She did the same. He thought he saw a longing in her eyes. She had to see the same in him. Ward knew he had to try. They kissed, melding together, holding each other tightly. There was no misunderstanding. When it was over, she rested her head on his chest

"I better go," she said. Then, she looked up at him and smiled. "Besides, I don't know where all of the surveillance cameras are in this place."

Ward smiled. "Understood."

He watched as she gathered her things to go, stopping only to give him a loving smile before walking through the door.

CHAPTER 39

9:08 a.m., Thursday, September 22, Amato Freight Lines Corporate Headquarters, Sacramento, California

Adler was glad that Estes had offered to come with. He was always an entertaining traveling companion.

"So, why don't they call you Doble E?" Adler asked. "It has more panache."

"I didn't give myself the nickname, bro," Estes replied. "I would have gone with something like Zorro."

Adler laughed.

Amato Freight Lines was just up ahead. This was a hastily arranged trip after a call from Parks. Adler had no idea what sort of reception he would get. He had explained the reason for the visit. The company would either comply with his request or not. And if not, he wanted to gauge reaction. The plan was to talk to whoever was in charge and ask for GPS records for their trucks for the last two years. It was a big ask, and he wasn't hopeful.

Adler drove through the gate and found a spot in front of the main office.

"Why, exactly, are we doing FBI's bidding?" Estes asked before they got out.

"They don't want to draw attention to their involvement,"

Adler replied. What he didn't say was that doing so made things more dangerous for Ward. That was Parks's concern, and he agreed.

"Understood," Estes said. "And we need the GPS records because every Mob case has a trucking angle."

Adler eyed his partner, saying nothing. The guy figured shit out.

"Let's go," Adler said.

"Right behind you, bro."

They entered the lobby. Adler approached the same receptionist he had encountered before and flashed his badge.

"Detective Joe Adler, Napa County Sheriff's Office," he announced.

"I recall," the receptionist said, her smile forced.

"And this is Detective Enrique Estes."

Estes gave her a nod.

"We're here to see Griffin Cooper," Adler said. He was told that Cooper had become the acting president of the company. Since Cooper called the shots, that's who he had arranged to meet.

"Is he expecting you?"

"He is," Adler replied.

"Have a seat. I'll let him know you're here."

A few minutes later, two men approached. One had the appearance of a man who had gotten his hands dirty, driven truck, maybe come up through the ranks. Adler assumed he was Cooper. The other was a suit and had the look of someone who was about to explain. Adler guessed him to be the company lawyer.

"Detective Adler?"

Adler stood. "That would be me."

"Griffin Cooper." The man extended his hand. Adler had guessed right.

"I'm the acting president of Amato Freight Lines," Cooper continued. "And this is our attorney, C. Barton Webb."

"Mr. Webb," Adler said, hand outstretched. The lawyer shook it, reluctantly, as if he might catch something.

Adler turned to his partner. "And this is Detective Estes."

Estes shook Cooper's hand and nodded at the attorney.

"So, I understand that you would like GPS records for our trucks," Webb began.

The explanation was underway. "That's correct," Adler replied, "for the last two years." He looked to Cooper. "I assume your trucks have GPS."

"They do," Webb answered. It was clear he intended to control the encounter. "May I ask why you need said records?"

Adler restrained himself from answering, *you may not, you pompous fuck.* "Of course," he replied instead. "Unfortunately, our investigation into the untimely death of your founder has stalled." He let that sink in for a moment. "We are just looking for anything that might produce a lead. You know, tying up loose ends."

"And how would this help?" Cooper asked.

Webb gave him a look that said, *let me do the talking.*

Adler directed his answer to Cooper. "What if one of the drivers was involved in something illegal? Maybe one of the trucks had an inexplicable departure from its normal route. What if Mr. Amato discovered that and confronted the driver?"

Cooper started to answer, but Webb cut him off. "That seems a bit of stretch," the lawyer said. "I've discussed this with management, and we are taking the position that you'll need to get a warrant."

And there it is, Adler thought. He looked at Cooper. "Is that correct?" he asked.

"I'm afraid so," Cooper replied. "It's just that..."

Webb interrupted. "What you're asking for is proprietary information that would disclose our client list, routes, pickup and delivery times, and other sensitive logistical information."

"We weren't planning to turn it over to your competitors," Adler shot back. He hadn't planned to get pissed, but now he was there. "You do understand that we're trying to find out who killed *your* founder?"

"Nonetheless," Webb replied.

Adler turned to Estes. "Let's go."

"That was a load of crap," Estes said when they were in the parking lot. "You think they're trying to hide something?"

"I don't know," Adler replied. "Cooper has assumed the reins of power. The company is uncooperative on the GPS records. That certainly makes him worth a look."

"Agreed," Estes said. "But that asshole Webb was driving the train in there."

"That's how it seemed," Adler said. "Or, at least, that's how someone wanted it to appear."

They got in the car. As soon as they were through the gate Adler, called Parks. She answered on the first ring.

"What happened?" Parks asked.

"It was interesting," Adler replied. He described the encounter, the company's reasons for refusing to comply.

"That's bullshit," Parks responded.

"I'm guessing that we don't have enough for a warrant?" Adler realized that the FBI almost certainly knew more than it was sharing with him.

"Not even close," Parks replied. "And even if we did, I wouldn't want to put it in an affidavit, not under the present circumstances."

"Understood."

"We'll have to find another way."

CHAPTER 40

11:16 a.m., Thursday, September 22, near Menfi Vineyards, Napa Valley, California

The Corvette rumbled through the Northern California countryside. Ward breathed in the fall air as he took in the rolling hills and sunlit valleys. It was a beautiful place; one he hoped to someday enjoy under different circumstances. His enjoyment of the scenery was interrupted by a call. He fished out his phone. It was Rowan.

"Hello," he yelled into the phone, knowing it would be hard to hear him.

"I take it you have the top down," Rowan yelled back.

"I'll pull over."

Ward found a spot on the side of the road.

"How's that?" he asked.

"Much better. Where are you headed?"

"Menfi Vineyards," Ward replied. "The owner is a guy by the name of Massimiliano Rizzo."

"Did you cold call this guy?"

"No. The owner of Three Peaks, George Reidel, arranged it. He said Rizzo wanted to meet me."

"Interesting," Rowan said. "Sounds like the word is getting out."

"I guess." Ward noticed that nothing was said about the night before. He considered bringing it up but thought better of it. Besides, he preferred to go with the version in which she wanted something to happen in the future, as opposed to the one in which she had second thoughts.

"If you can work it into casual conversation, I'd like you to ask him something."

"What's that?"

"Ask him what trucking company he uses."

"Do you know something about this guy that I don't?"

"No, nothing like that. But if it turns out that a bunch of these vineyards use Amato Freight Lines, that's a thread that might lead somewhere."

"And every Mob case, if that's what this is, has a trucking angle?"

"Something like that," Rowan replied. "Call it a hunch."

"Wouldn't Amato just turn over that information?"

"Adler was there this morning, asking for the GPS records for their trucks. Their corporate mouthpiece gave him some song and dance about it being proprietary information, turning it over would disclose their client list, routes, etcetera. Total bullshit."

"That's supposed to be some sort of trade secret?" Ward asked.

"So they claim."

"Seems suspicious."

"That's what I thought."

"I can ask him," Ward said. "I can work it into a discussion about the logistics of the supply chain."

"Do you think there's a way you can find out who the other vineyards use, the ones you've already visited?"

"That could be a bit trickier," Ward replied. "I suppose I could ask them if there is a trucking company they prefer to use, or if Coastal should consider using its own trucks, or maybe even contracting with another carrier. But first, I need to learn a little more about how the supply chain works in this industry."

"Don't do it unless you can bring it up, you know, without raising suspicion."

"Believe me, I won't."

"Okay." There was a pause. "David...stay safe."

"I will."

Ward ended the call. He pulled back onto the road. A few minutes later, he could see the entrance to Menfi Vineyards. A beautiful Spanish colonial home sat atop the sprawling estate, with a winery, in matching style, nearby. The vines, in their perfect rows, shimmered in the midday sun. A cobalt blue sky framed the picture. It was the scene one imagined when they thought of Napa.

Ward parked. A tall, distinguished-looking man approached. He was dressed in a guayabera, his dark hair combed back. The slacks were perfectly tailored, the sandals expensive. There was an air of success, and of being at ease with who he was. He stopped, stroking the Corvette as he smiled, lovingly.

"What a beautiful car," he remarked. "A '66?"

"Absolutely correct," Ward replied. He held out his hand. "Harley Ricard."

"Max Rizzo. It's a pleasure."

"You know," Ward said, looking around, "in my tour of the region, I can honestly say I have not seen a place more stunning than this."

"Grazie," Rizzo replied. "Please, let me show you our home."

They toured the house and grounds, then moved on to the winery. Rizzo was a man who took great pride in what he had accomplished, regaling Ward with tales of his humble beginnings in Brooklyn, how he and Gena had come west to build a life for themselves and their family. And what he had done was impressive. Ward had already visited several world-class vineyards, and Menfi's facilities were second to none. They finished at the wine bar as Rizzo poured a glass of Cabernet for each of them. Ward breathed in the aroma and then took a taste.

"Simply majestic," he said.

Rizzo beamed. "Grazie, grazie," he said, putting his hand on Ward's shoulder. "Please, I hope you can stay for lunch."

"I would be delighted."

They took the bottle and moved to the patio. Several guests were already seated there, enjoying their meals and wine. Rizzo found a table away from the patrons.

"Please, have a seat." He gestured toward one of the chairs. A waiter brought menus. As he considered the selections, Ward noticed a man coming toward them. He was hard to miss: large, thick, with a ruddy complexion. The man was a bull, the kind who could snap you in half if he were of a mind to do so.

"Boss," the man said as he drew near.

"Rudy," Rizzo replied. "Join us."

Ward stood to greet the newcomer.

"Harley Ricard," Rizzo said, "I'd like you to meet my associate, Rudy Moretti."

"How you doin'?" Moretti asked. He extended a bear paw of a hand.

The grip was as expected. Ward tried not to wince.

"Mr. Ricard is the buyer from Coastal Foods who I was telling you about," Rizzo said. "George Reidel was good enough to make an introduction." Rizzo motioned for the waiter to bring Moretti a glass.

"We are considering setting up an online platform to sell wine," Ward offered. "I'm scouting the more respected vineyards to see if they might be interested in getting in on the ground floor."

Moretti looked at the boss and nodded. "Sounds interesting."

"Interesting, indeed," Rizzo said. "And I hope Menfi Vineyards will be considered."

"From what I've seen, and tasted, here," Ward replied, "that seems likely."

Rizzo raised his glass. "*Salute!*" he said. "To our successful business endeavors."

They clinked glasses and drank. The waiter returned to take their orders. Ward ordered manicotti. When he was gone, Rizzo returned to business.

"How far along are you in the process?" he asked.

"Corporate would say we are still in the exploratory stage," Ward replied. He paused, smiled. "But I would characterize it as a bit farther along than that." He had to keep people interested while at the same time not creating immediate expectations.

Rizzo smiled. "Understood."

"As you can imagine," Ward said, "the logistics are considerable."

"I can imagine," Rizzo replied.

Ward saw an opportunity to do Rowan's bidding. "For example, the trucking. There would be regional distribution centers. Would the vineyards prefer to ship using their established carriers? Should Coastal consider using its own trucks? Or should we think about contracting with another shipping company?"

Rizzo nodded. "There is much to consider."

"If you don't mind me asking, who do you use?"

Rizzo glanced at Moretti, then back to Ward. There was a hint of something in the look, maybe concern. "We use Amato Freight Lines," Rizzo replied. There was a pause. "Have you heard of them?

"I see their trucks all the time," Ward answered. "I would guess that a large number of Coastal's suppliers use them."

Rizzo nodded, seemingly satisfied with the response. "I'm sure you're right."

CHAPTER 41

Moretti sat in his office, thumbing through the ledger. There were a couple of issues, both easily dealt with. Overall, it was a smooth operation. He preferred to keep it that way.

His cell was set to vibrate. He could feel it through the wood, buzzing as the screen lit up. The number was immediately recognizable. Moretti memorized phone numbers...well...some of them. Contact lists could lead to problems if you stored the wrong contacts. He had seen that happen. He picked up the phone.

"How's it goin'?"

"We might have a problem."

"How's that?" This was not a good way to start a conversation.

"That detective from the Napa County Sheriff's Office was here, asking for GPS records for our trucks."

"Not good," Moretti said. "Did he say why?"

"I heard this secondhand, but some story about looking for anything that might produce a lead, tying up loose ends. Said the investigation had stalled out."

"And you think it's bullshit."

"Like I said, secondhand. But when asked how it would help,

158

he said maybe one of the drivers was doing something illegal, departed from his route. Maybe Amato found out about it."

"Fuck me." Moretti knew he would have to tell the boss. He did not like to give Rizzo bad news. "What'd they tell him, this detective? What's his fuckin' name?"

"Adler."

"Yeah, Adler. What'd they tell him?"

"I guess Webb told him to get a warrant."

Moretti relaxed, a little. This was bad, but there was no way they had enough for a warrant. "Call me if you hear anything else," he said.

"You know it."

Moretti tossed the phone on the desk. He rubbed his forehead, thinking about what he was gonna tell the boss. But there was a nagging sensation, like he was forgetting something. Then he remembered. Ricard, the buyer from Coastal. He had asked what trucking company they used. That was it. A coincidence? Maybe. But most things that seemed that way were usually anything but. Moretti had learned to be careful, learned the hard way.

He logged onto his computer and did a search for Coastal Foods, quickly finding the corporate website. A directory of company officials gave him some names. As expected, there were no phone numbers for the head honchos, but there was contact information for some mid-management types. Moretti found one that might work, Donna Bauer, vice president of marketing for Northern California. He took a moment to conjure his cover story, then fished a burner phone out of his desk and made the call.

"Coastal Foods, marketing division."

"Hello," Moretti answered. "Can I speak to Donna Bauer?"

"May I tell her who is calling?"

"My name is Warren Geist," Moretti said. "I'm the owner of Geist Estates, a vineyard in Northern California."

"And what is this regarding, Mr. Geist?"

Gimme a break, Moretti thought. He wasn't calling the president of the fucking United States. "We were contacted by a representative of your company about participating in your new online wines sales program."

"I see. Let me check on Ms. Bauer's availability."

You do that, Moretti thought. "Thank you," he said.

There was a long wait. Finally, he heard someone pick up.

"This is Donna Bauer."

"Thank you for taking my call," Moretti said. "As I was explaining to the lady who answered the phone, my name is Warren Geist. I'm the owner of Geist Estates, a small vineyard in Napa." He hoped that she didn't try to pull it up online as they were speaking.

"And how can I help you, Mr. Geist?"

"We were approached by a buyer for Coastal, Harley Ricard, to see if we might be interested in being a supplier for your new online wines sales platform," Moretti said. "You know how it is these days, you can't be too careful. I just wanted to confirm that he was legitimate. An opportunity like this doesn't just come knockin' on the door too often."

There was a long pause.

"You say his name was Harley Ricard?" she asked.

"Yes."

"I'm sorry," Bauer said. "I've never heard of him. And I don't know anything about any online wine sales. That's something that has been discussed, but I'm not aware of any concrete steps to implement it."

"I see." Moretti could feel his hairs stand on end.

"But it's a big company," Bauer continued. "I work out of a regional office in Santa Rosa. Headquarters is in San Francisco. I'm afraid corporate doesn't always share with me what they're doing." She sounded annoyed. "You might want to call them."

"Understood," Moretti replied. "I'll do that." He noticed now that the area code he had called was 707, which was not one of those assigned to the city of San Francisco.

"Is there anything else I can do for you, Mr. Geist?"

"Not at the moment," Moretti answered. "Thank you for

your time." He terminated the call.

Moretti sat, thinking. The boss was excited about the prospect of doing business with Coastal. Best not to rain on that parade before getting more information. The situation with the GPS records for Amato's trucks, that was a different matter.

The sound surprised him, a popping, crunching noise. Moretti realized that he was cracking his knuckles. It was a subconscious habit, one that showed up when there was a problem that needed to get fixed.

CHAPTER 42

7:43 p.m., Thursday, September 22, Ward's undercover residence, Foster Road, Napa, California

The pizza had arrived moments earlier, and it was not pepperoni. When he had phoned in the order there was an uncomfortable silence on the other end, as if they were waiting for him regain his senses. Apparently, straight pepperoni just wasn't done in Napa, at least not at this restaurant. Funghi pizza was available, as were traditional toppings such as organic egg, spinach, eggplant, and sausage made from free-range chickens. The standoff ended when he ordered a pie topped with salami, Kalamata olives, and red onions.

Ward opened the box and took in the aroma. It did smell good, and he was hungry. A bottle of red Zinfandel was the choice to accompany his meal. He opened the wine and poured a glass, then slid a slice onto his plate. As he grabbed remote to pull up one of his favorite shows, another idea occurred to him. He would call Rowan and report what he had learned about the vineyards using Amato Freight Lines. Yes, it could wait. He knew that it was just an excuse to call her. Maybe he wanted to pretend that they were having dinner together, like last night. The memory was so fresh that he could feel her, smell her. Suddenly, he felt pathetic. But he knew that he was going to do it anyway.

Ward picked up the phone and called.

"Hi, David."

There was a hint of excitement in her voice. He hoped that it would always be so.

"Hi, Rowan."

"What are you up to?" she asked.

"Having my first Napa Valley pizza." He described the ingredients, and the menu choices.

"That sounds...interesting. I take it they were out of artichoke hearts and kale."

He laughed. "Exactly."

There was a pause. "I'm guessing you didn't call to discuss pizza."

He wondered if that might be an invitation to talk about the night before. Part of him was afraid to bring it up, afraid that she might declare it a mistake. "I just wanted to..."

"Yes?"

"I just wanted to let you know what I learned about who was using Amato Freight Lines."

"Oh...okay."

Was it disappointment he heard? Ward felt stupid, an opportunity blown. But now he didn't know how to recover.

"So, what did you find out?" she asked.

"Menfi Vineyards uses Amato," Ward said. "So does Three Peaks and Marroquin Winery."

"And, of course, we know Pavesi does." Parks was silent for a moment. "A bit of a coincidence," she finally said.

"It is a big company," Ward replied. "And it's headquartered in Sacramento."

"Still..."

"Yeah, I know. Every Mob case has a trucking angle."

"I just have a feeling that there's something there."

"Then I'll keep asking." Ward had learned to trust her intuition.

"Anybody seem surprised by the question, suspicious?"

Ward thought about the glance from Rizzo to Moretti. It probably didn't mean anything. He had been looking for some sort of reaction, maybe trying too hard to see one.

"I called Pedro Marroquin and George Reidel, the owner of Three Peaks. Obviously, I couldn't observe any reaction. But they didn't seem to be bothered by the question. Both completely bought into the explanation for it."

"What about the guy at Menfi Vineyards?" Rowan asked. "What's his name?"

"Rizzo," Ward replied. "He seemed to buy it. There was a look exchanged between him and a guy he introduced as his associate, Moretti. But I think I was just looking to read something into it. Probably nothing."

"His associate?"

"That's what he said. It caught my attention as well." She was quiet. He could almost hear her wheels turning on the other end of the line.

"Anything else?" she finally asked.

Ward took a gamble. He felt as if he were stepping off a cliff. "Wish you were here to share dinner with me." He held his breath.

"Yeah," she replied. "Me, too."

CHAPTER 43

8:11 p.m., Thursday, September 22, Menfi Vineyards, Napa Valley, California

Rizzo sat on the patio, sipping his Cabernet. It was just he and Rudy tonight. Gena was meeting with her book club. Everyone knew when she was gone. Even if only for a short while, the place seemed less alive.

"A little more?" Rizzo asked. He could see that his associate's glass was almost empty.

"Thanks, boss."

Rizzo poured. As he sat the bottle back on the table his phone rang. He checked the screen to see if there was a name.

"Ashton Cahill," Rizzo announced.

Rudy nodded. "Good guy."

"Ashton, how are you?" Rizzo asked.

"Great, Max," Cahill replied. "Yourself?"

"Rudy and I are sitting on the patio enjoying a lovely Cabernet and a beautiful starry night."

"Sounds nice," Cahill said. "Say, sorry about the short notice, but we're having a small wine and cheese party at my place tomorrow. I was hoping that maybe you and Gena could stop by. We're thinking around five."

"I'd love to," Rizzo replied. "Gena is not here, but I'm sure she would be delighted."

"Excellent," Cahill said. "And bring Rudy along with."

Rizzo looked to Rudy. "You're invited as well," he said. The announcement received a thumbs-up.

"Says he wouldn't miss it."

"Fantastic."

"If I can ask, who else will be there?"

"Stuart Boyd, George and Sara Reidel, several other couples you probably don't know."

"Always happy to meet new people," Rizzo said.

"Oh, and Harley Ricard, that buyer from Coastal. Have you two met?"

"I have," Rizzo said, "just this morning. But it would be good to see Mr. Ricard again. He's an interesting fellow."

CHAPTER 44

7:05 p.m., Friday, September 23, Cahill Estates, Napa Valley, California

Moretti sat at a table by himself, away from the others. He watched the crowd mingle, aware of how out of place he was in this well-heeled group. The boss, on the other hand, seemed to fit right in, like he was born to it. Moretti knew better.

Some of the guests had left, offering up dinner reservations or family commitments as excuses. But plenty remained, drinking free wine, sampling the array of cheeses. Stuart Boyd from *The Wine Observer* had already filled his plate a half dozen times. There had to be some serious digestive issues in his immediate future. Moretti hoped that it blocked him up like the Hoover Dam. Boyd was a weasel. The guy showed up at every freebie in Napa.

But the main reason he was there was to watch Harley Ricard, figure out what he was up to. It might be that the woman he talked to at Coastal was out of the loop. She said as much herself. But something seemed off. Moretti couldn't put his finger on it, but he had learned to trust his instincts on these things. After all, he had smoked out a few rats in his day; smoked them out and exterminated them.

Moretti saw Ricard look at his watch, heard him say something about needing to get going. It might be time to move. He had told the boss he needed to drive separate, that he was meeting a woman for dinner later. It was bullshit, but he couldn't tell Rizzo what he planned to do. Moretti hoisted himself out of the chair.

"Hey, boss," Moretti whispered, not wanting Ricard to hear, "I need to get goin'. You know, the date." He hated lying to the man.

Rizzo patted him on the shoulder. "Have a good time, my friend."

"I will, boss. Thanks."

Moretti headed for the parking lot. He wanted to be well down the road and out of sight before Ricard passed by. The Cadillac had been left at home. Too conspicuous. He had instead rented a nondescript black sedan for the tail, using one of the bogus driver's licenses he kept for just such moments. Looking back over his shoulder, Moretti saw Ricard shaking hands with Cahill, clearly saying his goodbyes. There was no time to lose. He quickly lowered his bulk into the car, started it, and drove out of the lot.

Moretti turned south, toward the city of Napa. Ricard would have to go that way. The road north led to a couple of obscure wineries up in the mountains. There was no reason for him to go that way. About a half mile down Moretti spotted a turnoff onto what appeared to be a little used side road. Trees lining the north side would obscure him from view. He drove just past the turnoff, then backed down the road. At fifty yards in he parked and killed the engine.

Moretti had seen the Corvette in the lot at the Menfi Vineyards and commented on it. The boss told him it was Ricard's. It seemed like a lot of car for buyer from a grocery store chain. Not impossible, but a lot. Still, that wasn't what made him suspicious.

It wasn't but a minute or two later when Ricard rumbled past. Moretti waited until he was a couple hundred yards down the road before pulling out. There was little traffic on this road. He would have to stay well back to avoid being spotted.

As they got closer to the city of Napa the traffic began to pick up. Route 29 was a four lane, allowing Moretti to use the other vehicles as cover. Ricard traveled south through town, eventually taking the First Street exit where he turned left, and then left again onto Freeway Drive. This is where it got tricky. Moretti fell back as far as he could while keeping the Corvette in sight. Fortunately, it was a vehicle that stood out. It continued south to Old Sonoma Road, where it headed west. Then, a few blocks later, it turned south again onto Foster Road and into a residential neighborhood.

Moretti knew that this was where he was most likely to be detected. He took a chance, bypassing the Foster Road turnoff, then finding a driveway where he could turn around and come back at it from the other direction. He would lose precious seconds but gambled that he could find the distinctive red Vette.

Moretti turned right onto Foster Road. He pressed on the gas, pushing the sedan forward, above the speed limit, but not so much as to draw attention. The gamble paid off. He caught up just in time to see the Corvette's tail end disappear into a garage. Two blocks down the road he pulled over and wrote down the address.

As soon as the garage door was down, Ward pulled out his phone and called Rowan.

"Hi, David. Where are you?"

"At the house."

"How was the party?"

"It was okay...but I think I was followed back here."

"Shit."

"Black sedan. Couldn't get a plate number. Too far away to even give you a make and model."

"Do you want to pull out?"

"Absolutely not."

CHAPTER 45

8:52 a.m., Saturday, September 24, Coastal Foods regional office, Santa Rosa, California

Donna Bauer had been fuming since receiving the call from Warren Geist. The thought that headquarters would have some guy out talking to vineyard owners in Napa Valley about supplying an online sales platform made her blood boil. Why wasn't she consulted? She was the vice president of marketing for Northern California. This was in her wheelhouse and on her turf. It was complete bullshit. The more she thought about it, the madder she got. Bauer wanted to know who approved this, and she was going to find out.

Bauer started her email. She had a mailing list for all the executives involved with purchasing and marketing, as well as certain senior management. Someone in that group had to know something.

So, it has come to my attention that we apparently have an employee by the name of Harley Ricard who has been talking to vineyard owners in Napa about supplying our new online wines sales platform. Needless to say, I was surprised to learn of this through an inquiry from one of said owners who was calling to confirm Mr. Ricard's bona fides. Anyone care to enlighten me?

Snarky? Yes. Did she care? No. There was a slight pause as

Bauer reread the message. Fuck it, she thought. She clicked send, then sat back to wait for the reaction. The phone rang a few minutes later.

"This is Donna Bauer."

"Donna, it's Howard Markham."

Bauer inhaled. Markham was president of the Northern California Division. Suddenly, the email did not seem like such a good idea.

"Good morning, Mr. Markham."

"Who made the inquiry?"

Oh boy, Bauer thought. Straight to it. Markham did not sound happy.

"I wrote it down," she said. "I have it here somewhere." Markham waited silently as she searched for the note. Every second was torture.

"Here it is. A fellow by the name of Warren Geist, the owner of Geist Estates."

"What did you tell him?"

"That I had never heard of Ricard and didn't know anything about any online wines sales," Bauer answered.

"Anything else?"

"I did tell him that it might be something out of headquarters in San Francisco, and that maybe I just wasn't in the loop."

"Which clearly annoyed you," Markham observed.

"I just..."

"Ricard is a recent hire. He answers to senior management," Markham said, interrupting. "And the online thing is merely exploratory at this point."

"Understood."

"Good."

Bauer felt sick. Her career started to pass before her eyes.

"When did you receive this call? Markham asked.

"Thursday afternoon."

"Did this Geist leave a callback number?" Markham asked.

"He did not."

"And did you ask him for one, offer to look into it?"

"I did not."

"I see."

"I just thought that..." Bauer heard him hang up.

Howard Markham pulled up a browser and searched for Geist Estates. There was no vineyard by that name. A similar search for Warren Geist yielded no one who appeared to be involved in the wine business. His instructions had been to call immediately if there was an inquiry. He hoped it wasn't too late.

Ward finished breakfast and began to clear his dishes. As he scraped the remnants into the garbage disposal, his phone rang. It was Mancuso.

"What's up?" Ward asked.

"We have a problem."

Ward sat down at the kitchen table. "Let's hear it."

"There was an inquiry at Coastal about Harley Ricard."

Ward rubbed his forehead. He had been concerned from the beginning about having civilians involved in his cover story.

"What happened?"

"Some marketing VP got a call from a guy by the name of Warren Geist," Mancuso said. "He claimed to be the owner of Geist Estates, a Northern California vineyard. Said they were approached by Harley Ricard on behalf of Coastal. I'm guessing you've never heard of him."

"I have not," Ward replied. "And I assume that this Geist and his vineyard do not exist."

"Correct."

"And let me guess," Ward continued, "this marketing VP said they had never heard of me."

"Again, correct."

Ward rarely got angry, but he was heading that direction.

"Your people assured me that the executives at Coastal would know what to say if asked. What the fuck happened?"

"The person called is well down the food chain and working at a regional office." Mancuso was silent for a moment. "We dropped the ball," he finally said.

Ward didn't respond to the admission. He didn't have to.

"How did this come to light?" he asked.

"Sounds like she was pissed about not being informed. Fired off an email asking if anybody had ever heard of you or plans for an online wine sales platform. One of the people in the know saw it and called her immediately."

"When was the inquiry?"

"Two days ago."

Ward now knew why he was followed the day before.

"The only positive," Mancuso continued, "is that this VP, her name is Bauer, told Geist that it might be something run out of headquarters in San Francisco, and she just wasn't in the loop."

"Not much comfort," Ward replied.

"I know. Do you want to pull the plug?" Mancuso asked.

For the first time in his life, Ward was tempted to say yes, just to reward the FBI for their stupidity. But sense of duty drove his response.

"We are not going to pull the plug."

CHAPTER 46

1:21 p.m., Saturday, September 24, Grumpy Toad Winery, Napa Valley, California

The Cadillac pulled in slowly and parked. There were few vehicles in the lot, and that was part of the problem. The place wasn't making money. And now payment was overdue, again. It happened before, a day or two, but this time it was coming up on a week. Moretti blamed himself. This is what happened when you cut a guy some slack, a failure to take the obligation seriously. It was time to send a message. There was a *pop*, another, then a *crunch*, like walking on gravel. Moretti looked down to find that he was cracking his knuckles.

He hoisted himself out of the vehicle and rumbled toward the main entrance. A sign greeted him: *Welcome to Grumpy Toad Winery*. Moretti liked the name, and the cute little mascot. But that wasn't going to help the owner. Alton Grant knew the terms and should have understood the importance of prompt payment.

Moretti walked into the tasting room, such as it was. It was a modest space in an equally modest operation. Grant was behind the bar, just finishing a pour for one of his scant customers. When he saw Moretti the color drained from his face. Grant sat the bottle on the bar, his hand already visibly shaking. It was exactly the reaction Moretti enjoyed. He jerked his head toward the door, indicating that Grant should follow him outside.

When Grant appeared, Moretti wasted no time.

"Let's go for a ride."

"But I have customers," Grant said. His tone was pleading.

"I think the two of them will be fine," Moretti replied. "Let's go." He walked to the Cadillac and got in, leaving his door open.

Grant followed, occasionally looking back over his shoulder as if someone might rescue him. Moretti grew impatient.

"Get in the fuckin' car," he ordered.

Grant slid inside, leaving the door ajar.

Moretti stared at him. "Shut the fuckin' door," he growled.

Grant did as he was told. Moretti slammed his door and started the engine. He drove out of the lot and turned right, a route that went up into the mountains.

"I'm sorry," Grant blurted out. "I can get the money to you tomorrow. I promise."

"Your promises don't mean shit," Moretti said. "We want our fuckin' money."

"I'll have it tomorrow," Grant whimpered. "Please don't hurt me." He began to cry.

Moretti scoffed. "It's always tomorrow with you. That's not the way this works."

They drove on. Grant rocked back and forth in his seat, holding his hands together as if praying. Moretti found a side road and turned off. He traveled another mile or so and pulled into a farm field entrance. There was no one in sight. He pulled out a gun, holding it in his lap.

"Oh my God!" Grant cried, staring at it. "Please don't! Please don't!"

"You don't seem to take me seriously," Moretti said. He lifted the gun and rested it on the bottom of the steering wheel. "You should. You will."

It was then that he saw the dark stain appear in Grant's crotch. What if it seeped into the seat? He was not going to ride around smelling piss.

"I can get it to you tonight," Grant pleaded. "I just need a few hours. I can get it. I promise. Please, I have a wife and kids!" He began to sob.

"Again with the fuckin' promises," Moretti growled. He was silent for a moment. "Tell you what, you got 'til seven o'clock. I'll be back then. If you ain't got the money, there will be an unfortunate accident."

Grant slumped forward, breathing heavily. "Thank you," he cried.

Moretti held out his slab of a hand, as if to seal the agreement. They started to shake, then Moretti clenched Grant's thumb, forcing it backward until it snapped like a dry branch.

"Ohhh God!" Grant howled. He doubled over, clutching his injured hand. Bone could be seen protruding through the skin. He turned green.

"Don't you fuckin' puke in my car," Moretti ordered.

It was too late. Grant's lunch exploded forth, covering the dash.

"Damn it," Moretti said. Now he would have to have the car thoroughly cleaned and detailed.

Grant whimpered like an animal caught in a trap.

"Get the fuck outta my car," Moretti growled.

Grant looked up at him, tears flowing. "It's miles back to the winery. I don't have my phone. I can't call anybody."

"Tough shit," Moretti said. "You've got 'til seven. Now, get the fuck out."

CHAPTER 47

6:35 a.m., Sunday, September 25, Ward's undercover residence, Foster Road, Napa, California

Ward gave up on trying to fall back to sleep. He was still upset over the call from Mancuso, the inquiry, the FBI's gaping hole in his cover story. Combined with being followed from Cahill Estates, he had to assume that someone suspected he was law enforcement. There was Jesse Morgan, the worker at Pavesi Vineyards, and Tommy Serra at Evans Creek. Both had some connection to the Mob, with Morgan possibly being a low-level associate of the Genovese family. But why would either of them have called Coastal? Why would they follow Harley Ricard? He had never met them, had done nothing to come to their attention. Could they have acted at someone else's direction? If so, who? Or was he completely off the mark? At this point, the possibilities were endless.

Still, two names wouldn't leave him: Rizzo and Moretti. Their interaction, Rizzo's reference to his *associate*. Ward recalled that both were at Cahill's party. Did Moretti leave before he did? He couldn't remember. But the guy's mannerisms, everything about him...

Ward grabbed his phone from the nightstand and called. It was only after three rings that he remembered the time.

"This better be good," Parks answered.

Ward cringed. "Sorry. I've been up for a while."

"I can understand why," she said. "We fucked up. I should have taken a harder look at the legend before putting you into this."

"Not your fault," Ward said. "Maybe it had to be set up this way. I know how to assess a cover. And I volunteered. You didn't put me into anything."

"That's generous." There was a pause. "What are you thinking?"

"I keep coming back to Rizzo and Moretti, the way they communicated, Moretti's whole persona."

"The associate thing."

"Exactly."

"I've been thinking about that, too."

"Can you have your contact in New York do some digging?"

"Already made the call. Asked him to see what he could find on both of them."

"Of course you did."

"I also want to put Moretti under surveillance."

Ward smiled. "It's like you're reading my mind."

He had another thought, picturing her in bed. He wondered if she could read that.

CHAPTER 48

9:02 a.m., Monday, September 26, Coastal Foods corporate headquarters, San Francisco, California

Howard Markham settled in at his desk and prepared to review sales reports for the stores in his division. Business had been good, but there were a few locations that had been underperforming for over a year now. It was possible that they might have to be shut down. He took a sip of coffee and started to scroll through the reports. No more than a minute into it, his cell rang. Markham checked the caller. It was Special Agent Mancuso.

"Good morning, Agent Mancuso," he answered. "I'm guessing this is about the call received by Ms. Bauer."

"It is."

"Again, our apologies. I wish there were some way I could fix it."

"That's exactly why I'm calling," Mancuso replied.

"What did you have in mind?"

"The FBI would like Coastal to put out a public statement announcing that it is considering development of an online wines sales platform. The press release should state that you are assessing the viability of such an operation and, as part of that process, have a buyer, Harley Ricard, who is contacting various vineyards to gauge interest."

Markham sighed. "This is a public company," he said. "It is one thing for a few of us to play along with your undercover agent's cover story, but quite another to make a public statement that we are planning to sell wine online. Such a thing can affect stock values. If untrue, that can have major repercussions."

"Let me be candid," Mancuso said. "Ms. Bauer's...*misstep* has created a significant problem. Our agent was followed shortly after she fielded that inquiry. Now, our operation, and his life, are in jeopardy. We expect to receive maximum assistance from Coastal in our attempts to rectify this situation."

Markham rubbed his forehead. This was going to be difficult.

"Let me make some calls," he said. "Perhaps, there is a way we can phrase this that will avoid problems for the company."

CHAPTER 49

9:23 a.m., Tuesday, September 27, the safehouse, San Francisco, California

Ward parked a good five blocks from the safehouse. He had taken the added precaution of renting a car for the trip. Whoever had followed him the previous Friday would not be able to do so when he was on his game. And he was on it, antennae up. There was no way he was tailed.

Rowan had already arranged a surveillance team. She thought it would be a good idea for him to meet them. He wasn't sure why. They would be watching Moretti. But Ward had learned not to argue with her. She had a reason, and that was good enough for him. That, and the fact that he wanted to see her.

Ward walked a circuitous route to the safehouse, occasionally checking the reflection in shop windows for signs that anyone was watching. Satisfied that he was alone, he headed for the building. As soon as he was in the entryway, he was buzzed in, no words spoken. The elevator took him to the seventh floor. Rowan greeted him. Her smile told him what he wanted to know.

"C'mon in," she said, her hand touching the back of his arm as she ushered him through the door.

Ward entered. Mancuso rose from the table to greet him, saying nothing, extending a hand. The way he did it was an apology. At least, that's how Ward took it.

"Coffee?" Rowan asked.

"That would be great," Ward replied.

He sat. Mancuso returned to this typing, still silent. It was odd.

Rowan returned with his coffee. "The others will be here in a few minutes," she said. "They called just before you arrived."

She sipped her coffee, the hint of a smile curling up one side of her mouth. She was up to something.

"Did you have breakfast?" she asked.

"No."

"Good. I was told they would bring it with them."

"Okay," Ward said. "That's good...I guess."

"I was assured you would like it."

Ward studied her. She was definitely up to something.

Just then, the intercom sounded. Rowan jumped up and checked the screen. She smiled, and then buzzed them in, slipping into the hallway to greet whoever this was. When Rowan returned, she was followed by two men, the first of whom Ward recognized immediately. He was carrying a pink box, which he slid onto the table.

"Hola, mi amigo!"

ATF Special Agent Cesar Cruz approached Ward, grabbed his outstretched hand, and then pulled him in for a bro hug.

"Ha ha!" Cruz laughed. "It is good to see you, my friend!"

Ward looked at Rowan, noticing her grin. There was even the hint of a smile on Mancuso's mug. Cruz had worked with Ward on Operation Knock Down, the infiltration and dismantling of the Earth Martyrs Brigade, an especially deadly eco-terrorist group.

"Does this mean what I think it does?" Ward asked.

"This is our surveillance team," Rowan replied. "ATF was only too happy to approve their involvement. And it seemed like the least we could do after the fuckup involving your cover."

The move gave Ward some comfort. Cruz was an ace. He

was grateful to Rowan for involving ATF. It was highly unusual for FBI to willingly bring in outside agents on their investigations.

Cruz stepped back. "Allow me to introduce Special Agent Thomas Cho. He's one of the best in the business."

Cho nodded to everyone in the room, then approached Ward. "I've heard a great deal about you," he said, extending his hand. "It will be an honor to work with you."

"An honor? Let's not get carried away," Cruz said with a laugh.

"So, what's in the box?" Ward asked, thinking he might know the answer.

"Ah!" Cruz retrieved the box and placed it on the table near Ward. "Your favorite pastries. You didn't think I would forget?"

A sticker on the box read *Achermann's*. Ward smiled. Cruz had once brought him coffee and pastries from the legendary bakery after a night drinking their way across San Francisco. In terms of a hangover cure, it wasn't a cheeseburger and a Coke. But it was the best apple fritter Ward had ever tasted. He opened the box. There they were, right on top, a half dozen apple fritters.

"Well done," Ward said. He grabbed a fritter, then slid the box to the middle of the table for the others to enjoy.

Cruz clapped his hands together. "Alright then," he announced, "let's get to work."

CHAPTER 50

9:31 a.m., Tuesday, September 27, Menfi Vineyards, Napa Valley, California

The morning sun illuminated the valley, making it feel warmer than the sixty-seven-degree temperature registered on the patio thermometer. Rizzo ate the last bite of his eggs Benedict, then took a sip of orange juice. He sat back and opened a copy of the *Napa Valley Courier*. There was little of interest on the front page, so he turned to the business section. The paper was known for its coverage of the wine industry and it was how he liked to start the day. Rizzo scanned the articles, his eyes quickly landing on one that grabbed his attention: *Coastal Foods Considering Online Wine Shop*. He read on.

> *San Francisco – Coastal Foods, the West Coast grocery giant, announced yesterday that it was exploring the possibility of adding wine to its online offerings. If they were to proceed with such a plan, it would immediately make Coastal one of the biggest players in a growing internet marketplace. Sources report that a buyer for Coastal has been contacting various vineyard owners in Napa Valley to gauge interest. The*

Courier reached out to the company for comment. Howard Markham, president of Coastal's Northern California Division, confirmed that they have had a representative in the field visiting some of Napa's major producers. Markham characterized the effort as purely exploratory at this stage, but something Coastal must consider given the explosion in online sales. "This is not something that can happen overnight," Markham said. "There are major logistical challenges, particularly in terms of shipping. That said, if Coastal determines to proceed, we will do it right, and we will be a major presence." Markham noted that until yesterday's announcement this project was known only by the company's senior corporate leadership.

Rizzo folded the paper in half, then in half again, so that the article was prominently displayed. He handed it to Rudy, who was just finishing off a sizable helping of waffles and sausage.

"What's this?" Moretti asked.

"Just read it."

Moretti's brow furrowed as he skimmed the piece. Then he let out a grunt.

"Seems a little too convenient to me," he said.

Rizzo didn't reply. He reached for his coffee, then settled back in his chair, sipping as he stared out over the vineyard that had become his life.

CHAPTER 51

2:21 p.m., Tuesday, September 27, Federal Bureau of Investigation, Santa Rosa Resident Agency, Santa Rosa, California

Parks scrolled through the forensic report on a computer they had seized as part of a child pornography investigation. The images made her feel sick, anxious, angry. How could somebody do this to a child? She decided to get up, go for a walk, try to calm down. As she stood to leave, her cell rang. Parks looked at the phone, deciding whether to answer. The area code was 212, New York City. That told her it was a call back on her inquiry about Rizzo and Moretti.

"Parks," she answered.

"Special Agent Roy Lambert, New York. Calling back on Massimiliano Rizzo and Nunzio Moretti. You got a minute?"

"Yeah," Parks said, thinking about the forensic report. "Actually, I could use a break from what I'm working on."

"Understood," Lambert replied. "Okay, Moretti first. He's from Brooklyn. We have nothing concrete showing that he's a soldier, or any other rank, in one of the families."

Parks knew that to become a Mafia soldier, or made man, an associate had to be of Italian descent and sponsored by another fully initiated member.

"Doesn't mean he's not," Lambert continued. "It's not like

they publish a list. But we do have pretty good intelligence on the rank and file."

Parks knew that to be true. "Anything on him that points to Mob connections?"

"I was getting to that," Lambert replied. "He has been employed at a number of businesses with known connections."

"Such as?"

"Waste disposal, cement, that sort of thing."

That was something, Parks thought. "Anything else?"

"Yeah," Lambert said. "He's got a DWI from 2003."

"And?"

"And...the passenger in the vehicle was a made Genovese guy."

Another Genovese connection. Parks started making notes. Now they were getting somewhere.

"What about Rizzo?" she asked.

"He's a mystery," Lambert answered. "Also from Brooklyn, but no known Mob affiliations."

"Other than his association with Moretti," Parks observed.

"Other than *maybe* his association with Moretti," Lambert replied. There was a pause. "Oh, one other thing," he added. "Rizzo's mother is Sicilian, born there. So..."

"So, maybe an Old-World connection," Parks noted.

There was a grunt of acknowledgment from the New York agent. "Exactly," he said. "Apparently, you think it's a Mob operation."

"I think there's what you know, and what you can prove," Parks replied.

CHAPTER 52

9:05 a.m., Wednesday, September 28, just south of Menfi Vineyards, Napa Valley, California

Cruz was set up a half mile down the road from Menfi Vineyards, tucked away behind a grove of trees on a little used turnoff. Cho was a quarter mile north of the main entrance. The first half day of surveillance on Moretti had yielded nothing. He had stayed on-site. The only thing they had established was that he lived in a guest house close to the main residence.

The decision had been made to use two vehicles. Moretti was a savvy target. Plus, his antennae would be up. It was thought that he had likely been the one to inquire into Ward's legend. Coastal Foods had put out a public statement regarding their possible move into online wine sales, but there was no guarantee that would calm Moretti's suspicions. If he was Mafia, he would always be on the lookout for a rat.

He and Cho were using two-way radios to communicate. Their channel had a dedicated, secure frequency, inaccessible to even those making a concerted effort to overhear. From where he sat, Cho would be able to see Moretti's Cadillac leave the vineyard and radio his departure. There was little to the north, so Cruz knew it was likely that Moretti would head his way. He would pick him up first, alternating with Cho as the primary tail. The secondary vehicle would drop far back, even turning off to an alternate tracking route when possible. They would have to be on their A game. Any slipup could have severe consequences. If spotted, it would heighten Moretti's suspicion of the man he knew as Harley Ricard.

The radio crackled to life.

"He's moving."

"Roger that."

Cruz put the car in gear, ready to move. He was in a black Toyota Camry, Cho a gray Honda Accord, two of the most nondescript vehicles on the road. If necessary, they would switch to similarly common vehicles during the surveillance to avoid detection. He picked up the radio and waited. Within seconds, the black Cadillac sedan flew by.

"Got him," Cruz said into the two-way.

"Copy that," Cho replied.

Cruz let the Cadillac go a good hundred yards before pulling out. Moretti was moving fast, and it was a lightly traveled mountain. That would complicate things. Cruz had to accelerate hard to get to a spot even two hundred yards back. He wondered if that was just how Moretti drove, or if it was a conscious effort to expose a tail.

"He's flying," Cruz radioed. "Stay with me."

"Copy."

Moretti wound through the canyon roads at a high rate of speed. As Cruz tried to keep up, he could feel the Camry start to lift as they took the curves. Would Moretti notice the black Toyota staying with him? It was a strong possibility. Soon, he would need to drop back, letting Cho take the lead. That meant the Accord would have to pass him, moving fast on a dangerous stretch of road.

"You, re gonna have to take it," Cruz radioed. "He's gonna spot me."

"10-4."

Cruz slowed. Cho roared up behind him, then deftly maneuvered around the Toyota as they approached another curve. Cruz puckered up as the Honda flew by. Thank God nothing was coming from the other direction.

Seconds later, Cho came over the two-way. "I've got him in sight."

"Copy that."

Cruz dropped back two hundred yards, far enough behind to be completely out of Moretti's line of sight on the winding roads. Now, it was Cho's ride.

They continued for another two or three miles. Cruz was thinking it might be time to again change positions, then Cho came over the radio.

"He's slowing down," Cho said. "No signal, but I think he's gonna turn. I'll have to pass by."

"On it," Cruz replied. He pressed down on the accelerator, pushing the Camry to catch up. He wanted to see where the Cadillac turned off in case Cho couldn't identify a road or landmark.

"He's turning off," Cho radioed. "Do you have visual?"

As Cruz came around the curve, he caught sight of the back end of the Cadillac disappearing behind a line of trees a good quarter mile distant.

"Roger that," Cruz said. "I've got him."

"Couldn't get a good look," Cho said. "Looked like a private drive. There's a large building about two hundred yards in."

"Copy that."

"I'll pull off about a mile down," Cho radioed. "Out."

Cruz slowed to a more normal speed, but not too slow as to be obvious. As he drove by, he could see what appeared to be a large factory or warehouse. There were a half dozen loading docks. The building was surrounded by a high fence, topped with barbed wire. A heavy steel gate covered what appeared to be the only entrance. It was just sliding shut behind the rear of Moretti's black Cadillac.

CHAPTER 53

6:23 p.m., Wednesday, September 28, at an undisclosed location, Brooklyn, New York City, New York

The meeting was in an abandoned warehouse, one fitted for the occasion. Security was exceptional. An army of soldiers from each of the Five Families guarded all access points. The boss of the Chicago Outfit had brought his own crew, as had Philadelphia. All of them were scary motherfuckers. Cameras recorded every movement outside the building, but nothing inside. There would be no recordings inside. Anyone who so much as thought about it would be dead. A plague of rats had been their scourge for years. Because of that, the Code was being enforced with renewed vigor. Messages had been sent.

These meetings were rare now. All of them were being watched, all the time. There had been some discussion of doing this remotely, their faces in little boxes on the computer screen. He hated that idea. Besides, they couldn't take the chance that someone would hack in. The feds were good at that sort of thing, something they had all found out the hard way.

It wasn't like the old days. At times, some of the families were even ruled by panels, no clear boss. That could make things difficult. Only one representative might attend. But tonight, at least, they all had someone there, all seven. It was a rare thing, a dangerous thing, but a good thing.

A tumbler of Scotch sat in front of most. For others, a glass of red. Cigar smoke wafted upward, sucked into the building's ventilation system. Much business had been discussed; some disputes settled. And that was the point, the reason this group had come to exist. Luciano understood the need. Really, they all did. But some complied with the rules better than others. And that was why certain actions were occasionally sanctioned. Tonight, that had proved unnecessary. An understanding had been reached. Now, they could engage in more relaxed conversation, enjoy each other's company. Barney sipped his Scotch, then took a draw from his Cohiba Robusto, the smoke slowly entering his mouth, lingering for several seconds before he blew it out. The process relaxed him like nothing else.

"So, how is the thing in Napa?"

Barney looked down the table. The question had come from Big Mike, a glass of Cabernet in his hand.

"Good," Barney replied. "Rizzo, he's a smart guy. Has things under control. No question about it." The Napa operation was profitable, an idea borrowed from the Sicilians.

"I like it," Big Mike said. "Reminds of the old days, bootlegging, the way it all began."

Lorenzo raised his glass. "Agreed," he said. "Our ancestors would be proud. *Salute!*"

"*Salute!*" they all repeated, then drank. Barney put his glass back on the table and poured another. He was enjoying this, a moment of peace, an appreciation of their lifestyle. Still, he knew as well as anyone how quickly things could turn.

"I understand there are some problem individuals out there."

Barney shook his head. "Nothin' we can't handle, Mickey."

"So, they have been dealt with?"

"In ways that leave no room for misunderstanding," Barney replied.

There were chuckles around the table.

"Rizzo has a strong enforcer, Rudy Moretti," Barney said.

"They understand the old ways."

"Rudy is a good boy," Big Mike chimed in.

"Understood," Mickey replied. "But Rizzo, I hear he has an ego, ambition. He needs to know that we call the shots."

Barney waved his hand. "He understands this. It's not a problem."

Mickey let out a snort. "We've all heard that before."

CHAPTER 54

9:02 a.m., Thursday, September 29, just south of Menfi Vineyards, Napa Valley, California

Cruz was just north of the vineyard entrance, waiting for Cadillac to emerge. Yesterday they had struggled to stay close. Cruz didn't think they had been spotted, but there was no point in taking the risk. They had swapped out those cars for two similarly common models, a black Honda Civic and a silver Ford F-150. Cruz was in the pickup, Cho the sedan.

There was a chance Moretti would head to the same building, but no way to tell. They had to be prepared for anything. This time, Cho was a good mile south. If necessary, he could get out in front of Moretti, slow him down. It was a two-lane road, hard to pass. They could use that to their advantage.

Cruz saw the Cadillac coming down the vineyard drive. He picked up the two-way. Moretti was already moving fast.

"He's on the way," Cruz radioed, "and coming hard."

"Roger that," Cho replied.

The Cadillac blew through the gate, skidding slightly as it righted itself in the southbound lane.

"What the fuck," Cruz muttered. He jammed the pedal down. The truck had some horsepower, but he would have to fly to keep up. Moretti was going to make it tough for them again. Was this just the way he drove? Or was it the practiced move of someone accustomed to avoiding surveillance.

"He's a rocket," Cruz yelled into the radio. "Wait a minute and then pull out. Stay just fast enough so he can't pass you."

"Copy that," Cho replied.

Cruz stayed a good hundred yards back, occasionally losing sight of Moretti through the twists and turns of the mountain road. He came around a curve just in time to see the brake lights flare. The Cadillac had slowed to avoid plowing into the back end of a Honda Civic. Cruz grinned. Then, as Moretti swung out to the left to see if he could pass, Cho sped up, just enough. This cycle repeated itself two more times until the Cadillac exploded forward, determined to get by. Cruz estimated its speed at ninety plus. But suddenly, Cho hit the brakes. At first, Cruz assumed it was to prevent Moretti from getting a good look at the driver of the Civic. Then he saw the semi.

The Cadillac jerked to the right, narrowly missing the front end of an oncoming Kenworth, then began to fishtail. Cho skidded to a halt. Cruz had visions of sitting in the SAC's office, trying to explain how the fuck they had managed to let this happen. But then, miraculously, Moretti somehow managed to keep it on the road. Cruz slowed as the semi roared by, the driver still laying on the air horn.

Cruz grabbed the radio. "You okay?"

"Fuck me," Cho said. "That was close. You got him?"

"Roger that."

Cruz swung out to the left as Cho pulled off on the side of the road. He pressed down on the gas, trying to catch up. Seconds later, he spotted the Cadillac, traveling noticeably slower. Apparently, the close call had even affected Moretti. Cruz stayed well back, no longer needing to push it.

Within minutes, they were approaching the entrance to the warehouse. Once again, Cruz saw the Cadillac slow down and turn in. He drove past, pulling off a half mile down the road. He pushed the talk button on the two-way.

"He pulled off," Cruz radioed, "same place."

"Copy that," Cho responded. "What's the plan?"

"We'll sit on him for a while," Cruz replied. "But tonight, I want to come back here, fly the drone."

It was a few minutes before seven. The sun was beginning to set. Cruz and Cho parked the Ford Explorer on a side road half a mile past the warehouse entrance. Inside the vehicle was a military grade drone. It was small, but fast and maneuverable. More importantly, it had a powerful camera. Cruz popped the hatch, removed it, and set it on the ground.

"This thing can be pretty loud," Cho said. "What if there's somebody outside?"

"It can get to an altitude where it's virtually undetectable," Cruz replied. "And the camera resolution is incredible, even from that high. Shouldn't be a problem."

"Can it zoom in?"

Cruz smiled. "Just watch."

The drone whirred to life, buzzing like a giant, angry hornet. Within seconds, it was airborne, on its way to the warehouse.

Cruz motioned for Cho to stand next to him. "Look at this." He caused the drone to hover, then zoomed in on a small shack between them and the warehouse. The images were crystal clear.

Cho nodded. "Impressive."

Cruz then continued piloting the drone in the direction of the warehouse, increasing altitude as it went. Soon, it was over the building. It was a large structure, nearly the size of a football field. Cruz flew the drone around the perimeter. There were no windows, but that was not particularly unusual for this type of industrial facility. What was unusual was the lack of anything stored outside. The only thing visible was a semi-trailer backed into a loading dock. Cruz positioned the drone so that they could get a better look. The camera zoomed in, revealing the name on the side: Amato Freight Lines.

"Well, that's interesting," Cho observed.

"Yes, it is."

Cruz piloted the drone back to their location and loaded it up. As soon as they were on the road, he pulled up the number for Rowan Parks.

CHAPTER 55

9:42 a.m., Thursday, September 29, Evans Creek Vineyards, Napa Valley, California

Ward had called the day before to set up the visit. Given the wine dump that had occurred there just two weeks earlier, he had been surprised when Henry Evans quickly agreed to the meeting. There was the presence of Tommy Serra on Evans's staff, and the kid's possible connection to the Lucchese family. All in all, this promised to be an interesting encounter.

Evans Creek was an award-winning winery, known for their Pinot Noir. But how much wine did they have to sell? There were earlier vintages, wine that they had held back from the market. But, according to Deputy Adler, thousands of gallons of this year's product had been lost. Evans was a businessman, a vintner of considerable success. Maybe he just couldn't pass on an opportunity to get his foot in the door for Coastal's launch of their online platform. But Ward felt there had to be more to it. He just wasn't sure what.

The Corvette swung through the gate and rumbled into the parking lot. Ward found a spot and parked. As he stepped out of the car, a man approached.

"Harley Ricard?" the man asked, a smile on his face.

"And you must be Henry Evans," Ward replied.

"The same."

They shook hands.

"Beautiful car," Evans said, admiring the Vette. "I had a '73. Sold it just last year, a decision I sometimes regret."

Ward nodded. "Understood." He patted the car. "This one's not going anywhere."

"Well, c'mon in," Evans said, gesturing for Ward to follow him. "Let me show you around."

They walked through the main doors, passing through a tasting room before entering the production area. Ward listened as Evans carefully explained each step of the process, what it was that made his wines different. The man had an obvious passion for his craft, the grapes, everything about winemaking. His pride was palpable, like a father describing a favorite child. It was the barrel room where Ward decided to bring it up.

"I heard about the wine dump," Ward said. "A real tragedy, especially with wine as good as yours."

The smile vanished from Evans' face, replaced by a wistful, distant stare. "Yeah," he said. "That was a tough day. The fermentation and barrel rooms were completely flooded. We lost thousands of gallons."

"Any leads?" Ward asked. He studied Evans, looking for tells, signs of deception.

Evans shook his head. "No. And I haven't heard much form the sheriff's office. I think they've hit a dead end."

Ward nodded. He was picking up nothing from Evans. If it was an act, it was a good one. The possibility existed that he was simply a legitimate victim.

"Enough of that," Evans said, the smile returning. "Let's head back to the tasting room. I'd like you to see, or I should say taste, what we're capable of."

"I'd like that," Ward replied.

When they reached the tasting room, Evans searched through the wine rack until he found the bottle he was looking for. He deftly removed the cork and poured a small amount in two glasses.

"Our most celebrated Pinot," Evans announced.

Ward breathed in the aroma, then took a small sip, using the tasting method he had by now perfected.

"Just tremendous," he said, and he meant it. What little Ward had learned about wine told him that this was truly something special. "The texture is velvety, to a degree I've never before experienced." He sat the glass down and looked at Evans. "Truly exceptional."

Evans nodded, clearly pleased. "Thank you." He raised his own glass in a silent toast. Ward reciprocated.

"So," Ward began, "if Coastal proceeds with an online platform, Evans Creek is a label we would like to carry."

There was a slight bow of the head from Evans. "That would please me greatly," he said.

"I have to ask," Ward continued, watching Evans closely, "given the accident, can you supply quantity, at least in the near term?"

There was no hesitation. "Absolutely," Evans replied. "We have more than sufficient reserves from earlier vintages."

Ward nodded. "Of course," he said. "But I would assume a gap down the road, when this year's product would have been ready."

"I don't foresee a problem," Evans assured him.

Ward wondered how that could be true but decided not to press it.

"As you can imagine," Ward said, "there are also significant logistical considerations."

"I'm sure," Evans replied.

"For example," Ward said, "the shipping. Coastal has regional distribution centers throughout its market area, and we could easily accommodate wines sales. But there is the issue of how to get the wine to those facilities, and how the costs would be handled. Would the vineyards use their established carriers? Should Coastal use its own trucks, contract out to another trucking company?"

Evans nodded. "Our preference would be to ship the wine to the distribution centers through our current carrier."

"Understood," Ward said. "If I may ask, who do you use?"

"Amato Freight Lines," Evans replied. "Their rates have been very reasonable."

One skill of the undercover operative was to suppress reaction, and Ward did just that. What he really wanted to know were the exact terms required by Amato's arrangement with Evans.

"I've heard of them," Ward said, downplaying it. "I believe one or two of the other vineyards may use them as well."

"I think that's correct," Evans replied.

Ward finished his wine. Evans reached for the bottle to add to his glass.

"No thanks," Ward said, holding up his hand. "I have several stops today."

"Of course," Evans replied.

Ward moved to leave. "Thank you for everything," he said. "You'll be hearing from us."

Evans tipped his glass. "I'll look forward to it."

Ward showed himself out.

As soon as he was in his car and out the gate, he pulled up Rowan's number and called.

CHAPTER 56

10:49 a.m., Friday, September 30, a quarter mile south of the warehouse, Napa Valley, California

They had been sitting on the building since following Moretti there earlier that morning. Cruz was south of the entrance, Cho to the north. Moretti had gone in at just after nine. Whatever he did for Menfi Vineyards, and for Rizzo, was apparently done mostly here. There had been little activity aside from the arrival of two trucks bearing the Amato Freight Lines logo. But what was being shipped? And why from here?

Just then, another one of Amato's semis rumbled by. Cruz picked up the two-way and radioed Cho.

"You copy?" he asked.

"Affirmative."

"I have seen three of Amato's trucks drive through the gate in the past hour," Cho said. "Are you sure they do the bottling at the vineyard?"

"Absolutely," Cho said. "Some of the big wineries have their own bottling line. But even the smaller ones have to do it on-site. They use a mobile bottling line that is brought in by semi. All the equipment is in the trailer. Think about it. There would be no effective way to get the wine to another location, and no reason to. The vineyard just buys the labels, corks, and bottles and it's all done right there."

"How do you know all this?"

"You asked me this the other day, so I looked it up."

"Roger that."

Cho continued to impress.

"And so, they would have to crate their product and ship from there."

"Correct," Cho said. "With no reason to make this extra stop."

"So, what the hell is with all of these trucks?" Cruz asked.

"Fuck if I know, bro."

CHAPTER 57

8:43 a.m., Saturday, October 1, Ward's undercover residence, Foster Road, Napa, California

Ward buttered his toast and poured another cup of coffee. He had already checked the news and now sat down to the latest issue of *The Wine Observer*, continuing to familiarize himself with the industry and its lingo. As he began to thumb through the pages, the phone rang. He glanced at the screen. It was Rowan.

"Good morning," he said.

"Good morning to you," she replied.

The tone was as if she had just awoken in bed alongside him and rolled over to welcome him to a new day. The thought distracted for more than a moment.

"And what are you doing?" she asked, restarting the conversation.

"I was about to flip through *The Wine Observer*. Always researching the role, you know?"

"I do know," she replied. "I know how you are."

He chuckled softly. Indeed, she did.

"So, what's up?" he asked.

"Well, you know how Cruz and Cho have been following Moretti to this warehouse all week?"

"I do."

"So, I decided to check into the building's ownership."

"And?"

"And it goes through a mysterious trail of shell companies that ends in the Turks and Caicos."

Ward sat up. "That's significant."

"No shit," she replied. "Whatever is going on here is something far beyond the Mob's typical loan sharking or shakedown rackets."

"Any thoughts?"

"I don't know," Rowan replied. "I just don't know."

CHAPTER 58

10:56 a.m., Saturday, October 1, just south of Menfi Vineyards, Napa Valley, California

Cruz looked at his watch. They had been waiting for nearly two hours. It was starting to look like Moretti didn't go to the warehouse on the weekends. Fortunately, he also didn't seem to be following Ward, the man he knew as Harley Ricard. That might be an indication that the FBI's remedial measures had lessened suspicions. Nonetheless, they would stay on Moretti until the operation was over or someone ordered them to pull out. Just then, Cruz heard the radio crackle to life.

"Eye on the prize," Cho announced. "He's moving, and today he's headed north."

Cruz grabbed the two-way and hit the push-to-talk button. "Roger that. On my way."

Within minutes he had Cho in sight. They were back in the cars from earlier that week, Cruz in the black Toyota Camry and Cho in the gray Honda Accord. Moretti was again moving fast. Cruz caught a fleeting glimpse of the Cadillac when all three vehicles briefly occupied the same straight stretch of road.

The cars weaved through twenty miles of mountain roads as Moretti continued to head north. Cruz was becoming concerned. It was a long time to have Cho in the lead. He keyed the radio.

"Do you want to trade off?"

"Hang on," Cho called back. "I see brake lights."

Cruz slowed, not wanting to get close until Cho gave the go-ahead.

"He's turning right into some winery," Cho radioed. "Name of the place is Coyote Pass."

"Copy."

"There was a small side road on the left, about fifty yards back," Cho said. "You might be able to watch him from there. I'll set up a couple hundred yards ahead."

"Roger that."

Coming around a curve, Cruz spotted the winery. He almost drove past the side road Cho identified as a possible surveillance sight, braking hard to make the turn. The location offered a clear line of sight to the winery's entrance and parking lot. He found a place to turn around and parked the Camry forty feet back from the intersection. A stand of trees blocked it from view. Cruz grabbed a pair of binoculars and slid up behind a large oak that offered a good vantage point. He focused on the Cadillac just in time to see Moretti emerge and enter the winery. A few minutes later Moretti returned, accompanied by a man wearing jeans and a yellow T-shirt. The shirt had a *Coyote Pass Winery* logo on the front. The man appeared nervous. Moretti said something to him and gestured toward the car. They got in. The car started, then backed out of the parking spot.

"He's moving," Cruz radioed, "and he's got someone from the winery with him."

"Copy," Cho shot back.

The Cadillac left the lot and turned right, heading north.

"Coming your way," Cruz said. He ran back to Camry, wondering if they might be forced to intervene in whatever was about to happen next.

A few seconds later Cho replied. "I've got him."

Cruz punched it to catch up. He spotted Cho's Accord and slowed to stay about two hundred yards back.

"He's turning onto a side road," Cho radioed. "I can't follow him without being spotted."

"Copy," Cruz replied. "Tap your brake lights twice at the spot where he turned off."

"Roger that."

Cruz saw the signal from the Accord. He slowed to maintain visual on the Cadillac for as long as possible. Then, just before he passed the turnoff, Moretti stopped and pulled into what looked like a farm field entrance. Cruz parked fifty yards ahead and hiked back to the turnoff, crawling the last ten yards to avoid being seen. He trained the binoculars on the Cadillac and watched.

Five minutes went by. Nothing happened. No one emerged from the vehicle. He radioed Cho.

"I've got him in sight. The car is pulled up to a gate into some farmland. It's just sitting there."

"Shit," Cho replied. "What if he whacks this guy, dumps the body there."

"Mob or not, I don't think he would do that here," Cruz replied. "My guess would be this visit is a not-so-friendly reminder of something."

"Debt collection?"

"Maybe."

Cruz saw the car start and back out of the field entrance.

"He's moving," Cruz said. "You got him."

"Copy that."

Cruz ran back to the car. He had it started and moving north before the Cadillac appeared in his rearview. As expected, it turned south, likely returning the man in the yellow shirt to the winery. Whatever the message was, it had been delivered.

Cruz raised a finger in acknowledgment as he saw the Accord coming back the other direction. Cho did likewise. Cruz found a spot to turn around and started back south.

"They're back at the winery," Cho radioed. "I'll find a spot down the road."

"Roger that," Cruz replied.

As he drove by Coyote Pass, Cruz saw the man in the yellow shirt stumble out of the passenger door of the Cadillac. He was holding his right hand against his chest, as if in pain. Cruz grabbed his cell and pulled up the number for Rowan Parks.

CHAPTER 59

9:14 a.m., Monday, October 3, just south of the warehouse, Napa Valley, California

The decision had been made to follow one of the Amato trucks as it left the warehouse. As he drove past the entrance that morning, Cruz saw two semis backed into loading docks. His guess was they would depart sometime soon. The plan was to tail one of the trucks for a few miles then hand off surveillance to Mancuso. He had come over to assist, allowing Cruz and Cho to stay on Moretti. If it was a long-haul delivery, Mancuso would employ agents from other field divisions as needed. They all knew this was a shot in the dark. But right now, they had nothing more than circumstantial evidence and intuition, and that wouldn't get you an indictment, let alone a conviction.

Cho was north of the warehouse. He had the drone in the air at a safe distance. Once one of the trucks started to move, he would give the signal. Mancuso was out on Route 29, the main state highway through the area. Wherever the delivery was headed, it would almost certainly have to travel 29 first.

Cruz unwrapped a sausage, egg, and cheese biscuit that was by now ice cold and hardening into a hockey puck. He took a bite and washed it down with some lukewarm coffee. Sad as it was, it was far from the worst meal he had ever choked down on surveillance. He took a second bite just as the two-way crackled.

"One truck on the move," Cho radioed.

"Copy that."

Cruz tossed the remnants of the biscuit onto the passenger seat and started the car. He edged forward, waiting for the semi to pass by. Soon, he could hear it coming, feel its approach. This would be a piece of cake compared to tailing Moretti.

"Got him," Cruz radioed as the truck rumbled by.

He stayed well back. There was no chance of losing the target, no reason not to play it safe. When they were within a few miles of Route 29, he keyed the radio.

"Mancuso, do you copy?"

"Copy."

"The target is headed your way."

"Roger that," Mancuso replied.

Minutes later, the Amato semi turned south onto 29.

"All yours," Cruz radioed. He pulled off and turned back toward the warehouse.

Mancuso was just north of the intersection. He quickly spotted the green and yellow Amato Freight Lines truck, then pulled into position, a good three hundred yards back. He had ditched his Charger for a gray Subaru Outback, a common enough vehicle for Northern California.

The truck continued south on Route 29, eventually passing through the city of Napa. When it got close to the airport, it went east on Jameson Canyon Road. Mancuso kept well back, tracking the semi from a distance until they approached Interstate 80. There, the truck merged onto 80 and headed northeast. Mancuso closed the gap between himself and the semi, knowing he could use the heavy traffic on I-80 as cover.

They passed through Thomasson, Fairfield, and Vacaville, then by UC Davis. Mancuso was beginning to wonder if this was going to be a long-haul delivery. If it went beyond Sacramento, he was prepared to hand it off to the Reno office. A contact there was waiting for the call.

As they neared West Sacramento, Mancuso waited to see if the truck stayed on the main interstate through the northern part of the metro, or took Business 80, also known as the Capital City Freeway. The semi stayed to the right, taking the freeway. That told Mancuso that he most likely would not need to contact Reno. At least one of the deliveries would be in the Sacramento area.

The truck continued east through downtown, then north as the Capital City Freeway turned that direction. It quickly exited onto the surface roads, eventually stopping at a place called Sactown Wines. From the looks of it, Mancuso guessed that it was a wholesale company. He did a quick search on his phone which verified that Sactown was a distributor and not a retail shop. This was starting to look like nothing more than a normal delivery of Menfi Vineyards wines. Apparently, they did use the warehouse as a loading and shipment facility.

Even though this was starting to look like a waste of time, Mancuso set up a block down the street from where the truck stopped to unload. From his vantage point he had a clear view to the trailer doors. The driver hopped down from the cab and entered the business. A few minutes later he returned, accompanied by someone from the distributor. There was an exchange of paperwork, then the driver opened the trailer doors. Mancuso focused a small set of binoculars, watching as they began to unload.

When the first box came out everything changed. Mancuso felt his jaw drop as he read the name on the side, *Evans Creek Vineyards*. Another box came out, then another, all with the same name. He pulled out his phone and called Parks.

"Anything interesting?" she asked.

"You could say that," Mancuso replied. He described what he was seeing.

There was a brief silence on the other end, then she spoke. "I'm going to put in a call to New York."

CHAPTER 60

9:57 a.m., Tuesday, October 4, the safehouse, San Francisco, California

Ward sipped his coffee. It was another strategy session to discuss the path forward. They all knew there was something here, but the evidence was circumstantial in the extreme. It was time to think outside the box, get creative. Along those lines, they were expecting a call at any minute. Special Agent Roy Lambert from FBI's New York office had done some digging and would share what he had found. Ward looked around the table. Rowan was seated to his left, close enough that he could smell her perfume. Mancuso, Cruz, and Cho were also present. Cruz had again brought pastries from Achermann's, and Ward had already eaten two of them. The only one missing was Detective Joe Adler. New York insisted they leave him out. Ward didn't like it, but it wasn't his call.

Ward turned to Rowan. "Did Lambert give you any idea what he had come up with?"

"No," she answered. "He just texted me that he has some ideas after talking with the Mob team out there."

"I'll take anything he's got," Mancuso said.

There were nods around the table.

Rowan looked at her watch.

"He's still got one minute," Ward observed, looking at the time on her cell. "I expect FBI punctuality."

Rowan rolled her eyes. Then, at ten o'clock, her phone rang. She gave Ward a smile and a shrug as she answered.

"Parks."

"It's Lambert."

"I've got everybody here," she said. "Okay if I put you on speaker?"

"Of course."

Rowan put the call on speaker and set her phone in the middle of the table.

"Go ahead."

"Any of you ever heard of the Italian Agromafia?" Lambert asked.

"This is Mancuso. I have heard of it."

"Then you may know how the Italian Mafia is involved in almost every aspect of the food chain there," Lambert said. "Sometimes it's nothing more than their typical loan sharking or the demand of *pizzo*, protection money. But it can also include almost every aspect of harvesting, production, and distribution, including grocery stores and restaurants. One of the biggest moneymakers is counterfeit food. Extra virgin olive oil is an example. They dilute the good stuff with sunflower oil or canola. The profit margins are incredible, better than selling drugs, and safer. There are estimates that up to eighty percent of the supposed extra virgin olive oil from Italy that is sold in the United States is fake."

"Wow!" Rowan said. "I'll remember that next time I buy some, or think I'm buying some."

Mancuso spoke up. "So, I guess I see where you're headed with this."

"Right," Lambert replied. "One of the other big moneymakers is counterfeit wine. They simply pass off the cheap stuff as top shelf product by slapping on a bogus label. When I heard about this delivery of Evans Creek wine from a warehouse associated with Rizzo and Moretti...Well, it raised some questions. My understanding is that Evans Creek is an award-winning vineyard."

"That's correct," Rowan replied. She looked at Ward, her eyebrows raised.

"I'm gonna put you in touch with one of my connections at the Anti-Mafia Investigation Directorate headquarters in Rome," Lambert said, "a Major Sergio Paletta. If what you have here is some sort of Agromafia-type scheme, he will be able to help."

"And you trust this guy?" Mancuso asked.

"With my life," Lambert replied.

CHAPTER 61

7:57 a.m., Wednesday, October 5, the safehouse, San Francisco, California

The call had been set up for eight o'clock a.m., five p.m. Rome time. Parks was to make the connection. It was just she and Mancuso this morning, the others having returned to Napa. She took a sip of coffee then tapped the phone app on her cell.

"You ready?" she asked Mancuso.

"Ready." He had his laptop open, prepared to take notes.

Parks punched in the number and placed the call.

"*Ciao*," came the answer. "This is Major Paletta."

"Major, this is Special Agent Rowan Parks, FBI. I have Special Agent Ralph Mancuso here with me."

"Ah, Mancuso," Paletta said. "A good Italian name."

"One hundred percent," Mancuso replied. He gave Parks a wink.

"Please, call me Sergio," Paletta said. "Special Agent Lambert has told me only a little of your problem. Perhaps you could tell me about your investigation and maybe I can be of some help."

"We certainly hope so," Parks replied. She summarized where they were at in the case, starting with the discovery of Raymond Amato's head and concluding with the delivery of Evans Creek wine earlier that week. Parks emphasized the apparent Mob connections of some of those involved.

"I see," Paletta said. "Yes, I think I can be of assistance."

"Lambert has told us a bit about the Agromafia there," Mancuso said.

"It is an enormous problem for us," Paletta replied. "One that consumes most of my time. Here, the Mafia is involved at every level of the food chain, harvesting, transportation, even in the, how you say, supermarkets. They sell counterfeit products, extra virgin olive oil, wine, cheese, many others. They own thousands of restaurants and collect *pizzo*, what you call protection money, from those they do not run. The extortion of food merchants adds up to billions of dollars each year. The counterfeit food makes them billions more. It is more profitable than even the drug trade."

"What about the wine?" Parks asked, thinking she knew the answer.

"It is, as you might guess, simply a matter of taking poor quality wine and placing a famous label on the bottle."

"So, how do you catch them?" Parks asked.

"Ah, that," Paletta replied. "And this is where I can be most helpful. Of course, we use many of the same investigative techniques that you would use, surveillance, wiretaps, that sort of thing. But here, it is difficult to convince victims to cooperate. The Mafia's influence is simply comprehensive. People are afraid. In that regard, maybe you have a bit of an advantage. But one way I think we are different is in the use of expert tasters. This is especially true for products such as olive oil and wine. They can detect a fraud with tremendous consistency."

"Do your courts accept those results as evidence at trial?"

"Sì, always. Their abilities are highly respected."

Parks looked at Mancuso, mouthing the question, *anything else*? He shook his head.

"Thank you so much," Parks said. "May we contact you again if we have additional questions?"

"Of course," Paletta replied. "I am only too happy to help."

Parks ended the call. She looked at Mancuso.
"I have an idea," he said.

CHAPTER 62

9:23 a.m., Friday, October 7, on Route 29, north of Napa, California

Today, Cruz would follow the Amato Freight Lines truck, taking the handoff from Mancuso. Cho would stay on Moretti. They had determined that the smaller trucks handled most of the local deliveries, while the larger semis were more apt to head cross-country. The goal was to simply pick a few bottles of Evans Creek wine that they knew had come from the warehouse.

"Headed your way."

It was Mancuso. Cruz grabbed the two-way.

"Copy that," he replied.

A few minutes later, Cruz saw the Amato truck approach the intersection with Route 29. A gray Subaru Outback was a quarter mile behind it. The truck turned south. Cruz pulled into traffic, staying well back.

"Got him," Cruz radioed. As he passed the intersection, Mancuso turned north and went in the opposite direction.

The truck continued south on 29 through the city of Napa, then on to Vallejo. South of town it picked up Interstate 80 into Berkeley. There, it turned east on University Avenue, eventually stopping at Berkeley Foods, a midsize grocery store.

Cruz circled the block until he found a good vantage point to view the back of the truck. He parked a block away, then grabbed a set of binoculars from the passenger seat. The driver entered the store, returning a few minutes later. He lifted the roll-up door and began to unload. The first few cases were a disappointment, all marked *Menfi Vineyards*. The driver loaded them onto a dolly, two at a time, and wheeled them into the store. Then, Cruz saw what he was looking for, a case with *Evans Creek Vineyards* plainly visible on the side, then another. But it was what appeared next that really got his attention. The driver pulled down two more boxes, both bearing the *Marroquin Winery* name.

Cruz lowered the binoculars. He waited as the driver finished wheeling the wine into the grocery store, closed the truck door, and departed. When the truck was out of sight, Cruz stepped out of the car and headed inside. On the way in he sent Parks a text, informing her of the Marroquin delivery. She replied a few minutes later, telling him to buy whatever he could, particularly the Cabernet.

Berkeley Foods had an impressive wine section for a grocery store of its size. Cruz found an employee stocking the shelves and approached. The young woman smiled at him.

"Can I help you find something?" she asked.

"Thank you," Cruz said, meeting her gaze and returning the smile. "Actually, yes."

She flipped a stray lock of hair off her forehead. There was a sparkle in her eyes. Cruz looked at her name tag, Erin.

"I was just walking in and saw that you received a shipment from Evans Creek Vineyards," he said. "I love their Pinot."

"Oh, an excellent choice," Erin replied. "Let me see if we have any out here."

Cruz followed her, realizing his mistake. He should have checked their store shelves first. A bottle already there may very well have come from the warehouse, but he couldn't take that chance.

"One bottle of the Pinot Noir," Erin announced, removing it

from the rack and holding it up for him to see.

"Excellent," Cruz replied. "But I'd like to get three."

"Well, I'm really not supposed to sell from the new shipments before they've been logged into inventory."

"I would really appreciate it, Erin."

She smiled. "Okay, maybe just this once."

As she started toward the storage room, Cruz spoke up.

"Oh," he said, "I almost forgot. What do you have from Marroquin Winery?"

CHAPTER 63

10:23 a.m., Saturday, October 8, Federal Bureau of Investigation, San Francisco Field Office, San Francisco, California

Parks sat in the conference room by herself, waiting. Mancuso told her it would be around ten-thirty. She looked at her cell, sitting there on the table. It had been a few days since she talked to David. He deserved an update, she decided, placing the call.

"Hello, Rowan."

She smiled at the sound of his voice. "Hi, David."

"What's the plan today?" he asked.

"Cruz managed to pick up a few bottles of Evans Creek Pinot," she replied.

"And you're going to try to determine if it's counterfeit."

"Correct."

"How?"

"We're going to do what the Italians do, use an expert taster."

"And where does one find such a person?"

"It is California, David. They're around."

"I see. Like on street corners...?"

"Funny," she replied. "But in this case, it's your friend from the training session. Mancuso said his name is Justin?"

"That's right," Ward said. "And Justin could tell the difference between a fake and the real thing."

223

"They're supposed to be here any minute."

"Let me know what happens."

"Will do," she said. "Oh, one more thing."

"What's that?"

"When the Amato truck made its delivery, it wasn't just Evans Creek wine."

"And I'm guessing that you're not talking about Menfi Vineyards," he said.

"No, I'm not. Want to take a guess?"

"Three Peaks?"

"Incorrect."

"Hmmm." He was quiet for a moment.

"Clock's ticking," she said. "Ten, nine, eight, seven..."

"Marroquin," he answered.

"Very good."

"I had a feeling about that guy."

"I'm sure you did." She was sure.

The door to the conference room opened. Mancuso and Justin walked in, the latter carrying a bag.

"I'll call you later," Rowan said.

"I look forward to it."

So do I, she thought, ending the call.

"I don't believe you two have met," Mancuso said. "Special Agent Parks, Justin Dodd."

"A pleasure," Justin said, stepping forward and extending his hand.

"Justin is a respected vintner and connoisseur of fine wines," Mancuso added.

"Sounds like just who we need," Parks said. "Nice to meet you."

"Well, should we begin?" Mancuso asked.

"Absolutely," Justin replied. He sat his bag on the conference table and removed four glasses, all with short stems and wide rims. Then, he removed a bottle of Evans Creek Pinot Noir and a bottle Marroquin Winery's Cabernet Sauvignon.

"I thought the bottles we collected were here?" Parks asked.

"They are," Mancuso replied. He walked to a cabinet and retrieved a box, placing it on the table. He then removed the wine purchased by Cruz.

"If I may explain," Justin said. "I was able to find two bottles submitted for a Napa Valley wine contest in which I was one of the judges. Obviously, a counterfeit would not be submitted for such an event."

Parks nodded. "Understood," she said. "And so, these were brought for comparison purposes."

"Precisely," Justin replied.

He removed a bottle of water and a small loaf of bread. Parks watched as he sliced off four pieces.

"To cleanse the palate between tastings," he announced.

Justin proceeded to line up four bottles, first the Evans Creek Pinot he had brought with him, then the suspected counterfeit, repeating the process for the Marroquin Cabernet. He then uncorked the wine, pouring a small amount of each into the glasses, which were then placed in front of the corresponding bottles.

The supposedly legitimate Evans Creek Pinot came first. Justine examined the wine, looking at it from all angles. He then gave it a swirl, hovering his nose over the glass. A few seconds later, he did it again. Then, he took a sip. Parks could hear a sound, almost as if he were sucking on it. Justin placed the glass back in front of the bottle.

"Excellent," he announced. "Clearly, a legitimate Evans Creek Pinot."

There was a bite of bread, then a drink of water, which he swished around in his mouth.

"Now, for the supposed imposter."

Justin repeated the process for the second glass of wine. There was a look of puzzlement after he sniffed the wine. When he tasted it, his brow furrowed. He turned to Mancuso.

"The aroma and bouquet are all wrong," Justin said. "And

the flavor is not remotely comparable."

"And we know it's not just a bad vintage?" Parks asked.

The look he gave her made her regret the question.

"My dear," Justin replied, "this is not a bad vintage, it's a bad wine."

He then moved on to the Marroquin Cabernets. The first glass resulted in an appreciative nod. The second, however, provoked a strong response.

"This," Justin said, holding up the second glass of Cabernet, "is little better than swill."

CHAPTER 64

12:37 p.m., Saturday, October 8, Bistro Bonita, Napa, California

"Try the fish tacos," Cahill said.

Ward gave him a purposely skeptical look. "I've never been a great believer in the concept of tacos involving fish," he replied.

"Seriously? You're one of those guys?" Cahill shook his head. "You don't know what you're missing."

The waitress approached. She gave Ward a smile.

"Do you know what you want?" she asked, chewing on the end of her pen.

She was cute, and about fifteen years too young, even if he was looking.

"I know it's Napa," Ward replied, "but I need a beer."

The waitress giggled. "Understood."

Ward picked a pale ale from a local brewery.

"And to eat?" she asked.

Ward studied Cahill for a moment. "The fish tacos," he said.

"Oh, they're the best," the waitress said. She turned to Cahill. "And for you?"

"Why, I'll have the same," he announced, grinning triumphantly.

"Very good," the waitress said. "I'll be right back with those drinks." As she walked away, she looked back over her shoulder at Ward.

"I think she likes you," Cahill observed.

"And I might have liked her," Ward replied, "when I was in college."

Cahill laughed.

"She's just trolling for tips," Ward added.

The drinks came moments later.

"Enjoy your beer," the waitress said, sliding the bottle in front of Ward. Her impish smile was accompanied by a seductively raised eyebrow. "Your food should be up in a few minutes." She turned and left.

"Trolling pretty hard," Cahill said, watching her walk away. "But I don't think it's a tip she's trying to catch."

Ward laughed. They drank their beers, surveying the crowd.

"There's Pedro Marroquin," Cahill said, nodding toward a table on the other side of the patio.

"How well do you know him?" Ward asked. Rowan had called him a half hour earlier to report on Justin's conclusions.

"Not well," Cahill admitted. "Aside from hosting the Harvest Gala, he mostly keeps to himself. I've often wondered where his money comes from."

"What do you mean?" Ward asked.

"I'm sure the winery is profitable," Cahill said. "But the grounds there, the buildings...And then there's the cost of the Gala. I can't imagine what that amounts to."

"He puts up all of the money for that himself?" Ward asked.

"That's what I've been told."

Ward studied Marroquin for a moment, wondering how deep his involvement might go.

"I overheard a strange conversation between him and Rudy Moretti one time," Cahill said, lowering his voice.

"Oh?"

"It was at last year's Gala," Cahill said. "There was no one else around. Moretti asked Marroquin when he was going to get him the labels. Then he said they would take care of the transportation."

Ward took a sip of beer, mostly to prevent showing any reaction.

"I thought it was odd," Cahill said.

Ward nodded. He did, too. But he wasn't going to say so.

CHAPTER 65

3:22 p.m., Saturday, October 8, a quarter mile south of the warehouse, Napa Valley, California

They had followed Moretti to the warehouse over five hours ago and nothing had happened. Cruz was struggling to stay awake. He leaned over and grabbed an energy drink from a small cooler in front of the passenger seat. It was his third of the day, a bad habit that was taking its toll. As he popped the tab and took a slug, the warehouse gate started to slide open. Seconds later, Moretti's black Caddy appeared, already accelerating toward Mach 1.

"Shit," Cruz exclaimed. He tossed the can in the general direction of the cooler as he put the car into gear and grabbed the two-way.

"He's moving," Cruz said, watching Moretti turn north. "Headed your way."

"Copy," Cho replied. A few seconds later the radio crackled. "I've got him."

Cruz crushed the gas pedal, needing to keep Cho in sight. It would be another difficult tail because of Moretti's pace, and because they were headed up into the mountains where there would be less traffic.

"You on him?" Cruz asked.

"Roger that," Cho replied.

Soon, Cruz caught a glimpse of the back of Cho's car. He was still driving the same Accord. Cruz hoped that hadn't been a mistake.

"How far back are you?" Cruz radioed, worried that Cho might get made.

"Not far enough," Cho said. "Maybe two hundred yards. Hard to stay with him."

They traveled up into the Vaca Mountains on Route 121, then turned east where it intersected 128.

"Let me take the lead," Cruz radioed.

"Roger that," Cho replied.

Cruz accelerated hard. He got behind Cho and waited for a straight stretch of road where he could pass. When his opening came, he hammered the gas and flew by the Accord. Cruz glanced at the rearview as Cho dropped far back.

The Cadillac appeared in his sights as 128 turned north. A few minutes later, a lake and several boat docks appeared out the driver's side window. Cruz caught glimpse of a sign: Lake Berryessa. He stayed tight on Moretti as road suddenly veered to the right, then sharply back to the left. The road then curved slowly to the east before passing along the south end of the dam that created the reservoir. About five miles later, Cruz saw the Caddy's brake lights come on.

"He's turning south on Pleasants Valley Road," Cruz radioed. "There's a bridge that crosses the creek. I'll drive past the turnoff. Pick him back up."

"Roger that," Cho replied.

Cruz found a spot to double back. In the rearview he could see Cho turning south and crossing the bridge.

"Got him," Cho replied. A few seconds later, he radioed again. "He's turning onto a private drive. Looks like a pretty place."

Cruz pulled off the road. "Shoot me the coordinates," he said, "and an address if you can see one."

Cho texted him the information. Cruz copied the text, forwarded it to Rowan Parks, then called her.

"Did you see my…"

"Reading it right now," Parks said, cutting him off.

"Can you pull up who lives…"

"Already on it," Parks interjected.

"Okay then," Cruz said. He waited.

It was a minute or two before Parks spoke. "Well, this is interesting," she said. "The property is owned by Griffin Cooper."

"And he is…?"

"He is…the acting president of Amato Freight Lines."

"That is interesting," Cruz agreed. "Given the deliveries we've seen, there is no way that someone higher up at Amato isn't in on this, whatever this is."

"Agreed," Parks said. "And when Detective Adler from the sheriff's office tried to get GPS records for Amato's trucks, it was Cooper and the company lawyer who refused."

"I'd love to hear the conversation between Moretti and Cooper," Cruz said.

"So would I," Parks said. "But there's no way to make that happen, at least not yet." She paused. "Any other vehicles on-site? We should rule out the possibility that it's just a little get-together for some of his clients."

"Just a second," Cruz said. "I'll radio Cho."

Cruz picked up the two-way. "Any other vehicles there?" he asked. "Any signs of a party?" He held the radio up so Parks could hear the answer.

"Negative," Cho replied.

CHAPTER 66

6:29 p.m., Saturday, October 8, Menfi Vineyards, Napa Valley, California

Moretti stood on the patio, watching the sunset cast a golden hue over the vineyard. At times he missed Brooklyn, his old haunts, the crew. But he had to admit, this place was special. It could even bring some measure of peace to an old warhorse like himself.

"How did it go with Cooper?"

Moretti turned to see Rizzo approach, a bottle and two glasses in hand.

"Not so good," Moretti said.

Rizzo uncorked the bottle and poured them each a glass. He was calm, not immediately responding to the comment.

"What do you mean by *not so good*?" he asked, handing a glass to Moretti.

"Cooper says handlin' our…special deliveries is cuttin' into his bottom line. He says the increased shipments are pullin' too many trucks away from their regular routes and customers."

"Increased shipments are good," Rizzo replied. He held up his glass in salute.

Moretti did likewise.

Rizzo took a sip, then spoke. "Cooper needs to understand

that these are his regular routes. And we most assuredly are his regular, and most important, customer."

Moretti nodded. "I think I conveyed that message."

"I'm sure you did," Rizzo replied.

"I explained that it would be unfortunate if there were some losses to their fleet," Moretti said, "seein' as how it is stretched so thin and all."

"The response?"

"Cooper insisted he needed a new arrangement."

"I see."

"That's when I spotted the family photo on the bookshelf. I picked it up, mentioned it was probably real hard on Ray Amato's family, not knowin' what happened all that time, then him bein' found the way he was."

"And did that resonate with Mr. Cooper?" Rizzo asked.

"I believe it did," Moretti replied. "And I told him I better not have to make a return visit."

"Good," Rizzo said.

"There's somethin' else," Moretti said. He hated to bring it up now, but no time was good.

"What's that?"

"I think I was followed."

Rizzo's face dropped; his eyes grew intense. "What do you mean, followed to Cooper's?"

"Possibly," Moretti said, looking away from the boss's glare. "There were two cars, maybe switching off. I don't know. I mean, Cooper lives in a pretty out-of-the-way location."

Rizzo looked away, his face expressionless. Moretti couldn't read him, and that was unsettling.

"Feds?" Rizzo asked.

"Or the Napa County Sheriff's Office," Moretti replied. But he knew the FBI was more likely. His mind once again went to Harley Ricard.

"Has it happened before?" Rizzo asked.

"I don't think so."

Rizzo turned back, staring him in the eye. "You don't think so?"

Moretti could feel himself take a step back. It just happened, involuntarily. He couldn't remember telling his legs to do it.

"I mean...I don't think so." Fuck. Why did he say that again?

Rizzo put his hand over his forehead, then ran it back through his hair. He took a breath, then seemed to step back from the edge.

"Maybe we need someone to come in and watch the watchers," he said.

"I can arrange that," Moretti said.

"No," Rizzo replied. "I'll arrange it."

Moretti nodded. "Whatever you say, boss." He was insulted.

Rizzo studied him for a moment, then turned and leaned against the patio wall, looking out over the valley. "Quite a place, isn't it?"

"Definitely."

"I'm not going to lose everything that I worked for," Rizzo said. "Understood?"

"Understood," Moretti replied. He started to get angry in a way he never had with Rizzo, wondering what had happened to everything *they* had worked for.

CHAPTER 67

9:08 a.m., Monday, October 10, the safehouse, San Francisco, California

Ward had come in the night before, staying at the safehouse. He got up early and found his way to Achermann's. It was his turn to bring breakfast. Now, the coffee was on. He expected the others to arrive shortly.

Cruz and Cho arrived first. Ward buzzed them up.

"I apologize, my friend," Cruz said as he walked through the door. "I didn't have time to..." It was then that he saw the pink box on the table. "Ha ha!" Cruz laughed, slapping Ward on the back. "You are a good man!"

Cruz and Cho helped themselves as Ward went to get coffee. When he returned the video intercom system crackled to life.

"Mancuso and Parks."

Ward checked the screen. Mancuso was looking up and down the street, checking for followers. Rowan, on the other hand, winked into the camera. Ward smiled. He buzzed them in.

Rowan entered first. "How was your stay at Hotel Fed?" she asked, smiling cutely.

"No complaints," Ward replied.

"Not much of an establishment," Cruz chimed in, his mouth still full of apple fritter. "Guest had to provide his own breakfast." He pointed at the box.

"I got up early," Ward added.

"Nice," Rowan said. "Don't mind if I do." She selected a scone. "And if you could get me a coffee," she added, waving a finger toward the kitchen.

"My pleasure," Ward said. He turned to Mancuso. "Anything for you?"

Mancuso held up his to-go cup. "I'm good," he said.

They gathered around the table as Ward returned with Rowan's coffee. As he sat the cup down, she took it, letting her fingers slide along his. She looked up and met his gaze, an impish smile on her face. Ward instinctively glanced around to see if anyone noticed, though he wasn't sure if he cared.

"All right," Mancuso announced, opening his laptop, "Let's get down to it."

"Yes, let's," Rowan said, eyeing Ward. It was that same look.

Mancuso looked up, studying Parks. He glanced at Ward. Cruz was watching all three of them.

Ward took a drink of coffee and stared at the table, trying not to laugh. He thought he heard the hint of a giggle. *Provocative* was an adjective that described Rowan Parks in all respects.

"Yes, let us not forget why we are here."

Ward looked up to see the raised eyebrow and knowing grin of Cesar Cruz. He looked at Rowan out of the corner of his eye. She bit her lip. He looked back at Cruz, his grin still present.

"Can we just get started?" Mancuso asked, shaking his head.

"I'm ready," Cho said, licking icing off his fingers. He seemed oblivious to what was happening.

"Thank you," Mancuso replied.

"As I've said before, there's what you know, and what you can prove," Rowan began. "We all know what's going on here, but we're a long way from having enough to indict, let alone convict."

"Agreed," Mancuso replied. "So, what do we do about it?"

"We have enough for a search warrant," Cho noted, "At least for the warehouse."

"But that would expose David," Parks said.

"I agree," Cruz added.

"But maybe not if we don't include his information in the affidavit," Cho explained.

"It would still make it difficult to maintain any undercover component once we alert them like that," Mancuso observed. "I think that has to come later."

There were nods of agreement around the table. Ward felt it was the right call, at least for now. There was more to learn from the inside. He was sure of it.

"I think we need to flip somebody," Ward said.

Rowan gave him a puzzled look. "That could alert them as much, if not more, than a search warrant," she said.

"Maybe not," Ward said. "I have an idea."

Mancuso looked up from his laptop. Rowan leaned in.

"How well do you trust Detective Adler?" Ward asked her.

"He's solid," she replied.

"Cooper seems like the weak link," Ward said. "He's also the least likely to be mobbed-up."

"How does that work?" Mancuso asked. "I'm not big on sharing info with the locals."

"That's obvious," Ward replied. "Look, I get the risk. But this guy should have had more involvement in this investigation. Besides, it's my ass on the line."

Ward caught a wink and a slight nod of approval from Cruz.

"I agree," Rowan said. "If David's okay with it, I'm okay with it."

"But back to my question," Mancuso said. "How does that work?"

"Assuming Adler doesn't tell us to fuck off, which I don't think he will, we have him approach Cooper as part of the local investigation."

"And say what?" Mancus asked. "Cooper is not gonna roll

easy. How does Adler say enough to make Cooper believe that his ass is on the line without potentially exposing the operation and putting them on high alert?"

"He doesn't have to say much," Ward explained. "He needs to approach Cooper somewhere when he's alone, away from the company lawyers. All he needs to tell him is that they know Amato Freight Lines is involved with some questionable shipments, and that Raymond Amato's death was a result of that. Doesn't matter that we can't prove it. Then he throws around words like *accessory* and *obstruction* and tells Cooper that this is his chance to help himself. If Cooper's sitting naked without his lawyer, I say he shits his pants. There's some risk with this, but there's always some risk. And we need to do something to get this moving."

"What if Cooper tells his minders that he's been approached?" Mancuso asked. "Maybe he's more afraid of them than the Napa County Sheriff's Office?"

"Understood," Ward replied. "Again, there's always some risk. But Adler makes it clear to him that if he doesn't keep it to himself, there's a good chance that the people involved might see him as a weak link and make him disappear. After all, he already knows somebody killed Ray Amato."

For a moment, nobody spoke. Then Cruz rapped his knuckles on the table. "I like it," he said.

"Me, too," Rowan added.

Cho nodded his agreement.

They all looked at Mancuso.

"Adler better stick to the fuckin' script," he said.

CHAPTER 68

5:06 p.m., Monday, October 10, Menfi Vineyards, Napa Valley, California

Rizzo stood on the patio, away from the crowd. He was told to expect a call around five o'clock. He poured a glass from a bottle of one their better Cabernets and proceeded to wait. It had been a while since he had dealt directly with New York, and he needed some fortification. After two sips, the phone rang. He looked at the number. The area code meant nothing. He assumed that the call was made from a burner.

"Hello," he answered

"We just landed in Reno," the voice on the other end announced. "Should be there in three or four hours."

It was a distinct Brooklyn accent, one that brought back memories, not all of them good.

"Why Reno?" Rizzo asked. Sacramento and San Francisco International were much closer.

"We still have friends here," the man said. "Arrangements have been made."

Of course, Rizzo thought. He regretted the question.

"You know the job?" Rizzo asked.

"To an extent," the man answered. "We were told you would provide the details."

"We think Moretti is being followed," Rizzo said, "maybe by the feds. I want you to look for a tail, find out who it is."

"Can do."

"How many of you came in?" Rizzo asked.

"Three."

"There's another man," Rizzo said, "goes by the name of Harley Ricard, a possible alias. He may be a plant."

"You want us to take care of him?" the man asked.

"Nothing like that, at least not yet. First, I want to verify who he is."

"Understood. Anything else?"

Rizzo thought for a moment. "Yes," he said. "There is something else."

CHAPTER 69

12:27 p.m., Tuesday, October 11, Sacramento, California

It was just like the FBI. They only contacted you when they needed something. Joe Adler was not too thrilled at the prospect of being their errand boy, but he was a pro, and he wanted the case resolved. The task was to reach out to Griffin Cooper and see if he might be willing to cooperate with what was to be described as a purely local investigation.

Adler had tracked Cooper to a local café where he was having lunch, alone. That was the key. Make sure that no attorney was in the vicinity when he was approached. Adler recalled the suffocatingly pompous C. Barton Webb, Amato's corporate counsel. He needed to be kept completely out of the loop.

The café was not busy. Adler entered and ordered a coffee. He kept his back turned to Cooper who was at a table in the corner, away from the other patrons. It was perfect for an approach.

The coffee came. Adler paid and gave the barista a healthy tip. He walked toward Cooper who had not looked up from his tablet.

"Congratulations on your promotion," Adler said. He was aware that Cooper had been formally installed as the president of Amato Freight Lines.

Cooper looked up, a smile on his face until he saw who it

was. The smile vanished. "What do you want?" he asked.

"Mind if I have a seat?" Adler asked.

Cooper looked around, apparently to see if anyone was listening, then gestured at the chair.

"Well?" he asked.

Straight to the point. That was fine with Adler.

"We know that Amato Freight Lines has been involved with some highly questionable shipments, and that Raymond Amato's death was a direct result of that."

Cooper started to squirm. He leaned in. "Do I need my lawyer?" he asked, his tone hushed.

"Why would you?" Adler asked. "Did you do something?"

Cooper looked around the room. "Please," he said, "keep it down."

Adler leaned forward. "I don't think you were involved in the murder," he said, "but I think you know things, things that could be...helpful."

Cooper started to breathe heavily. There was a panicked look. Adler could tell that he had struck a nerve. "Maybe I need a lawyer," he said.

"That's up to you," Adler replied. "But I want you to think about some things before you make that choice. The first one would be that you don't know who to trust."

Cooper's head dropped. Clearly, he had been having the same thoughts.

"I don't want to use words like *accessory* and *obstruction*," Adler lied, "but this is a chance for you to help yourself."

Cooper did not look up. He appeared as if he was about to be sick. "I need to think about it," he said under his breath.

Adler pulled out a business card and slid it across the table. "Call anytime," he said, "day or night."

Cooper nodded, almost imperceptibly.

Adler got up to leave, then remembered something. He sat back down.

"A bit of advice," he began. "Keep this to yourself. If the

people involved know you've been approached, they might see you as the weak link and...you know...make the problem disappear."

Cooper looked up and met his gaze. The fear was unmistakable.

CHAPTER 70

9:22 a.m., Thursday, October 13, just south of Menfi Vineyards, Napa Valley, California

Moretti had been lying low for a few days, not leaving the vineyard. Cruz was getting bored. He and Cho had been sitting on the place night and day that entire week. It might mean nothing, but it also might mean that Moretti knew he was being tailed. Either way, they were doing nothing to move the investigation forward.

Cruz wondered if Cooper had said something after his conversation with Adler, spilled his guts about being approached. That would be magnificently stupid, but hardly unprecedented. Maybe Mancuso was right. Maybe Cooper was more afraid of whoever was pulling the strings than he was of anybody with a badge.

Cruz took a bite of an inferior donut that he had bought at a nearby convenience store. He washed it down with a slug of similarly disappointing coffee from the same place. Tomorrow he would bring better provisions. He lifted the donut for another bite when the two-way crackled.

"He's moving," Cho radioed. "Headed your direction and coming fast."

Cruz tossed the donut on the passenger seat. "Roger that," he replied. He put the car in drive and started to nose forward just as Moretti's Caddy flew by before he was in position.

"What the fuck?" he said out loud. Moretti always drove aggressively, but Cruz estimated him to be at least thirty miles per hour over the speed limit. He pulled out and accelerated hard, straining to keep up. Soon, he had the Caddy in his sights. Cruz wondered if Moretti was purposely trying to expose anybody following him. He grabbed the radio, steering with one hand as Moretti rocketed along the winding mountain road.

"You think he's trying to draw us out?" he radioed Cho.

"Wouldn't surprise me," Cho replied, "especially after he's been sitting tight all week."

Cruz tried to stay close without being spotted, but it was difficult at this speed and on these roads. If Moretti saw any vehicle staying with him for even a short period, he would have to suspect that something was up. After a half dozen miles Cruz wanted to hand off the lead to Cho, but he wasn't sure they could execute the switch without losing their target.

"Can you take the lead?" he radioed.

"I can try," Cho shot back.

When he saw Cho in his rearview Cruz slowed, drifting onto the right shoulder to give him room to pass. Cho flew by. Cruz started to pull back onto the road. It was then that he saw the black SUV coming up fast.

"Shit!" Cruz yelled, jerking the car back onto the shoulder. The SUV roared by, nearly taking the left side of his car with it. His stomach dropped. Cruz hit the gas, trying to catch up, trying to verify what he already knew. At a hundred yards back he slowed, maintaining surveillance. It was obvious that the SUV was staying with Cho and Moretti. He grabbed the two-way.

"Pull off," Cruz radioed. "We're made."

Parked a half mile off on a little used side road, Cruz waited for Cho to join him before making the call. A few minutes later, Cho approached. Cruz pulled up the contact info for Mancuso.

He was not going to be happy.

"What's up?" Mancuso asked, straight to the point.

"We're made," Cruz replied. He described what had happened.

"Fuck," Mancuso said.

There was nothing but silence for a minute, then two, three...

"You're gonna have to pull out," Mancuso finally said.

Cruz felt sick. This was a first for him, a low point in his career. Abandoning the mission went against his every instinct. But he knew Mancuso was right. They were compromised. He looked at Cho, his partner's head hung low.

"I'm sorry," Cruz said. He ended the call.

CHAPTER 71

9:58 a.m., Thursday, October 13, on the surface roads of Napa, California

Ward was headed north to meet another vineyard owner as Harley Ricard when he received the call. The contact info showed Mancuso.

"Ward," he answered.

"Where are you?" There was an urgency to Mancuso's voice.

"Just leaving town," Ward said, "visiting a vineyard up near Yountville."

"Keep your eyes open," Mancuso said. "Cruz and Cho were just made."

"Damn it. What happened?"

"Moretti was driving hard, trying to draw them out. There was an SUV behind him looking for a tail. Our guys didn't see it until it was too late."

"Where are they now?"

"I told them to pull out...permanently."

Ward could only imagine how Cruz and Cho felt at that moment.

"Any ideas on who it was?" he asked.

"No," Mancuso replied. "California plates, but that doesn't mean anything. My guess would be out-of-towners, maybe from the East Coast."

"That could mean a lot of things," Ward said. "A lot more than just looking for a tail."

"Agreed. Like I said, keep your eyes open."

Ward ended the call as he checked the rearview. Nothing immediately jumped out. He began a circuitous, clockwise pattern through a residential neighborhood. There was one vehicle, a dark gray Chevy Tahoe, that stayed with him through the last two turns. Ward pulled to the curb. The vehicle turned off. He then began a counterclockwise pattern. The Tahoe popped up again on the third turn. Whoever it was, Ward thought, they had only moderate skills in surveillance.

CHAPTER 72

11:09 a.m., Thursday, October 13, Menfi Vineyards, Napa Valley, California

They sat in Rizzo's office. The boss eyed his longtime associate. The news was not good.

"So, you were definitely followed?" Rizzo asked.

"No question about it," Moretti replied.

"Feds?" Rizzo asked.

"Has to be."

Rizzo pressed his hands together, resting his chin on his thumbs as if praying.

"They'll back off for now," Moretti assured him. "But I'd be real careful about what I say over the phone."

"I already am," Rizzo replied, not looking up. Did the man think he was stupid? The wiretap was a tool that had almost destroyed Cosa Nostra.

"There's somethin' else," Moretti said.

Rizzo placed his hands on the desk and just stared, saying nothing.

Moretti shifted in his seat, appearing uncharacteristically nervous. "It's about Griffin Cooper," he said. "I got a call last night. He was approached by that deputy from Napa County, Adler."

Rizzo knew the answer but asked anyway. "About what?"

"They want him to cooperate," Moretti replied. "Told him they knew Amato Freight Lines was makin' some questionable shipments, and that Ray Amato's death was because of it. Started using words like *accessory* and *obstruction*."

"Sounds like a desperate bluff. If they know so much, why do they need Cooper?"

"Maybe it's a bluff, maybe it's not," Moretti replied. "But Cooper is definitely a weak link."

"Still, he came to us."

"That's because he's more afraid of us than he is of them," Moretti said, a satisfied look on his face.

"For now," Rizzo said. Maybe Cooper was trying to show his loyalty, but how long that would last was another matter. The FBI was still involved. They had interviewed Pavesi, and they didn't just quit. Sending Adler to work on Cooper sounded like a ploy. Rizzo went quiet.

"What do you wanna do?" Moretti finally asked.

"He knows too much," Rizzo said. He knew that was all he would have to say.

"Understood."

"Let's use the Brooklyn crew," Rizzo said, studying Rudy.

"If that's what you want," Moretti replied. "I'll set it up."

Rizzo shook his head. "I'll do it." He could see that the comment displeased Rudy. Was he simply offended because these tasks usually fell to him, or was it something else?

"Whatever you say...boss."

There was something in the way he said it. Rizzo started to think about who would have the most to gain from talking to the feds.

"If you'll excuse me," Rizzo said, "I need to make some calls."

Moretti appeared taken aback, as if wondering what calls could not be made in front of him. Rizzo rallied, realizing his mistake.

"Gena," he said. "She's in San Francisco. Been trying to get ahold of me."

Moretti nodded. He stood and left without a word.

Rizzo watched the video feed from the surveillance camera mounted in the hallway outside his office. When Rudy was gone, he reached into the lower left desk drawer and removed the burner phone that had been acquired for this purpose. He punched in the numbers.

"Yeah," came the answer.

"We have a problem," Rizzo said. He told them what they needed to know about Cooper, no more.

"We'll take care of it." The Brooklyn accent assured Rizzo that they would.

"And I want you to stay on Moretti," he said.

There was a slight pause. "I don't think they'll tail him, at least not for a while. They know we spotted them."

"Do it anyway," Rizzo said.

"You think he's a rat?"

Rizzo didn't respond.

"Understood."

CHAPTER 73

2:23 p.m., Friday, October 14, Napa County Sheriff's Office, 1535 Airport Blvd, Napa, California

Adler put the finishing touches on a report concerning the burglary of a residence the night before. The place was just east of Yountville, off Silverado trail.

"If I had a dollar for every burglary I've typed up," he said, looking up. Double E had just entered the room.

"This is true," Estes replied, handing Adler a fresh coffee.

"Gracias, mi amigo." Adler picked up the cup and took a sip, letting out an audible sigh. "I needed that." It was just like Estes. The man was a good partner, always anticipating what was needed, be it a cup of coffee or stopping the next move of a suspect who was about to go for your gun. Adler remembered that night, now four years ago. Estes had likely saved his life.

"I might take a run over to that pawn shop on Pueblo," Adler said. "Wanna ride along?"

"Absolutely."

As he was about to get up, Adler heard his cell ring. He slipped it from his jacket, which was hanging over the back of his chair. The number was unfamiliar.

"Adler," he answered.

"Detective, this is C. Barton Webb, general counsel at Amato

Freight Lines."

Adler immediately remembered the pompous fuck. What the hell was this about?

"What can I do for you, Mr. Webb?" he asked.

"It concerns Griffin Cooper," Webb replied.

Adler had been wondering about Cooper. He had not heard from him since their conversation three days earlier.

"What about him?" Adler asked.

"Well, he didn't show up for work today," Webb replied. "And I can't reach him on his cell, which is unusual."

"Does he have family?" Adler asked. "Have you contacted them?"

"Yes," Webb replied. "His wife hasn't seen him since last night. She is very upset. He left to meet someone right after dinner and never returned. She was about to call the police. I told her I would phone you."

Adler felt ill. He was sure no one had seen him talk to Cooper. He must have told someone. Why didn't the man heed his advice?

"Can you give his wife's name and number?" Adler asked.

"Of course."

Adler wrote down the information, thanked Webb, then ended the call. He scrolled through his list of contacts and found the number.

"Parks," she answered.

"We have a problem."

CHAPTER 74

6:23 p.m., Monday, October 17, at an undisclosed location, Brooklyn, New York City, New York

It was unusual to have another meeting this soon, but it was necessary. Barney had called them together, on short notice. There would be no representatives from Chicago or Philly. Tonight, it was just the Five Families. But they were all that was needed.

Bottles of the best Cabernet from Menfi Vineyards had been opened; glasses had been poured. This was the real stuff, from their vineyard, not the swill that was passed off under the labels of those they controlled. He raised a glass.

"*Salute*," Barney said, acknowledging every man in the room. He took a sip. "Ah, *delizioso!*"

"*Sì, magnifico*," Big Mike agreed. "I take it our thing in Napa is going well."

Barney took a draw from his Cohiba Robusto. The smoke entered his mouth, then lingered before he slowly blew it out. All eyes watched him, waiting for the answer. When it didn't come, looks were exchanged.

"Something is wrong," Mickey said.

Barney nodded. He looked at each of them, then spoke, "We have a problem."

CHAPTER 75

8:03 p.m., Tuesday, October 18, Menfi Vineyards, Napa Valley, California

Rizzo sat under the patio lights, about to enjoy a late dinner. The chef had prepared veal Marsala. It was paired with a nice Sangiovese. A perfect combination, and one of his favorite meals.

The guests were gone. The staff had left for the night. Gena was still in San Francisco. Tonight, it was just him, alone with his thoughts, and that was fine. Everyone needed time to themselves, time to think. That was as true now as it had ever been.

There was a chill in the air, the temperature dipping to near sixty degrees. A patio heater had been placed nearby. The heat from it warmed him, making the night comfortable. Rizzo cut into his veal, raising a bite to his mouth.

"Looks delicious."

Rizzo immediately recognized the voice, the Brooklyn accent. It was the man from the phone, part of the team from out east. He sat his fork back on the plate, the bite of veal uneaten.

"Care to join me?" Rizzo asked, turning in his chair.

The gun, with silencer, was leveled at his head. The man, in black, looked fit, serious...lethal. Rizzo knew immediately who had set him up.

"I'll pass," the man said. He took aim. "Rudy sends his regards."

CHAPTER 76

4:10 p.m., Wednesday, October 19, on Interstate 80, southwest of Sacramento, California

The trip had yielded nothing. Adler had offered his services to the Sacramento PD in their search for Griffin Cooper, disclosing only what he could. The Solano County Sheriff's Office was also involved. FBI resources were being utilized independently, a fact Adler was not allowed to share with local law enforcement. So far, all efforts had yielded nothing. Cooper had vanished in much the same way as Raymond Amato, and possibly with a similar fate.

As he approached Vacaville, Adler's cell rang. He picked it up off the passenger seat and looked at the screen. It was Double E.

"What's up?"

"I just took a call from Geneva Rizzo," Estes said.

Adler felt his back stiffen.

"She came back from San Francisco this morning," Estes continued. "Her husband was not at the vineyard, and nobody has seen him since last night."

CHAPTER 77

2:33 p.m., Friday, October 21, Dash Estates, Napa Valley, California

Moretti had timed the visit to avoid the lunch crowd. There had been no need. The parking lot was empty, a fact that explained why there had been no payment. The events of the last few days made him want to lay low. And he and Gena had already been interviewed by that detective, Adler. But business was business. Cutting any slack on due dates would be bad for his reputation. Stone had his thirty days. Now it was time to collect.

A rental had replaced the Caddy earlier that day. Moretti was sure he was not being followed, but it seemed a reasonable precaution. There had been no signs of a tail since the feds' fuckup the week before. Still, he stopped after getting out of the car and looked around for anything suspicious. Seeing nothing, he walked toward the entrance.

Stone stood behind the bar in what passed for the tasting room. He was alone. When he saw Moretti there was something like a whimper.

"It don't look like business is so good," Moretti said. "Maybe you wasn't such a good investment."

"I just need a little more time," Stone pleaded. "I've got most of it."

Moretti smirked. "What's most of it?"

Stone looked down. "Almost a hundred thousand," he said softly.

"You ain't too good at math," Moretti said. "A hundred ain't one-fifty."

Stone looked up, his eyes red, moist. "Just give me a week," he begged. "I've got a '65 Mustang. It's cherry. I'm sure I can get fifty for it."

"Oh, a '65 Mustang," Moretti said. "That's real nice." He slowly slipped the leather sap out of his jacket, the weight of it heavy in his hand. "Yeah, that might get fifty."

Moretti smashed the sap down on Stone's knuckles.

"Ohhh God!" Stone wailed. He clutched his hand as he bent down over the bar.

"Do I look like I'm in the fuckin' used car business?" Moretti asked. He delivered another blow to Stone's forearm, then grabbed him by the hair and collar and hauled him over the bar.

Stone howled in pain as Moretti delivered blow after blow to his back and upper arms. But when the kicks to the ribs began, the old actor grew silent. Moretti rolled him over to see if he was still breathing. He was barely conscious, but still alive. Moretti kneeled and clenched his face, mere inches between them.

"I'll be back tomorrow," he spat. "You'll have it all or things won't end so well."

Moretti pushed Stone away, causing his head to bounce off the floor. Then, he stood and walked toward the door.

Cruz lowered the binoculars when Moretti got in the car. Mancuso had told him to back off after he and Cho were made, but then Cooper went missing, and Rizzo. Somebody had to stay on this guy. Besides, no fucking FBI agent was gonna tell him what to do.

Something had happened inside, and Cruz had a pretty good idea what it was. He was going in.

As soon as Cruz was in the door he saw a man on the ground, bloody and beaten. He ran over to him and checked for a pulse. The man was alive was alive. Cruz called 911 and asked for an ambulance. His next call was to Parks.

"What's up?" she answered.

"I followed Moretti," Cruz admitted.

"I thought Mancuso told you not..."

"I don't have time for that," Cruz said, cutting her off. "Moretti made what I assume was a collection visit. He just left. The place is called Dash Estates. It's owned by a former actor, a guy named Rory Stone."

"Why do you think it was a collection call?" Parks asked.

"Because there's a guy lying on the floor who I'm pretty sure is Stone, and he just had the shit beat out of him."

"You went in?" Parks asked.

"Good thing I did," Cruz replied. "I just called for an ambulance."

There was a brief silence on the other end of the call, then Parks spoke. "Okay," she said, "this is going to force our hand, but it also gives us something to work with. Is he conscious?"

Cruz kneeled at Stone's side. He gently nudged his shoulder, trying rouse him. There was a soft moan, then the eyes started to open. A look terror swept across Stone's face. Cruz realized that he probably couldn't focus and thought Moretti was still there.

"You're gonna be okay," Cruz said, trying to calm him. "Help is on the way."

"See if you can get him to talk," Parks said.

"Who did this to you?" Cruz asked, leaning in so Stone could hear him.

Stone shook his head, tears forming in his eyes.

Cruz knew he was afraid to talk. There was no choice. He pulled out his badge and held it close so Stone could see.

"We can protect you," Cruz said. "Please help us catch him."

Tears now streamed down Stone's cheeks. He was in agony, but also clearly terrified of the consequences should he talk.

"Who did this?" Cruz asked again.

Stone's mouth started to form the words. Cruz had to lean in close to hear.

"Don't know his name," Stone whispered. "Mobster."

An ambulance siren could now be heard in the distance.

"Did he loan you money?" Cruz asked.

Stone nodded, then closed his eyes.

CHAPTER 78

7:02 p.m., Friday, October 21, the warehouse, Napa Valley, California

They had been forced to act fast. Fortunately, Parks had kept a running summary of the investigation on her laptop in anticipation of just such an event. She had updated the affidavit within minutes of the call from Cruz. United States District Court Judge Constance Emery had shown little hesitation in signing off on the search warrants. Teams were in place at the warehouse, Menfi Vineyards, Marroquin Winery, Evans Creek, and Amato Freight Lines. The Menfi warrant included Moretti's residence and vehicles. It had been an effort to pull together the personnel on a Friday night, but they got it done. Now, it was go time, the key being to execute all entries simultaneously.

Parks had Mancuso, Ward, Cruz, Cho, and Joe Adler on conference call. Ward would stay back to protect what was left of his undercover identity. FBI and ATF had support from both the Napa County Sheriff's Office and the Sacramento PD. They were all waiting for the signal from Parks.

"Let's move," she announced, giving the signal to the warehouse entry team. Three SUVs carrying a dozen agents stormed the gate. They were prepared to dismantle it or blow it, whichever was necessary to gain entry. But a lone security guard approached the commotion. When he saw what he was up against, he simply raised his hands.

Parks stepped out of one of the vehicles, flashed her badge and held up the search warrant. "Open up," she commanded. The guard quickly complied.

They were through the gate and in the building within minutes. The agents spread out, fully briefed on what to look for. It soon became clear that the warehouse was nothing more than a large bottling operation. Wine had been shipped in, all of it in bulk stainless-steel tanks. From the quantity, it had clearly come from numerous vineyards. Here, it was simply being bottled and labeled.

"Parks," one of the agents yelled. "Over here."

She walked to the end of the bottling line where the agent was standing.

"Take a look at this," he said.

Parks had expected to find labels from Marroquin and Evans Creek, but what she saw stunned her. There were labels from over two dozen vineyards, several of them well known. She pulled out her cell and called Mancuso.

"What's up?" Mancuso asked.

"We've got something big," Parks replied. She shared what they had found.

Mancuso let out a low whistle. "Well, we also have something big," he said.

"What's that?"

"One Nunzio Moretti," Mancuso replied. "And he does not seem happy."

Parks smiled. "I'll be right there."

Moretti lived in a small guest house near the main residence. Parks was there in a matter of minutes. When she entered, an agent pointed her toward the bedroom. There, she found Mancuso and two other agents standing next to Moretti. He was handcuffed behind his back, sitting on the edge of the bed, a smug look on his face. Parks was instantly determined to make that vanish. Parks pulled Mancuso aside.

"Did you Mirandize him?" she asked. "I mean, he's cuffed. He's not free to go. And we'll have to arrest him, or he'll flee."

Mancus nodded. "I was waiting for you. Thought I'd give him the opportunity to volunteer anything he wants to share."

"And?"

"A couple of *fuck yous* and some other choice expletives."

Parks gave a snort. "So be it."

She approached Moretti. "I'm going to read your rights," she said.

"Am I under arrest?" he asked. "What for?"

"We'll get to that," Parks replied.

"Kiss my ass, bitch."

Parks smiled. "You have the right to remain silent," she began. "If you give up that right, anything you say can, and will, be used against you in a court of law. You have the right to an attorney, and to have an attorney present during any questioning. If you cannot afford an attorney, one will be appointed for you. Do you understand these rights?"

"Fuck you," Moretti answered.

"I'll take that as a yes," Parks said. "Let me tell you a little bit about the position you're in." She summarized most of what was in the search warrant affidavit presented to Judge Emery, holding back a few key details.

"Any interest in talking to us, maybe helping yourself out?" she asked.

"I'm no fuckin' rat," Moretti replied.

"We pulled your cell data," Mancuso said. "It has you showing up at some interesting places at some interesting times, especially around when Ray Amaro went missing."

"Coincidence," Moretti said. "Big fuckin' deal."

"Then there were the calls to Jesse Morgan and Tommy Serra," Mancuso added. "Yeah, we pulled their records, too."

He turned to Parks. "Now, why do you suppose he would want to call a couple low-level workers at Pavesi Vineyards and Evans Creek?"

"And the timing," Parks said. "Curious."

She turned to Moretti and shook her head. "Sloppy."

"Ever heard of a burner phone, dumbass?" Mancuso asked him.

Moretti's façade cracked a bit. He broke eye contact, stared at the floor. "I want a lawyer," he said.

"Fair enough," Parks replied. "But here's a little food for thought before you talk with your attorney. We followed you to Dash Estates. We know what happened there."

Moretti was silent, the smug look gone.

"And, yes," she finally answered. "You are under arrest."

CHAPTER 79

9:43 a.m., Wednesday, November 9, Phillip Burton Federal Building & United States Courthouse, San Francisco, California

Assistant United States Attorney Amy Gao went through her notes one final time. This was the biggest case of her career. She did not intend to miss a question. When the arrests were made, the indictments unsealed, there would be a media firestorm. This case needed to be tight. Some of the most expensive mouthpieces in the defense bar would pick it apart, looking for any weakness that could be distorted into reasonable doubt. After all, at trial they only needed one juror's vote to get a mistrial. She needed all twelve to convict. But trial was a long way down the road. Today was about building a case, a case that, she hoped, would ultimately net the biggest of fish.

The grand jury was finishing up with testimony on a local heroin dealer. Shortly thereafter they would vote to return an indictment, the document that formally charges a defendant with a crime. Gao could not recall an instance of a no bill, that rarest of occasions when they would refuse to approve charges. There were always members who came into the process thinking they would expose the heavy handedness of the feds, protect the innocent. But by the time they had served a couple months of their year-long stint, they just wanted to know where to sign, shocked by what was going on in their community. Gao had long thought that if everyone had to serve as a grand juror it would be a better country. As for this group, they had no idea what was coming. They were about to hear from the first witness of many in a case that would shake Napa Valley to its core. And that first witness was quite possibly the most important.

There was a knock at the door.

"Come in," Gao said.

The door opened to expose two large Deputy U.S. Marshals standing on either side of an equally large man clad in the tan inmate garb of federal detention. He was handcuffed, shackled at the feet. Several additional deputies could be seen in the hall outside of the witness room. Gao knew that a dozen more were on high alert, stationed at various points around the building. There was no reason for anyone to know that the witness was here today, but he was a member of an organization that had its sources, its ways of reaching out.

"Mr. Moretti," Gao said, "have a seat."

Moretti sat. A smallish man in an expensive-looking black suit took the seat next to him. It was Moretti's lawyer, Sam Campbell, a man readily capable of defending anyone against any accusation, no matter how vile. Campbell was well known to the U.S. Attorney's Office, and roundly despised.

"Mr. Campbell," Gao said, barely looking up.

"Ms. Gao."

"I assume your client fully understands what is required of him?" she asked.

"He does," Campbell replied. "I think you will find Mr. Moretti to be quite forthcoming."

"He better be," Gao said. "If any one thing he says in there turns out to be false, the deal is off, and he will be indicted on all readily provable charges, of which there are many." Gao watched Moretti, almost hoping for a smirk. There was none.

"And immediately after his testimony he will be placed in witness protection," Campbell said, "with *no* charges filed."

"Correct," Gao replied, choking back her disgust. Moretti deserved the worst that the Department of Justice could throw at him. But he was exactly the kind of witness that WITSEC had been designed for.

"The Marshals Service will facilitate his entry into the program as soon as we're finished," Gao continued. "If and when we need him again, he will be transported back under our safe passage."

There was a snort from Moretti. Gao eyed him coolly. "If you follow the rules," she said through gritted teeth, "you'll be fine."

"So you say," Moretti replied. "You don't know these people like I do."

Campbell placed his hand on Moretti's shoulder. It had the desired effect.

Just then, one of Gao's colleagues, Rich Ripley, stuck his head in the door. "They're ready for you," he said.

Gao stood, gathering her file. She jerked her head toward the door. "Let's go."

CHAPTER 80

8:27 a.m., Thursday, November 10, Pavesi Vineyards, Napa Valley, California

Parks stepped out of the driver's door. Adler exited from the passenger side, Estes from the back. It was only appropriate that they be along for this. She and Ward had insisted. Her plan was to let Adler slap on the cuffs.

No call had been made ahead of time. The element of surprise was imperative. All the arrests were being made at the same time: Henry Evans, Tommy Serra, Pedro Marroquin, and several others. That would prevent anyone from being tipped off.

As they walked from the parking lot toward the entrance Martin Pavesi appeared on the patio. He came toward them.

"Good morning," Pavesi said. "Do you have news?"

"Oh, there's news," Parks answered. "Where's Jesse Morgan?"

A puzzled look appeared on Pavesi's face. "I think he's down in the barrel room."

Adler gave a snort. "How appropriate."

The three quickened their pace.

"Is there a rear exit?" Parks asked.

"There is," Adler replied. He motioned for Estes to go around back.

"What's this about?" Pavesi asked, trying to keep up.

"Just stay behind us," Parks said.

They drew their weapons. Morgan was unpredictable. Outside the barrel room, Parks peeked in.

"There he is." She turned to Adler. "You do the honors."

Adler smiled. "My pleasure."

They entered the barrel room. When Morgan saw them, he immediately looked toward the rear exit.

"Don't try it," Parks said. "We have people outside. It won't end well for you."

Adler holstered his weapon. Parks kept hers trained on Morgan.

"Turn around," Adler said. He pulled out his handcuffs and snapped them tight on Morgan's wrists. "Jesse Morgan, you are under arrest for the murder of Raymond Amato."

"What?" Pavesi asked. He leaned against the barrel rack to steady himself.

"You have the right to remain silent," Adler began. "If you give up that right, anything you say can, and will, be used against you in a court of law. You have the right to an attorney, and to have an attorney present during any questioning. If you cannot afford an attorney, one will be appointed for you. Do you understand these rights?"

"That fuckin' rat Moretti," Morgan said. He opened his mouth to say something else, then seemed to think better of it.

"Do you understand these rights?" Adler asked again.

"I want a lawyer," Morgan said.

"You're gonna need one," Adler replied. "I'll let Special Agent Parks explain the federal charges on the way to the jail." He spun Morgan toward the door and pushed him forward. "Let's go, asshole."

CHAPTER 81

5:59 p.m., Thursday, November 10, KSFZ TV Studios, San Francisco, California

The countdown began. "Five, four, three, two, one, and we're live." Marilyn Chen smiled into the camera and started the broadcast as she always did. "Good evening, and welcome to the KSFZ TV Evening News." She focused on the teleprompter. "Tonight, we lead with the follow-up to a KSFZ TV exclusive."

"That's right, Marilyn." Co-anchor Mark Lane took the lead. "In August we reported on the details of a brutal murder in wine country. The severed head of Raymond Amato was discovered inside an oak barrel stored in the aging room of Pavesi Vineyards. Amato had been a co-owner there along with Martin Pavesi. Now, following a lengthy investigation, numerous arrests have been made, including for the murder of Amato. We go once again to Miguel Santos who broke the initial story."

"Mark, we are just outside the Phillip Burton Federal Building here in San Francisco," Santos began. "In a story that has rocked Napa Valley, numerous individuals, including several prominent vineyard owners, have just appeared in court on charges related to marketing counterfeit wine. Sources tell us that the murder of Amato is related to this scheme."

So, Miguel, how did this work?" Lanes asked.

"We've been told that inexpensive wine was bottled as high-end product using identical bottles and counterfeit labels. Indications are that this activity was widespread. In fact, one of those arrested was Henry Evans, owner of the highly regarded Evans Creek Vineyards. Their wines have won numerous awards, particularly their Pinot Noirs."

"Miguel, I understand that there was an incident at Evans Creek in September," Chen said. "Something about a wine dump?"

"That's correct," Santos replied. "We've learned that thousands of gallons were emptied from the tanks there, flooding the facility. No one was arrested for that offense, and the crime remains unsolved."

"And what about the murder charges?" Lane asked.

Santos nodded. "Earlier today in Napa County Superior Court an individual by the name of Jesse Morgan had his initial appearance on those charges. His bond is set at two million dollars, partly due to ties to the East Coast. And that's where it gets even more interesting. On condition of anonymity, unofficial sources have told us that this may be a Mob operation."

"As in the Mafia?" Lane asked.

"Correct."

"Just incredible," Lane observed. "We'll stay on top of what is shaping up to be a huge story out of Napa. Thank you, Miguel."

"You're welcome. This is Miguel Santos, KSFZ TV, reporting live from the United States Courthouse."

EPILOGUE

7:05 p.m., Friday, November 25, Lolo, Montana, just south of Missoula

Ward leaned against the railing on his back deck, watching the Bitterroot River roll by. The temperature had dropped below freezing, but the cold night air invigorated him. His thoughts went to the operation in Napa, what Moretti had disclosed, where it all might lead. But who exactly gave the orders, the connection back East, those things were tough to prove. The Mob was good at this sort of thing. They spoke in code, used players who were unknown to each other, and killed those who might talk. The FBI still had not found the bodies of Rizzo and Cooper. That was information that the hit team from Brooklyn had not shared with Moretti. Ward believed him on that point. Why would they?

It turned out that Ray Amato had wanted to back out, terminate the use of the trucking company that he had worked so hard to build. And that is what had cost him his life. According to Moretti, Marty Pavesi had been kept in the dark. That was likely the only reason he was still alive. All of those who had been arrested were cooperating or had indicated a desire to do so. The one exception was Jesse Morgan. He had expressed no interest, nor would there be an offer. It was he and Moretti who had whacked Amato and stuffed his head in the wine barrel.

Ward heard the sliding door open. He turned to see Rowan emerge onto the deck. She had a glass of wine in one hand, the other was behind her back.

"Believe it or not," she said, "I've decided to have a Chardonnay. I guess I developed a taste. Would you like one?"

"Anything but Chardonnay," Ward said. "In fact, I'm taking a break from wine."

Rowan smiled. "I thought so." She removed the beer from behind her back and handed it to him. "Cheers!" she said, raising her glass.

Ward tipped the bottle toward her, then took a swallow. She had arrived on Thanksgiving morning, making him truly grateful.

She came to him. He put his arm around her as she rested her head on his shoulder. "What are you thinking about?" she asked.

"The case," he replied.

"I know," she said, reaching around his waist and giving a squeeze. "I just wanted to see if you'd admit it."

Ward chuckled.

"Sometimes, you give these people a little push and they take care of the problem themselves," Rowan observed.

She was right, he thought. Not the most satisfying conclusion, but often the best you could hope for.

"Dave, you comin' or not?"

Ward turned to see Jim McNeal, hands outstretched, as if to ask, *anytime soon?* The ritual had begun. The band was set up in the basement, awaiting his arrival.

"After you," Ward said, gesturing for Rowan to go first.

After she entered the house, McNeal turned to Ward. "Thank God you got her back," he said.

Ward put his hand on his old friend's shoulder. "I couldn't agree more."

* * *

11:48 a.m., Wednesday, May 17, somewhere in Utah

Moretti stared at the TV, flipping through the channels, looking for something to watch that didn't make him want to gouge his eyes out. This was every day, life in the middle of fuckin' nowhere. He hated it, hated the whole state. Fuckin' Utah, and not even Salt Lake City. They stuck him in a pissant town that was close to exactly nothing. Sometimes he thought it would have been better to just take the rap and do his time, even if it was life. At least on the inside he could have commanded some fuckin' respect. This place was torture. There wasn't a decent Italian restaurant within five hundred miles. Well, not exactly true. Las Vegas was 277 miles away. He'd checked the map. There were plenty of times he gave serious to slipping onto Interstate 15 and making the trip. But showing his face in Vegas would be a death sentence. No doubt about it.

It was a week until he was scheduled to testify. There would be people waiting, watching, looking for an opportunity. Those who wanted to take him out were patient, determined. And they had their people everywhere. Moretti hoped that the Marshals Service knew what the fuck they were doing. Bad as it was, he didn't want to die. Not that there would be many who would give a shit if he did. Arlene had divorced him long before the move to California. Their daughter wanted nothing to do with him, wouldn't take his calls. He missed the old crew in Brooklyn, but they would all shun him now...or worse. His aunts and uncles, his cousins, they were all he had left.

Moretti turned off the TV and hoisted himself off the couch. It was lunchtime. He would drive downtown, if you could call it that, and eat at one of the same five restaurants. Maybe the Mexican place. The waitress there had seemed receptive to his flirtations the other day. That, or she was just trolling for tips. Either way, it was something to do. Moretti grabbed his wallet and keys. He walked through the kitchen and out into the garage. The old F-150 sat waiting. It was red. He hated it. His handler told him it would help him fit in. As he began to climb in there was a footstep, a scuff on the garage floor behind him.

"The Commission sends its greetings."

Moretti knew the accent, pure Brooklyn. He turned. The man was well-dressed, his suit north of a thousand dollars. There was a smirk on his face. The gun, with silencer, was pointed at Moretti's chest.

"You shouldn't have called your cousin Sal," the man said.

Moretti grunted, an acknowledgment. The Marshals told him, no contact with anyone from your previous life. Follow the rules and you will be okay. It was one call. One fuckin' call.

"What did you do?" Moretti asked.

"No worries," the man said. "Sal's in good health." He raised the gun, pointing it at Moretti's head. "But he's not okay with havin' a cousin who's a rat."

Moretti gave a snort. Sal always was a fuckin' punk. He should have known better.

"You see," the man continued, "the Code of Omerta still fuckin' means somethin' to some of us."

"Easy for you to say," Moretti replied. He closed his eyes and waited for the shot.

ACKNOWLEDGMENTS

A Word of Thanks

As always, I gratefully acknowledge my many friends and former colleagues in law enforcement who contributed to this work. They have taught me much about duty, honor, and public service.

Thank you to my wife, Karen, who continues to encourage and support me in my various endeavors, including the long experiment of trying to become an author; to our children, who actually do think it's cool that their dad writes books, even when they won't admit it; and, of course, to Eric Campbell and Lance Wright at Down & Out Books who gave me the opportunity to tell my stories to a wider audience.

JOEL W. BARROWS is an Iowa district court judge who regularly oversees both criminal and civil trials. Prior to his appointment to the bench he was a practicing attorney for nearly twenty-three years; the last eighteen of those spent as a state, and then federal, prosecutor. As an attorney, Joel regularly argued before the United States Court of Appeals. His cases have been as diverse as white collar crime, environmental crime, cyber-crime, child exploitation, narcotics and firearms offenses, immigration crimes, bank robbery, health care fraud, public corruption, civil rights offenses and threats against the president, and have included many high profile prosecutions.

He has traveled extensively in Central America. He lives with his family in eastern Iowa along the banks of the Mississippi.

(The views expressed in this novel are those of Joel W. Barrows alone and do not reflect those of the Iowa Judicial Branch.

BOOKS

On the following pages are a few
more great titles from the
Down & Out Books publishing family.

For a complete list of books and to
sign up for our newsletter,
go to DownAndOutBooks.com.

Groovy Gumshoes
Private Eyes in the Psychedelic Sixties
Edited by Michael Bracken

Down & Out Books
April 2022
978-1-64396-252-8

From old-school private eyes with their flat-tops, off-the-rack suits, and well-worn brogues to the new breed of private eyes with their shoulder-length hair, bell-bottoms, and hemp sandals, the shamuses in Groovy Gumshoes take readers on a rollicking romp through the Sixties.

With stories by Jack Bates, C.W. Blackwell, Michael Bracken, N.M. Cedeño, Hugh Lessig, Steve Liskow, Adam Meyer, Tom Milani, Neil S. Plakcy, Stephen D. Rogers, Mark Thielman, Grant Tracey, Mark Troy, Andrew Welsh-Huggins, and Robb White.

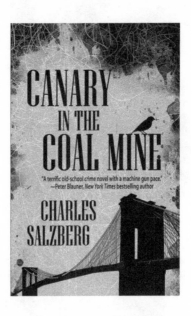

Canary in the Coal Mine
Charles Salzberg

Down & Out Books
April 2022
978-1-64396-251-1

Pete Fortunato, a NYC PI who suffers from anger management issues and insomnia, is hired by a beautiful woman to find her husband.

When he finds him shot dead in the apartment of her young boyfriend, this is the beginning of a nightmare as he's chased by the Albanian mob sending him half-way across the country in an attempt to find missing money which can save his life.

The Damned Lovely
Adam Frost

Down & Out Books
May 2022
978-1-64396-253-5

"She wasn't pretty but she was ours…" Sandwiched between seedy businesses in the scorching east LA suburb of Glendale, the Damned Lovely dive bar is as scarred as its regulars: ex-cops, misfits and loners. And for Sam Goss, it's a refuge from the promising life he's walked away from, a place to write and a hole to hide in.

But when a beautiful and mysterious new patron to the bar turns up murdered as the third victim of a serial killer terrorizing the local streets, Sam can't stop himself from getting involved. Despite their fleeting interaction, or perhaps because of it, something about her ghost won't let go…

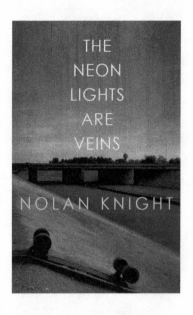

The Neon Lights Are Veins
Nolan Knight

Down & Out Books
May 2022
978-1-64396-265-8

The underbelly of Los Angeles, 2008; a place where hard-lucks scrounge for hope in gutters.

Alvi Drake is an aged pro skateboarder whose lone thrill is a pill-fueled escape from the terror of past ghosts. When news hits of the disappearance of an old flame, he sets out to find her—the biggest mistake in his track ridden life.